Downieville

Nevada City

Auburn

Sacramento

Yuba River

Feather River

Sacramento River

SIERRA NEVADA

D1505468

THE THIRTEENTH

Also by Steven Nightingale

THE LOST COAST

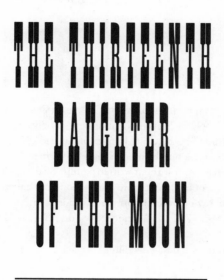

THE THIRTEENTH DAUGHTER OF THE MOON

STEVEN NIGHTINGALE

ST. MARTIN'S PRESS ❧ NEW YORK

This book is dedicated to
Leon Nightingale,
my father, my friend.
Your strength matched your gentleness.
In Memoriam

Endpaper design by Ellisa Mitchell

Library of Congress Cataloging-in-Publication Data

Nightingale, Steven.
  The thirteenth daughter of the moon   /   Steven
  Nightingale.
    p.   cm.
  ISBN 0-312-16911-6
  I. Title.
  PS3564.I3637T48   1997
  813'.54—dc21   97-15593
                                              CIP

First Edition: November 1997

10   9   8   7   6   5   4   3   2   1

ACKNOWLEDGMENTS

At St. Martin's Press, my editors Thomas Dunne and Neal Bascomb gave me critical support and comment. They are tough professionals, ideal for a writer, and I am fortunate to have them.

My agent Robert Stricker has shown throughout my readings and my writing the most aggressive support for my work. This is a man who never stops working for the stories he believes in. He labors for the benefit of books and writers; and for the delight of readers.

A special thanks to Ellisa Mitchell, who created the map for the endpapers of both *The Lost Coast* and this current book. Ellisa reads closely, so that the maps have a reflective, detailed, direct relation to these texts. She draws with a studied and brilliant whimsy.

Elizabeth Dilly read this manuscript as it took form, and at every turn brought her considerable gifts to bear. She has a natural and learned understanding of storytelling—the larger questions of form, as well as the minutiae of pacing and phrasing and proportion. She is honest, intelligent, amused, and marvelous.

Lexine Alpert is the admirable photographer whose work graces the cover of this book, as it did my previous book. She is patient and artful in her seeking out of just that light and timing and composition that make an image live.

My friends Kelly Cash and Graham Chisholm and their son Ian, by sheer force of liveliness and goodwill, make a man want to tell stories. As if that weren't enough, they took me in one night after a terrible auto accident and brought me back from the dead with hot food, jokes, and general rollicking.

Michael Sykes and Zoë Alexis Scott of Great Basin Books are

friends to writing and to writers, and I am lucky to know them. Writers themselves, publishers, photographers, booksellers—in addition to all this, they have uncanny instincts for finding places of beauty and making places beautiful.

In my traveling to give readings for my previous book, *The Lost Coast*, I had remarkable and affectionate support from Douglas and Diana Wilson in Denver; and from Rachel Jacoff in Boston. May they have always two companions: contentment and celebration.

My trustworthy, longtime dear friend Marci Brown, working in support of this book, did important research in the bars of San Francisco.

A lucky chance brought me to the fine novelist Monique Laxalt Urza, a fellow Nevadan and a devotee of good prose. Her friendship and her thoughtfulness are a delight to me.

A writer can have time to work only if he has people in his life of rock-solid reliability and helpfulness and good spirits. Joyce Ousley and Vernon Campbell are those people for me. My deepest thanks to each of them.

Tom Gregory, Spook, the North Yuba, the Great Basin: may you live and thrive.

Most, and first, and best: the classical scholar Andrea Wilson Nightingale, my beloved wife: she is a life-giver. Wise in the ways of language and of loving; faithful, strong, ardent; a teacher, a blessing, a genius.

A Paradise.

ONE THING SURE about rivers: they run in the direction of heaven.

In the town of Downieville, California, Cookie stood on the banks of the North Yuba River. She watched the willful shining waters. She memorized the pattern of its flashing, she called to her company those paradisiacal greens. These were messages of light and color she needed, because they marked out subtle pathways that led to the Land of the Dead.

Cookie was going to find her murdered husband.

All in all, a common circumstance: a cowgirl headed downriver, following instructions given her by Great Basin Shoshone and Paiute Indians, to find the spirit of the man she loved. You can't shoe horses and mend fences *every* day.

Just behind Cookie, Izzy tooted the horn of the old station wagon they had packed up.

"C'mon, woman! Can't you see it's time to get on the road?"

Next to them, leaning out the window of the pickup truck, Ananda did her part:

"We're ready to ramble! Let's go for it."

Sitting next to Ananda in the pickup, Chiara gave Cookie her practiced the-world-is-tasty-and-we-ain't-seen-nothin'-yet smile.

As if the women weren't provocation enough, the cowgirl found by her side a muscular, fragrant Jamaican—Muscovado Taine.

"You probably think you heard me sing all my songs, huh? No way. Once we get rolling, I got outlandish tunes I want to hum in your ear. I hum slow. I hum smooth," he said with an easy look.

"How did I ever get mixed up with this bunch?" she asked the river.

The river took a deep breath and reminded her:

In Eureka, Nevada, she had ducked into a bar. There, wouldn't you know it, she met Chiara, a dark-haired mercury-minded professor on the run, who was accompanied by her sixteen-year-old daughter, Izzy, opalescent, amorous, bemused. Now Izzy in her easy, brazen way in that bar gave herself over to be wooed by Muscovado Taine, and he did more than merely woo—he handed over all his tropical heart to the girl. He wanted to taste Izzy so long and deep that he could run his tongue along the edge of the girl's soul; and sure enough, before long her body was like a Caribbean meadow full of flowers that opened in the sunlight of their lovemaking—but before we get too carried away with Musco and the nubile Izzy, let's get back to that bar.

It was there Cookie had met Ananda, jazz trumpeter and austere Los Angeles securities attorney. She had hair like dawn light. And what had since happened to Ananda? Without going into the details we must confess that her mornings came now to her with a surprise: for she awakened with her hair spread in sunny languor over the olive skin of—who else?—the delighted and willowy Chiara, by her side naked and no less astonished by their embraces and their—but we digress.

In that original bar, of course, was also our Renato, a painter of houses and of canvases. We will refrain from any account of his adventures. Still, it should be mentioned in passing that on their trip across the Great Basin Renato ended up in bed—these things can't be helped—with a black-haired woman named Maria-Elena, who was, he should have known, one of the Daughters of the Moon; and in the radiance of her pleasures he saw a life he had hoped for always. Renato wanted to live as the man entrusted with her delectations . . .

But let us return once more to the bar in Eureka, for there was one more traveler there to be met, one more lover: there was Juha, our Cookie's beloved Juha, a contractor built like a mountain. Juha was a man whose heart was shy and delighted, and whose manner was hopeful and boisterous. And not only that: Juha loved animals. And in that very bar he had let loose a bountiful selection of his famous animal cries, including the neigh of a big stallion and the peep of the little cheechee bird; he followed with an excellent wolf-howl; he passed shamelessly on to the communications of a cheetah, a turkey, an ape. This performance, though only a small part of Juha's throaty repertoire, was now a legend of the Nevada barrooms and remembered by animals everywhere.

All in all, a cast of characters to be met with in any little town of the high desert.

They had embarked together on a trip across Nevada, moving toward the Sierra. Nothing much had happened. True, they had met a Shoshone who had told them a story of the progress of the soul in the form of a coyote; and it must be admitted that they had visited a ranch house inhabited by angels, and at Pyramid Lake heard the music of death and resurrection—but it was Nevada, they were never too far from a bar, so why worry? They went right on to meet more of the same plain-living types: a peacock who was trying to find out about the Wild Light of God, a rancher named Beulah who was mother to a lightning bolt named, very reasonably, Bolt; all twelve of the Daughters of the Moon; and so on and so forth, some rambles just turn out like that, but all of it was no surprise to Cookie: she knew that once you're mounted, you have to ride.

And ride: Cookie married Juha in a bar in Gerlach, Nevada, in a ceremony attended by the very cosmos. They were so much in love the coyotes sang to them. They were so much in love the moon stopped to watch the wedding.

And then all of them together, following an imperative of the countryside, had rambled on, moving west toward the Sierra Nevada. They felt confident, since the peacock and the coyote had joined up with them for good. Once they hit the mountains, though, these pilgrims could not help themselves: they founded the Improvisational Hurricane Theater Troupe, which put on a few shows, until summertime came along. Then they all left each other to their labors and adventures and old-fashioned sweat-and-cinnamon sunlit couplings. So did our travelers live and love there in the North Yuba Canyon.

Until by the side of the river Juha was murdered.

Two months had passed. Cookie had finished the beautiful little cabin that she and Juha had been building in a meadow at a bend of the North Yuba. There had been a search for the killers, and interviews with the sheriff. At first, the sheriff had the idea that one of the Hurricane Troupe had killed Juha in some lovers' quarrel. Then again, Juha had been shot so many times it might have been one of the crackpot survivalists who tuck themselves away with their weapons, in small enclaves in the Sierra. But a search had turned up nothing. And the killing was still unsolved.

Cookie watched the river a minute longer, then turned to her friends.

It was time to go.

Off a dirt road, camped on a far promontory that overlooked the Yuba canyons, Tabby and Grimes sat together in their camp and remembered Juha's truck. On the back of the truck there had been an elaborate house, gabled and balconied and ornamented, that the big contractor had built all the way back in Eureka to house his newfound friends. And in which Cookie had with her loving cowgirl aggressions combed out Juha's muscles by sheer pressure of savory attentions.

It hadn't been easy, getting rid of Juha. Maybe it had been a mistake, they had to face it; but he looked so crude and dangerous. A big, meaty guy, so big they knew right away he was a monster. A threat, anybody could see that. You had to strike hard. Tabby and Grimes had been bold and stylish, as was customary to them. Tabby had a lean physique and an uncommon grace of movement, very persuasive; Grimes was shorter and coiled round with muscle tissue he had won with years of workouts; his demeanor spoke of burly, unbound energies.

They reminisced, the two of them, leaning back against a couple of ponderosa pines. They had done so much work together. It had brought them closer.

"That big fella did look surprised, didn't he?" said Tabby.

"Like he'd seen a power. Someone superior."

"They don't feel any pain. Shock."

"Took the whole magazine! Standing there! How did he do it? Thirty cartridges!"

"Gravity. That was one big shithead."

"Think of all the people we saved."

"It had to be done. The best way to protect people is to do what they all want to do, if they had the guts. You have to deal with every threat, every evil. No waiting or compromising."

"Remember the truck?"

"It didn't look real."

"So funny-looking."

"It had all that frilly shit."

"Cutie-pie shit."

"I guess we remodeled it."

They remembered how they'd strode over to their tarp, thrown it back, got some grenades they had been saving. It was like war games. They had run around in the meadow, met, whispered together, got on their bellies, and practiced the SWAT team drills they knew. They got closer and closer and in throwing the grenades had pulled off a nice bit of synchrony that blew the house to high heaven. They grabbed for each other when it went off.

Not long after, they had gone over to the other side of the canyon to their present camp, in a meadow up above Downieville.

They lounged around for a few hours, shirts off, taking it easy.

Tabby, lanky and energetic, was thinking how much had happened. And how close he was to Grimes. They had come through for each other; nothing bonded men like combat memories.

"I've been thinking of Angelica," Tabby said. Angelica had been their favorite whore in San Jose. Grimes had loved her dark violet lipstick. They had protected her; even now it hurt Tabby to remember how abused she had been. And by Tabby's own father!

"I'd like to see her with short hair. I'd cut her hair off, and then cut her clothes off and fuck her," said Grimes, laughing. "She'd be so grateful."

"She's just not the one for me anymore," confessed Tabby. "That black-haired girl I met by the road in Sierra City, I can't get her out of my head. Beautiful! What did they call her? Stizzy? Fizzy? She's part of the dream. All she has to do is be loved. It sounds like a fairy tale; but look at all the people we've helped. I want to tell her my story. I'm her chance. Her chance to be loved by someone who could stand tall and keep his word and stay clean."

But the patter of Tabby and Grimes was interrupted by a well-dressed, good-looking young woman who came out of the trees waving at them and carrying a video camera. She came steadily at them, filming, talking; lithe and friendly she came.

Nobody was foolish enough to try to comfort Cookie; they too had stood around the dead Juha. But they were a band of lovers; they knew what there was to lose.

Our travelers headed along Highway 49, toward Nevada City. Beside them ran the North Yuba, green with bounty and blessings. They had their beat-up station wagon and an old pickup truck. In the wagon, Cookie and opalescent Izzy and the Jamaican Muscovado Taine all rode up front. In the pickup were the smitten Ananda and Chiara, and stretched out on Ananda's thigh was Tupelo, the soft gray cat that had traveled with her through their adventures in Nevada. In the bed of the pickup lay Renato and his lover Maria-Elena, the Daughter of the Moon, who was in her lunar way beginning to look rather pregnant. Between Renato and Maria-Elena slept the peacock.

They knew little about the road ahead, except that they had to try to get to Lost Coast, a stretch of wilderness coastline in northern California, north of Mendocino. They carried on with a high-hearted uncertainty, having from their adventures a momentum of heart, a hopefulness that there was a homecoming in this new life. It was as though, on the day they had all met in that little bar in central Nevada, some fuse had burned down, and they had now in their days a detonation of possibilities.

Not a one of them could understand how Juha could be gone. They had loved him so much; they loved him still. Through the storytelling and laughter of the journey through Nevada, it had seemed that they were beyond loss: there had grown upon them a sense of invulnerability, of surety, of sweet, unstoppable acceleration. Now, with one blow, all that was destroyed. They knew that they must go on; and that Cookie had her own responsibilities to Juha. But their going forth now had a wariness, almost an ignorance—for they did not know how to protect the joys visited upon them. Now, as they traveled, it was just this art of protection they needed to learn. And more than that: they needed to make sense of Juha's life and death; they needed to honor him; they needed to find the ceremony that matched the pain of missing him.

Just now, driving down Highway 49, through the North Yuba Canyon, they talked and hummed and sang, they swapped tales and jokes. In the back of the pickup, Renato sat close to the sleeping peacock, who draped his tail languorously over the legs of Maria-Elena. Renato was curious about the baby that already tumbled and whispered in his lover.

"How do you know it's going to be a girl? Are there no sons of the Moon?" he inquired.

Maria-Elena laughed in the soft, cherishing heat of autumn air. "There's no man subtle enough, for now. Maybe someday."

"A subtle baby?" inquired Renato skeptically.

"She'll be a dark-eyed, moonstruck baby." And Maria-Elena leaned up close to Renato, she leaned as she had when first they had met and danced together, the night before the wedding of Cookie and Juha in the Jalisco Club in Gerlach, Nevada. She and Renato had danced their way out the door and down the street under the stars to a motel room.

Up in the cab Chiara was razzing her lover Ananda.

"Yep, I'm a woman with a ragged heart. Been around, seen how weird and tough it can get. But it's worked so far. We'll just make it up as we go along. It'll be razz-ma-tazz comedy. Enough of dignity. It's time to get lurid. What's Indian summer for?" She tossed her black hair, which gave forth its silver lights. She could not have predicted any of their trip across the Great Basin—not the stories nor the animals nor the metaphysical high jinks. And certainly not the late afternoon in a little room on a ranch in the Smoke Creek desert, falling into bed and falling in love with this blond, experimental lawyer. Now the two women lived in the learned certainty of their affections. Epigrams, memories, stories, pleasures, hopes took them over, and they talked in great bursts—freshets of affection. Just then they were bringing one long exchange to a close, with laughter and the brushing of fingertips.

But the radiant Ananda had shadows on her thoughts. "What if we just stopped all this wandering around?" she asked, and there was a pleading in it. She had been full of admiration and affection for Juha; and she had thrilled at the way Juha's fierce loving of Cookie had left the cowgirl loose-limbed with satisfaction and delight. How could he be gone? "You know, I could set the two of us up in Los Angeles for a while. So much has happened, maybe it's time to look back amazed; maybe it's time for . . . for safety. Do we have to risk everything for a life we don't even understand yet?"

Chiara, thoughtful, ran her hand through the blond ribbons of hair that swirled down over the shoulders of her lover. "I know," she said softly, "I know. I'm worried too. We've got to stay loose." She was thinking helplessly of the two boys who had threatened Izzy by the side of the road in Sierra City.

Tupelo, Ananda's gray cat, got up from Ananda's lap, lifted herself high, and rubbed her soft cheeks along the necks of both women.

In the old station wagon Muscovado, sitting between Izzy and Cookie, sounded off:

"What's a boy like me doing headed down the road, surrounded by wild females? I'm scared. I got no more antics left. I'll just get passive. I'll be a lapdog."

"Keep that lapdog down," suggested Izzy.

The rivers swirled round, the pine needles gilt with noon pointed the way down the canyon, brushy cirrus stroked the sky, light with the soft velocities of autumn bolted down the Sierra ridges and blew bright passages through the air.

They were ready for a story, and when they pulled into Nevada City, they wandered the streets, on the lookout. But it was not until they entered the Blue Dream Cafe, and trouping noisily through went to the back and out the door into the little courtyard, that they saw the old woman in denim overalls. Throughout their travels, they had come upon storytellers in bars, mechanic's shops, on ranches. And now in the cafe, they gathered expectantly, ready to listen.

The old woman's name was Nattie, and she was sitting there like a piece of blue afternoon. Next to her, with his usual wily and weathered look, sat Antelope on the Moon. The Antelope, of course, was well known to them as the man who way back in Austin, Nevada, had told them the story of the coyote's visit to the House of the Winds. Antelope could do entertaining and useful things, such as turn into an animal (the golden eagle was his favorite); and he knew the way mountains moved when they were making the passage a man must follow to the Land of the Dead.

"It's about time you all showed up," complained the Antelope. "I'm so wired up from these coffees that if you gave me a stroke, my veins would sound off like guitar strings."

"I'll do it. I'll try it," piped up Izzy.

"You are *such* a volunteer," commented Musco.

"Now I'm here 'cause I was thinkin' that it was about time for another coyote story," the Antelope went on.

"Of course," mused Nattie, "I could tell them the story of the Music of the Spheres. Everybody needs that story. Especially, they need to hear it from me. I've got a helluva delivery, ya know?"

The Antelope looked appreciatively at her, as one would at a compatriot of long standing. "I think they should have to wait to find out about the Music of the Spheres. They're still mostly slack-brained fools. They should have to earn it," he suggested mischievously.

"Sure," said Chiara, "what do we have to do? Stand on our heads and play the kazoo? Juggle cinnamon buns? Do I have to put on a fluffy dress and square-dance?"

"She has to, I'll bet. And I'd love to see it. She could use more fluff in her life," observed her daughter Izzy.

Nattie chuckled and tsk-tsked and turned to Antelope. "Are they always making cracks like this?"

The Antelope was shaking his head. "It's *so* adolescent."

"I think you're right: they should have to earn the Music of the Spheres," agreed Nattie. "I'll just wait and see how they do."

"I've got it!" said Izzy brightly. "We'll put on a fashion show; you know, dress up like peacocks and swagger around grinning like idiots. Then you'd have to tell us, huh?"

"I resent that!" said the peacock.

"Will you all just pipe down!" said Nattie. "This is the way it's going to work: I'll tell the story of the Music of the Spheres when you're by the Pacific, headed up the coast, on the way to Lost Coast—I'll tell you this story under one condition only."

"Yessss?" oozed Muscovado Taine.

"That you're able to get that far without being killed," finished Nattie cheerfully.

All of our travelers fell silent. Finally Cookie said, "Ain't goin' to be no more killin', if this cowgirl has anything to do with it.

So we'll get that story when it's time. Meanwhile, let's hear 'bout the coyote."

And they gathered around Antelope on the Moon, and the Antelope told them

THE STORY OF COYOTE AND THE HOUSE OF GREAT WATERS

"Once upon a time there was a coyote that had visited the House of the Winds. Now, why would a coyote do a crazy thing like that? Because this coyote jes' didn't like being himself. It didn't make sense. There he was, a mangy coyote, and all around him was a blessed, astonishin' world. Why in tarnation, I mean, why in a million years would he want to stay himself? No way he would. With so many beauties out there, so many singin' strange places, he jes' wanted to give himself away, to get inside the world, to make himself a part of what he saw.

"So, as I was sayin': coyote, after his usual sneakin' around and shenanigans, his roundabout tricks, had visited the House of the Winds. And there, he had got himself a little education. He was taught by the Winds how to move clear and far over the earth. And he said to hisself, Oh, boy, am I ever goin' to do some tricks now! Why, nobody will ever have seen such a strong, fast-movin', far-travelin' coyote! Watch out, everybody!

"So's he had to think of what to do. And he thought of the natural thing. He thought he'd go to the beach. Jes' like a coyote, lazy damn thing. So's he jes' leapt into the air, and sure enough, he zipped right over to a beach out there in California, place called Lost Coast."

"Oh, fer chrissakes, this isn't all goin' to start fittin' together and makin' sense, is it? Lost Coast!" complained Cookie.

Antelope on the Moon looked at Cookie. "A man can't help but like you, you're so belligerent."

"Are we going to make it to Lost Coast?" asked Muscovado Taine, who was still bothered by Nattie's monitory comments.

"Search me," answered the Antelope. "Crazy-ass bunch like this, you'll be lucky to make it to dinner. But jes' in case against all the odds you do make it, you're goin' to need this story." And he looked around and harrumphed and went back to his yarn.

"And so there the coyote was, Lost Coast, lookin' out over the ocean, and he ain't never seen the like. All that spittin' and crashin', that hissin' and rumblin', standin' up and layin' down; all that noise! Now everybody knows how smart a coyote is: he jes' looked and looked at the big sea, an' he said, 'Nope, it sure ain't the desert. It don't look right. It ain't much at all. It's all wet. Kind of monotonous. Nothing to do here. I'm gettin' out. I'm goin' home.' And so forth, you know how them coyotes like to chatter on."

"If ya ask me, coyotes ain't the only one," observed Cookie.

But the Antelope paid Cookie no mind.

"Exceptin' as there was jes' one thing keeping the coyote from headin' right back to his desert. Jes' one thing."

"It was a pretty German shepard bitch that turned up just then," guessed Muscovado.

"No, no, no! It was the ocean started talkin' to the coyote! An' makin' fun of him! And coyote was a-listenin' and a-listenin', and the waters came for him with all kinda high-hearted invitations and mockery, an' all of a sudden he had that same old feelin'— that being himself jes' wasn't enough! There's no use being alive if you're stuck with yourself! Same old coyote every mornin'— what a drag!

"And 'cause he had these thoughts, he followed those funny beckonin' voices of the sea down along Lost Coast. They led him down along the sands and around a headland to a hidden cove. And lookin' at it all, coyote, who thought in his cocky way that he had seen everything, was jes' about knocked over, 'cause the water in the cove was no ordinary ocean color. It was unnatural blue. It was a bright burnin' phosphor of a blue: a movin' sky-come-alive blue; it was a firestorm of blue. And more than that: right beside that blue fire, on the sands of the cove, he saw a small house. And next to the house an old woman, motionin' for him to come to her. What on earth was she doin' there? She looked so wild and sure. What was a coyote to do? Well, he should have skedaddled for home. Headed off to the nice safe, quiet desert.

It was the right thing to do. That's what coyote wanted to do. But, first of all, he was jes' so damned curious. And most of all, he loved old women."

Old Nattie beamed at the Antelope.

"So's he went rippin' on down the hill, going faster and faster, until with the speed of that dashin' he did something just as foolish as we coulda hoped: he threw himself straight off the edge of the bluff and thudded down like a bag of sand right at the feet of the old woman who lived in the cabin at the edge of the perilous waters.

" 'I just knew you'd do that!' said the old woman with a smirk. 'You're just so curious!'

"And coyote, as he got to his feet and brushed the mud from his coat, said with dignity, 'It was not curiosity. It's my courage and resolution.'

" 'Yeah, and you're full of coyote shit too!' exclaimed the old woman, smiling.

"And coyote had to admit she was right. He looked at her beat-up little cabin.

" 'It is the House of Great Waters,' said the woman quietly. And she led him in.

"Inside the house there was nothing but a table with some bottles holding various clear liquids, and a very old silver cup. And on the other side of the room, an enormous stone basin full of water and fed by a little channel that led to the mantic azure waters of the cove. The water in the basin glistened, but it was calm.

" 'House of Great Waters! Humph! Don't look like much to me!' said coyote in his cocky way.

"And that was when the old woman, whose eyes were as blue as the deep blue sea, went over to the table and picked up the silver cup. And coyote could hear, louder than ever, the roarin' of the waters. And the old woman looked at him, and coyote was terrified.

" 'Don't look like much, huh?' said the old woman. 'Well, it just happens to be the home of all the waters on earth.' And she walked straight for the glistenin' water of the big stone basin; and as she got near it, the water moved and flashed and seethed, it turned violently upon itself, and . . ."

Antelope on the Moon fell silent. Our travelers stared at him. He looked nonchalant. They waited. He looked lackadaisical.

"Don't tell me we have to bribe you again to get the ending! Haven't you made enough money off of us?" said Ananda crossly. She felt how surely the story was going to lead them out onto the road.

"Nope, I ain't takin' no bribes. Nope, you'll just have to wait to find out what happens," said Antelope on the Moon smugly. And he got up to leave.

"If you tell us now, I'll invite you to dinner," suggested Muscovado. "Rum and jambalaya."

"Done deal!" said the Antelope hungrily. "I'm crazy for jambalaya!" And he settled back into his chair, lit up a cigarette. He looked at Muscovado.

"Okay, okay," said Musco. And he went inside and got Antelope on the Moon a glass of rum. "Sort of like a down payment," observed the Jamaican as Antelope took a deep, satisfying slug of the dark liquor. The tale moved on.

"And the old woman with eyes blue as the deep blue sea stood with her silver cup before the glistening pool of water.

" 'Here,' she said quietly, 'is the homeland of waters. You will see.' And she dipped her cup into the strange bright liquid and then led the coyote out onto the sand. 'You will see all the ways of water on the earth.' And she threw the water from the cup into the air, and all at once the woman, the coyote, and the cove were enveloped in a violent ocean storm—the sea rose, the trees bent and shook, rainwater blasted them and rocked the mountainside and blew both of them down on the sand.

"Then, just as quickly, it was over.

" 'How did you do that!' exclaimed the soaked coyote.

" 'That was one of the ways of water,' said the mischievous old woman. And they went back inside the House of Great Waters, she went again with her silver cup to the stone basin, dipped once, then led coyote into the woods a little ways. Among the big fragrant trees she poured the water on the ground. And right there bubbled up a beautiful clear, sweet mountain spring.

" 'Storms and springs . . . two of the ways of water on this earth.'

"And the old woman kept coyote there all day, dippin' from the stone basin with her special cup. Sometimes she would pour the water, sometimes toss it in the air, sometimes hurl it into the cove. And coyote saw all the force fields of seawater and freshwater and the water of the skies. He saw along the mountainside the surging of big springtime rivers; he was buffeted on the sands by hailstorms and white squalls and the feathery tumbling of fog, and he saw in the cove the massive silent rush of ocean currents. He saw the spinnin' rain of cyclones and the misted rain of deserts: everything that water could be was given him by an old woman who stood there in front of her cabin in a little cove along the Lost Coast.

"And what was the coyote to do? What to do? Well, it was time to decide, because the woman turned to him and said, 'Coyote, you've seen enough! Now get away from here! Go skulking back to your desert! You think you can understand the House of Great Waters? The stories of river and sea and spring and rain? The stories of water wandering everywhere, making everywhere a home, working a way everywhere inside of life? Not you, coyote! You could never live like that. You will never be the one who can go everywhere and in that place give life. You want to stay a coyote. You visit the House of the Winds, and what do you turn into? A flying beach bum! Get on away! Just you blow on back to the desert!'

"Now what was our simple coyote to do?

"In her blue eyes he saw what to do.

"He followed her back into the House of Great Waters and she kissed and stroked him. And then he walked into the calm glistening pool, and as soon as the water enveloped him, he heard the roaring: he gave himself to the waters and he felt the ocean currents in his blood and the big storms inside his bones and the life-giving springs that rose in his flesh. And when he

1 5

was ready, he went further, into the blue cove and down into the shining waters. He gave himself away to learn all the stories of water, taking them into himself, down and down he went until the coyote who had learned the ways of the Winds now came into possession of all the powers of Water. Down into the roaring he went, and how did coyote return to us? Where is the coyote to be found?"

And our travelers looked above and saw the swirling of the sky.

"Are you ready for coyote to bring you the stories he learned in the House of Great Waters?"

There was a roaring all around the cafe.

Clouds billowed in the courtyard, there was a thundering as of waterfalls, a rumble of rivers.

"What are the stories of water? When are you going to learn?" yelled the Antelope on the Moon. "How many chances do you think you have? How many lives?"

A storm of all their days broke over their heads, the sky turned around them like a cyclone, they held each other tight, the door to their courtyard swung violently shut.

THE DOOR HAD shut, of course, behind Nattie and Muscovado Taine, who had retreated inside the Blue Dream Cafe to begin their leisurely cooking of the jambalaya.

"Are they going to be okay out there?" asked Musco, motioning with a big knife to the back courtyard.

"Don't mind them," said Nattie, "they've gone off into the raptures. And the Antelope loves to watch people in such a state. He's sort of a mystical voyeur."

"When do they come back from the raptures?" Musco asked. They had traveling to do; he had a meal to prepare.

"Now how would I know?" she replied intemperately. "The important thing, anyway, is to have a lot of good chow along the way."

Muscovado spiraled some olive oil into a big iron pot; he sliced garlic, carrots, onions, and celery, flung them in; and then spread out on the counter moist, shining tomatoes and gnarly okra. Naturally enough, he thought of one of the tenets of analytical philosophy: if a man can make a meal delicious, his lover will find his soul delicious. With such reflections he cored the tomatoes, cut and opened them roughly; he set them out in bright irregular array. The old woman watched him.

"Izzy is too young to understand that you love her as rain loves earth, hawks love wind; as the night sky loves stars. She cannot understand that you would never leave her except to go out to work: work which is a gathering of beauties you would bring home to her. And that you would not have that gathering end, not ever, not in this life nor any other."

All this took Muscovado's attention off the okra.

"I know, I know. What can I do?"

"Ask the sea along the Lost Coast, if you make it."

Musco smiled. "Imagine Iz by the side of the sea! Those waves would rise up and take a look. They'd hold themselves high and just watch that girl."

"How about some journalistic detachment, Musco?"

"Let me finish cooking." Musco grinned as he poured in some stock and added the tomatoes and okra, then began heating some golden oil for the roux.

"If only we had some bammy," he lamented, thinking of the wonderful cassava flour, pressed into flat loaves, eaten throughout Jamaica.

And Nattie promptly walked over to the freezer, rummaged around, and then from within a cloud of frosty mist, returned, carrying a huge cardboard box filled with enough bammy to last the long trip to the sea.

"When folks get as strange as this bunch, you got to cater to their appetites," she noted in her soft, musical, meditative old-woman's voice. "Let's fry these up, finish simmering the jambalaya, and eat. Where is everybody, anyway?"

The young woman with the video camera was done up very neatly. There were inelegant sweat marks from the climb up to the meadow where Tabby and Grimes were camped, the lipstick was a little botched from a brushby of fir branches, but all in all she was coiffed and decorous. Pants suit, painted nails, firm body, and in her soul that acceleration felt by a reporter in the field.

"Who the fuck are you?" demanded Tabby as he moved his hand toward the shoulder holster. This shooting people, was there an end to it? And the corpses! It would be cool if, when you shot somebody, they just disappeared.

"I'm Dorothy Gallagher from KICU television in San Jose. I've been trying to find you, and I got a tip from a woman named Angelica that you were up here in the Yuba canyon. I know how much you love Angelica. I know you were attacked by your own father. I want to tell your story."

The camera started to roll. Tabby calmed down. It was as though he could feel himself being set down on film; there was a security and a happiness to it. He knew just how he looked; and how he could look, if she would just keep that beautiful camera rolling.

Grimes, though, was still scared that they were being ambushed. He looked around at the trees that surrounded the clearing.

"Why should we trust you?" he demanded.

"Because I know your story."

"So what is it?" asked Tabby. This was exactly what he had been hoping to find out.

Dorothy lowered the camera and looked at them.

"Two kids made to steal and lie by a preacher, Tabby's own father, Ben, a violent man. A hypocrite. They have to go along because of his threats, but they know it's wrong. This knowing, this wanting to do good, not even the preacher can extinguish. It's hard on Tabby, because it's his own father selling corpses to morticians and hospitals and medical schools, his own father collecting the churchgoers' money and taking it for himself. He's an abuser. He abuses his only son, he cheats his congregation, he beats up prostitutes. With your pal Grimes you try to protect these women. You spend time together in the gun shop of Grimes's parents, you learn about guns because you need to. You're threatened. You're alone. You want justice."

Dorothy paused for a breath. She loved this; she could tell she had it right. Tabby and Grimes were rapt.

"You go to the dump for gun practice. There's going to be a

confrontation. You're scared. It keeps you up nights. You want to defend the prostitutes. Poor, desperate women."

Dorothy hit her stride.

"The day comes. Tabby and Grimes. Two boys who want to do right. You come into the church to find Tabby's father hitting the prostitute Angelica. You know he's going to kill her and sell her body. You go to help her. There is a fight. It takes all your strength to overcome Benjamin, he attacks you, he wants to kill you too. He wants you dead, he's pistol-whipping his own son, he wants to murder his own son over a half-dead prostitute. You fight to save your lives, to save a woman. You don't mean to do any damage; but you have to defend yourselves. He goes down; he's hurt. And now you're scared. You know Benjamin will recover and come after you. You know he'll never let go of his scam. You're just two boys. What can you do?"

Dorothy looked at them so directly, with such admiration.

Tabby elbowed Grimes. "She knows so much," he said with relief.

"You can do the right thing with the life you have left. You go to the safe in the church and get the money Ben has stolen. You give a handful of cash to Angelica, you kiss her and tell her you love her. She's so grateful, she's in tears. But she knows you have to get away.

"You hit the road for northern California. It's there you give all the money away, every dollar of it. A carpenter down on his luck. A waitress working her way through school. A woman collecting for dying children. Lonely people. People working hard to restore the beautiful forests. A lumberjack hurt in a fall.

"It's what you can do: turn evil into good.

"But afraid. You know you'll be chased. And so you drive into the Sierra to hide yourselves."

Dorothy walked up and put her hand on Tabby's arm, on the bare skin where the muscles came from beneath the cutaway T-shirt. And she gave her other hand to Grimes. She looked at them each in turn, directly and sincerely.

"I've talked with Angelica. I've been to Eureka and Arcata and talked to everyone you gave money to. I know you two. You're heroes. I'm here to tell you that you don't have to be afraid. Station KICU in San Jose wants to tell your story. You're young, you stood up. We want to tell a story of heroes."

Dorothy's eyes were shining. She was so happy to find them. It was the break she'd been hoping for, these last many years. The real thing: a story the public needed to know, about someone who saw how tough it was these days for everybody; who refused to take the bullshit.

Later, headed off for sleep in their campsite, the thrilled Tabby said to Grimes:

"I knew it! I knew it! Fantastic! Didn't I tell you? Sooner or later the truth comes out. I knew we were like that! Just how she says. God, I just wish the girl I love could hear it. Black-haired beauty! Do you think she'll see me on television? Do you think? She's got to. That's how I'll find her, I know it. She'll come with me this time. She'll see I can rescue her."

"It's a love story," suggested Grimes.

Tabby went right on, "It's just like we hoped. Everybody will be able to see the truth. And besides that, you know we get to fuck that sweet-talking television babe. When's the last time she got to fuck a hero?"

With a clanking and a strain of the music inside all storms, with riff and scat-song and a last shining laughter as sunshine broke through the tumult of the storm—with these signs and good-byes the weather swept out of the back courtyard of the Blue Dream Cafe in Nevada City.

Nattie put her head through the courtyard door. "Dinner is served," she said with feeling.

And the Hurricane Troupe rose to go inside.

"This is *some* sabbatical," said Iz, elbowing her mother.

"How I love seeing people get educated," sighed Maria-Elena

the Daughter of the Moon. She was one of twelve daughters, all of whom had new moons for eyes. So she already knew all about coyote.

"Will our child fly through the sky as a baby? Or is it a learned skill?" Renato wanted to know.

"She'll just be an ordinary squalling baby," replied Maria-Elena.

"I resent that," said the baby from the womb.

The old woman and Muscovado Taine brought over to a long table a great cauldron of steamy circus-colored jambalaya, and a plate stacked full of steaming bammies.

"Excuse me while I put on the backround music required in all distinguished restaurants," said Musco. And soon reggae flared in the room.

Cookie stood to make her toast:

"To Death! I thought you were somethin', Death, but you ain't nothin'. You think that you can do anything 'bout the man I love, you think you can send him away from me, keep us apart. Well, I got somethin' to tell you: you ain't shit. You get attention, people ooh and aah, you ain't shit. You got people shakin' in their shoes, people cryin' and fallin' all over themselves to get out of your way, you ain't shit. You think you got a chance of keepin' my Juha away from me? You got no chance. I'm goin' to the coast to find my true love Juha. You got no way of changin' what we had, me and Juha together, goin' to face everythin' hand in hand. You got no way to stop me and Juha from workin' side by side. You just try, you just try, an' if you want to try, you come and find me, this is Cookie, here I am, an' I say you ain't shit."

Maria-Elena noticed a handsome man, who had been sitting in the corner of the cafe with a cappuccino, stand up and regard them all thoughtfully. He was, of course, instantly recognized by all as a Messenger from Death. Anyone marked by Death may have such a visitor, come to draw the mark deeper. When someone is to die, he is the one who starts the darkness. The Messenger noted Cookie's outburst, then with dignity walked out the door.

Our travelers, determined to keep their spirits up, breathed deep and got brazen.

"Maybe he just wanted some bammy," said Muscovado hopefully to his beloved Izzy.

"You *need* some fortification for these love-and-death sagas," said Iz.

"Let's get him back here," said Renato. "I'd like to paint the bastard."

"I'd like to see him myself," said the peacock. "I'll heckle him with the proverbs of God."

"Let me propose a toast," said Chiara, getting to her feet. "An instructional toast, before we get rolling towards the ocean."

"That's my mom," said Izzy, "always planning. A real professional dame."

Chiara went on briskly, for she had a sense of the work to come. "We need to look ahead. Fortunately, it's the only way we *can* look. It's as though we *have* died."

"That was quick," complained Musco. "So much rum, so little time."

"Shoot," threw in Ananda, "I was hoping to go on back to work and tell them all about my vacation. I'll say: a cruise, lots of organized social events, and cribbage at night." Ananda loved to gibe at Chiara, once her lover got started on a riff.

"So now we're ready," mused Cookie.

"Right!" said Chiara. "The lives we had before were rehearsals. It was a gas, it gave you fits, it may have been memorable, distinguished, rowdy, or even now and then one lalapalooza of a blowout: but it was a rehearsal. Now it's showtime."

"Yes, ma'am!" boomed Muscovado. "Yes, ma'am, I is born again!"

"Makes sense," said Renato. "Set aside one life, get on to something else. Why dillydally?"

"Happens to the moon every month," noted Maria-Elena.

"Remember, Death is still hanging around. He'll probably leave us notes, fer chrissakes," observed Cookie.

"Yikes!" said the peacock.

"In fact, he did leave a note," said Nattie as she looked at a fine piece of stationery handed to her by one of the waitresses. The paper had an elegant script. "It says: 'To the Hurricane Troupe: See you in Berkeley and Mendocino. Look sharp. Good luck. Once I start the darkness, it's up to you to stop it.' "

3

THERE WAS SILENCE in the cafe. Nattie looked at them all curiously. Izzy was staring at her wide-eyed. Ananda, having her own premonitions confirmed, looked a question at Chiara. There in the womb, Maria-Elena's baby stopped kicking and cavorting and pressed her ear against the side of the placenta. Even the peacock shut up. And sure enough, the coyote, who never missed anything, ambled in the door and sat down by the side of Iz, brushing her cheek against the soft brown arm of the girl.

Of course, Nattie treated this news from Death as the perfect setup; it was her chance to loosen them up and do her part to put this crew in a mood to move on and make do. "Anybody who's got a rendezvous with Death has got to have some stories to take straight into the fight," she said. "So just relax a minute, and I'll tell you

THE STORY OF GENESIS AT LAST; OR, WHAT A DADGUM MYSTERY IT IS GETTING FROM HERE TO THERE; OR, YET ONE MORE IRRESPONSIBLE SPECULATION ON THE RELATION OF BODY AND SOUL

"I begin," said Nattie, "with the origins of the world."
"I'm going to need another drink," said Cookie.

25

"Terrific. First the House of Great Waters, then the origin of the world. Pretty soon we'll move right along to hog farming and beer swilling," added Chiara hotly. She hated being threatened.

"Couldn't you have kept the old gal in the kitchen?" queried Izzy of her lover Muscovado Taine.

"I have never seen a chattier bunch. It's like having a goddam flock of magpies for dinner," razzed old Nattie. But she was heartened to see the Hurricane Troupe still had attitude.

"Is this going to be the *original* origins of the world?" asked Iz.

"Yep," said the woman. "It's a romance."

"Go for it," urged Iz.

"Our world came into existence because of a love affair. There was no one around in those distant days, no one at all. So there wouldn't seem much of a chance, really, to party. But there was always the hope that the only two living things would meet. And since these two really did get around, they did meet. You may already have guessed their names."

"Ken and Barbie," speculated Ananda.

"Not Eve and that stupid Adam!" protested Cookie.

"I've got it! Bob Marley and Emily Dickinson," offered Muscovado.

"Nope," said old Nattie. "Time and Space."

Everyone groaned.

"A real bodice-heaver of a tale, here," noted Iz.

"Rock 'em, sock 'em romance!" gibed Musco.

"It went like this: they met, they supped, they tippled, they bedded," said Nattie with satisfaction.

"Very touching," said Maria-Elena.

"And Space, now she was destined to be the mother of life, to give birth to all living things. Their offspring would roam all through the world, they would have like all children the qualities of both their parents. Question was, how were these lives to be put together? Easy. Everyone would have a part that was permanent, just like Space. And everyone would have a part subject to the movements of Time. And this is why all creatures have a soul and a body. Neat, huh?"

"The things that happen in bed!" exclaimed Muscovado.

"After they got all that figured out, things were just simple as food," the old woman went on. "The soul, partaking of the nature of space, became the dwelling place of the beauties of heaven and the earth. A rather obvious move—it just had to be: space contains all things, space is where time tells its stories, all together and one after another. And all these stories of time have an end."

"Don't remind me," said Cookie.

"Think of what a terrific deal this was for Time. Stories need a place to happen, they need coast and meadow and mountain, rivers and rain and all the things of this world, which is the message bearer of beauty. Now Space, the wife of Time, loved him so much! And she loved her sons and daughters, all the living creatures, cougars and black bear, parrot and porpoise, men and women. Just as she had given them life, so did she make sure that they had a place for their living—the wide-open spaces of the world. These are, of course, the same as the wide-open spaces of the soul."

"What I want to know is, why did I have to come to the Sierra Nevada to find this out?" asked Chiara. "I was at the university. We had a philosophy department. If you even say the word *soul* to them, they get chicken pox."

"It still doesn't quite add up," said Iz thoughtfully. "C'mon now. Give us more. So she makes sure all the things of earth, her dear ones, can live out the stories of their lives. But what about her? What are the stories she herself tells?"

"Oh, she's just got her one story. It includes all the others," said Nattie.

"What a lot of flimflam!" said Chiara.

"Bunkum!" said Renato.

"Hokum!" added Ananda.

"She's got to be right," said Cookie.

Everyone turned toward the cowgirl.

"And why so?" asked Izzy.

"Because she knows the one story that has no end," said Cookie.

"Which is?" asked Nattie, who knew that Cookie knew.

"A love story," said the cowgirl.

Dorothy Gallagher, crack young reporter for KICU television in San Jose, had led Tabby and Grimes to a specially beautiful meadow just up above the North Yuba. She needed footage. The tapes she had shot when she had found the two boys had been terrific: the dirt, the sweat, the muscular forms, their fear and wariness. And then their time afterward, their all building a campfire among the pines and their twilight conversation in the resinous air of the Sierra, and then under a night sky criss-crossed with candent meteor trails. She had been right about them. They loved that whore Angelica. Tabby's father—a monster.

In the meadow Tabby posed for the camera; for hours she shot tape while he flexed and posed and told his story. It was so good for the two boys: a woman who can recognize a hero. Angelica wasn't the only one.

Tabby had *known* this would happen.

Dorothy mounted the camera on a tripod and started it rolling. She checked herself: down jacket, crimson scarf, hair neat but not too neat—she was ready to go:

"And now, a special report from the field, exclusively for KICU—Our News Is *the* News!"

"We all remember the shocking revelations of corruption in a downtown San Jose church. A preacher stealing money from his congregation and spending it on prostitutes and drugs, a man who said he had been called to the Lord, dealing off bodies to morticians, medical schools, pig farmers: whoever made the highest bid. A man of the church practicing embezzlement, fraud, extortion, statutory rape.

"All of us in San Jose wanted to know—what happened to his son Tabby, missing with his friend Grimes? I traced these young men to the town of Arcata, in northern California, and from there I reported to you the incredible story of their giving money to the needy, the desperate; giving money to save the forests, to women working their way through school. But where did they go after that? These boys who took the ill-gotten gains of a corrupt preacher and turned them back to the people—where are they now?

"Just yesterday I found them, here in a meadow above Downieville, in the North Yuba Canyon. And they're ready to tell their story."

She showed off some shots of the boys—in clean shirts, nice and contoured so you could see how well built they were. Talking, working out, looking around the countryside. Their movements were natural and impressive, once the camera was rolling. They felt more secure; more real.

Tabby at the edge of a meadow, sitting on a tree, he was saying:

"I always knew I'd have to fight him. It was up to me to set things right. But he was my dad!" And here Tabby paused, he brooded, he looked off into the distance, he sighed. "He was my Dad and I loved him. I thought he was a man of the church; a humble man, a helper. There when it counted. And then I . . . I found out what he was really doing. And . . . and . . ."

"And what, Tabby? You can tell us. We're your friends," threw in Dorothy.

"I wanted to stand up. To count for something. I didn't mean to hurt my dad. I wanted to stop him from hurting anyone else. I wanted to be the one to . . . to save, to defend . . ."

Grimes stepped close to Tabby.

"It's about sticking together. It's about brotherly love," he said.

Dorothy let a little silence run; then:

"From a quiet meadow here in the Sierra Nevada, this is Dorothy Gallagher, reporting for KICU television."

The taping over, Dorothy turned to the boys. "That was terrific. Now let's shoot the alternative ending." She turned the camera on Grimes, who had moved over to stand by the side of one of their gun racks. Across the tops of a nearby row of old corral posts he had put targets: a plate, a picture of a fashion model from a magazine, a shirt on a stick, a dead raccoon he had scraped off the road.

Grimes looked into the camera.

"I think we *can* help," he said.

And he whirled and with a sweet little Beretta shot the plate off its post; he swept up an autoloader carbine and took out the model with a blast; with a Force 5 Thunderpistol he blew away the shirt and knocked down the carcass of the 'coon; then reaching into his belt, he took out four throwing knives and whipped them one-two-three-four into the end post.

Grimes stood silhouetted, peaceful, satisfied.

"Fantastic, fantastic," congratulated Dorothy. "I'll splice that scene in for some of the Christian cable channels. Maybe even some of the adventure channels will take it for late-night slots about crime-fighting. We have to keep track of what markets we're playing to. It's just the way news works these days."

Dorothy looked at them. The two boys couldn't have any idea how happy they had made her. They were *material*. She loved it. The workings of instinct that determine what matters to the public, the narcotic rush when a story falls into place, the rigorous and persuasive fitting together of facts—to exercise these fateful skills was her joy.

All storied out, that night in Nevada City, our lovers, moving with a delicious after-feast certainty, went to dance the dance they knew best.

Who is it who has in her blood not just movements of heart, but the suggestions of rum?

A lover with opal eyes, our Izzy, who turned with her Muscovado as though salt waves lifted them toward the sun, then slid them down a smooth bank of moving pleasures—they were never still, these two lovers. They had come into a cadence of seagoing tropical languors: they were lovers who called spiced winds to blow softly through their bones.

And what did he say, our Muscovado Taine, to his Izzy, who in the candlelight shone with their sweat?

He touched and kissed her and he whispered, "Look how you shine, my love. It is like the sunlight shining on the tropical seas. In the meadows of Jamaica watching that light so many years ago, I was loving you, Izzy. There across the sea spread the lotion of light I have now in my hands. There was the world and the warmth I wanted to bring you, my beauty. And now you shine with sweat, the light is in love with you, my beauty, my lover," and Muscovado Taine stove his hands into her hot black hair and kissed her and kissed her again, he kissed her eyes and lips, he ran his fingertips along the lines of her face as she watched him, all down her cherished skin, along her many-and-variously pleasured body he moved his hands, until he put his fingers gently into her nether lips, moving there as he watched the gold come and go in her opal eyes. He brought that hand to his own lips and took a taste of her, then in her mouth he put his fingers, and he said, "That is the musky sweetness you bear, my lover. You taste like flowers and blood and smoke and cinnamon. The taste of you so bright within me, my beauty, my lover—I have made your pleasures my homeland; and you are my shining one."

Izzy took his face in her hands and looked at him so long and wildly that he could feel the opal light playing over his skin.

The black hair of Maria-Elena the Daughter of the Moon was twisted around Renato, and she held him close. He could feel against his belly the wild, hard life of their baby.

And Maria-Elena said, "I knew the first time you talked about your painting that you would be my lover, making move in me the colors you hold in your hands.

"You paint so slowly. It is as though you can see a beauty in me. And you with your touches so long and sure, with your long, slow strokes you fuck my beauty into its full sure colors.

"You know now what I can do: our bed is full of moonlight, it is a radiance I give only to the man I love. I make that radiance from a brightness I bear from the moon, who is mother of my eyes. I make it from beauties I learned in my lunar way in my beloved desert. And you, I make it from you, I use your cum, so bright and savory, inside me it spreads and shines like moonlight concentrated. It is the thick white paint that contains all colors. Renato, my lover, my cocksure nightlong deep-brushing lover, how I love you, stay inside me, paint me with these pleasures, my lover, my lover."

And Renato was rocked by the surge of moonlight in their room; for Maria-Elena now gave forth her light with a newly fierce radiance—because her daughter, taking slowly on within her a divine form, now added her pure infant shining to the mature luminosity of her mother.

"Marry me by the side of the sea," said Renato.

Maria-Elena sat up and took him by the shoulders. "What makes you think I'm going to marry you?" she asked sharply.

Ananda and Chiara took to bed. Brushing up against them, passing her gray, soft fur along the bodies of both women, was Tupelo the cat. She purred, she rubbed her cheeks on them.

The two lovers understood the brightness of the past and the darkness of the future and so lay in the warm twilight of their lovemaking.

What is desire, and when is it beautiful?

When desire is the introduction to love, just as the body is the introduction to the soul; when two women hold each other in high-hearted deliverance; when the longing of women brings their lips to a temperature of musky readiness; when two women feed each other their names; when they taste each other so long and lovingly that it tastes like trust; when two women become learned in the tenor and cadence, the coasting and quickening of pleasure as it turns through the beloved face each of them touch into place.

When the arch of a back matches curve of river; turn of a thigh recalls to a lover the turn of music at midnight in a bar, the turn of the morning into the sun. When two women have to hold on tight because they don't know where they might go on high curves of a dangerous sweet speed; when after two hours they smell like gunpowder and honey . . .

Then they might have made a beginning to the promise of desire.

"Let's set up house together. Soon," whispered Ananda.

Cookie was in the local coffee shop with Nattie, who had been questioning her.

"But surely you have heard of the Music of the Spheres?" she asked.

"Well, yeah. Are they goin' to set up a bandstand or something?"

"What did you think of the Time and Space story?" asked the old woman.

"Well, I already knew all that. I jes' never put it that way."

The next day our high-hearted travelers set out from Nevada City, with the Great Basin of so many beloved deserts at their back, and at their back the Sierra in its ransacked, ragged beauties, the Sierra known to the desert but facing the sea.

Nattie and Antelope on the Moon were with them. The two of them surrounded Ananda and Chiara.

"You two have got some looking around to do," advised Nattie.

"We're good at it," shot back Ananda.

"Do you know what you're looking for?" inquired the Antelope.

Ananda and Chiara were silent.

"Then I guess you need Nattie's riddle," he observed.

And Nattie rang out:

> *This young woman calls with her music*
> *Children of the sky to her fingertip.*

Flowers and forests move with her beauty—
Do tall trees watch her? Does Nature see?

"Okay?" inquired the Antelope. "Is that clear enough now?"

"That's all we get to go on?" asked Chiara skeptically.

"You must find both of them. They need you; and you need them," said Nattie.

In the wagon and in the pickup they headed down Highway 49, away from Nevada City toward Auburn. Ananda and Chiara stayed in the pickup, with Renato and Maria-Elena in the back; Izzy, Cookie, and Muscovado Taine sat irresponsibly in the front seat of the wagon, which, with its ancient bullet holes and wonderful listing to starboard, looked like an automotive version of a pirate ship.

As they approached Interstate 80, they noticed the change in the air. They had grown used to the incandescence of the light in the valleys of the Great Basin, used to the Sierra canyons where mountain light plays like a child among marvels. All this began to change in the foothills around Auburn, and a little way down the interstate, when Sacramento became visible before them, the air took on a thick, cadaverous gray.

"There's been a nuclear war. We missed it," hypothesized Izzy.

"What the fuck is going on?" asked Cookie, who had never been out of Nevada before. "Is that smoke? Are they burning that city down?"

"It's just the air," said the worldly Muscovado Taine. "It means they're busy."

"How can they see what they're doing?" asked the pragmatic Cookie.

"Good question!" said Iz. "Maybe they don't want to see." She thought a minute. "Maybe they think it's romantic."

They all looked dubiously at the muck.

* * *

34

In the pickup, Ananda and Chiara looked at the skyline of Sacramento, holding like a septic tank its immense political power; and they began a long academic deliberation on whether to stop in the city. They weighed the pros and cons, they spun out this or that skein of reasoning, they judged their luck and assessed their fitness for such a stop. It went like this:

"Speed up, for chrissakes! Head for the coast! Don't even downshift! Pedal to the metal until we hit the Berkeley Hills!" cried Ananda in her lawyerly way.

And they zipped on, right into

The Story of the Two Men Who Hitchhike the Roads of History; or, How Junk Can Get Even More Interesting Than It Already Is

They recognized the first hitchhiker right away. He was rough, gnarly, singing. It was Homer.

The poet clambered in the pickup.

"I thought we left you in Downieville," said Chiara.

"Enough of the rural solemnities," said Homer acerbically. "It's been too long since I got to see hatred, greed, pride, death, mayhem. It's a stench I like. Give me Sacramento, Berkeley, San Francisco, Los Angeles. It's terrif! Corruption, political murder! Good men who do evil, gunfire in the streets! People like bags of skin stuffed with money! What narrative possibilities! Besides, the ice cream is better."

"How could a blind man see all this, anyway?" asked Ananda suspiciously, especially since Homer was gazing at her in so direct and appreciative a way. He had, in fact, in the enthusiasm of his speech, managed to stroke the back of Ananda's hand with an ancient but electric charm.

"I can see you very well, bright one!" said Homer. "Standing in the light, tall and golden, like a poplar in autumn, swaying with wind coming in from the country to praise you with its passage."

"You can see!"

"Of course I can! After a certain stage, you have complete

control over your senses. I become blind when I speak my verse, so as to concentrate on the shape and texture of sound, the parade and savory concealments of sound."

"And then . . . ?" said the fascinated Chiara.

"And then I take on sight again and go out to the world and witness. I am your witness, my dear women, and your servant. This is the way I love you, the way I've found that you'll have me. And even as you have given me, a lonely traveler, a ride, so would I honor any wish you have, should you but say what it is that I may do."

Ananda and Chiara looked at each other.

"We'll think about it. For now, how about if you just stop in for coffee now and then?" suggested Chiara.

"Done!" said Homer immediately.

"What do we do if we want to see you?" asked Ananda.

"Just wanting, in this case, is enough. In the meantime, take this and give it to Muscovado," said Homer, handing them an old but burnished knife. The knife had a metal handle encircled with gold bands, and the blade was sharp enough to make the air bleed. "It's something he'll need."

Ananda silently took the knife.

"And one more thing," said Homer. "Give this to Cookie, she'll have to figure out what to do with it." And he handed them an angular, battered piece of wood.

"We knew some junk dealers in Nevada, so we're used to weird objects," observed Ananda.

"These things are excellent examples of the junk in the world, for you have in your hands the knife of Achilles, and a piece of wood that was—well, that's a secret. That's for Cookie," said Homer with a grin. "Good luck to you! Be careful!" And with a wave he guided them to the side of the road, and when they slowed, he jumped out.

"And don't forget, it's lucky to pick up two hitchhikers in a row," he yelled as they were pulling away.

Not two miles down the road, a bearded man appeared with his thumb out and winked at them. Muscovado Taine, so as to make sure that Ananda and Chiara didn't get to have all the fun, pulled straight over. The man, carrying a dirty satchel, leapt right in.

"You look just like Saint Francis of Assisi," said Izzy.

"Thank you," replied the man. "I *am* Saint Francis of Assisi."

"I knew we were going to have fun in California," rejoined Iz delightedly.

"Many of my brothers and sisters in Jamaica spoke of seeing you," said Muscovado.

"I am often in Jamaica," Francis said. "I love to wear my hair in dreadlocks. I mean, all that time as that little lamb of a saint. In my dreads, I feel like the rest of the Rastas: the Lion of God."

"How is it we can sit four across in the wagon?" demanded Cookie.

"I take up only as much space as I want to," said Francis. "Everybody knows that."

"So what are you doing here?" asked Izzy. "Aren't there some required fireworks and a whole lot of hoopla before the dead get their bodies back? Not to mention Armageddon, which was supposed to get everyone's attention."

Francis sighed. "All that is the horsepucky of mere doctrine. Monotheism, c'mon! It has rather too often been used as a pest extermination program. What were you all thinking?" Francis shook his head, then went on, "Have we got a surprise in store for you!"

"A return to paganism?" guessed Izzy.

"Not exactly. But I do chat about that with my friend Homer. We often hitchhike together."

"The blind and the bearded. I bet you have to stand in the rain a lot," cracked our Cookie.

"I like the rain. It washes our thoughts," replied Francis immediately.

"You think that the divine should be more widely available?" followed up our Iz.

"It always has been," noted the saint.

"Well, since you're here," said the opportunistic Izzy, "why don't you go ahead and tell us something about, say, the immortality of the soul?" Iz thought this information would be useful when she applied for college.

"It's easy," said Francis. "Only the soul is alive. Even a figwort knows that. Of course, some humans, less than figworts, think *they* are alive. What a joke. It's like a tree thinking, as the wind blows over it, that it's swinging its own branches."

"Moving right along . . ." insisted our Iz.

"As you live, the story of what you love is written on your soul. Everybody knows that, even a salamander. At death, the body is unwrapped and inside is a book of love. It is this the world reads; and by the story it finds there, the world then takes you deep inside itself, and you are granted the forms and range and life of what you have loved. Nothing more, nothing less."

"So what happened to you?" asked our brazen Izzy.

"Oh, me, I got lucky, because of my lover—"

"Your lover!" exclaimed Izzy.

"Moving right along . . ." said Francis. "As I say, I got lucky. I can become anything; I mean, anything in the world. Singing birds, light on water, anything. Jesus, I once did a stint as a singer in a rhythm-and-blues band."

"No!" Even Muscovado Taine was astonished.

"Yep, you should go to Larry Blake's on Telegraph Avenue in Berkeley. We used to play in the basement."

"So how was your love lucky? And who is this woman?" asked the irrepressible Izzy.

"That's another story. But I'll be glad to tell you, if we could meet later in a bar in San Francisco. I like to be in my own city and just sit around and swap tales. I believe you all have experience in this field."

This seemed rather practical to Cookie. "How do we know you're Francis?"

"I happen to have my halo right here in the satchel." He reached in and withdrew a tarnished ring of light.

"How does it look?" Francis asked, putting it in place over his head and giving them a few profiles, a few beatific looks, and some rather virile frontal shots.

"It becomes you," said Izzy, and with affection she gave him a kiss.

The saint looked at the opalescent girl, he breathed in the heat and spice of her hair and skin, he looked upon her amorous, lithe form—sinuous as wind on a warm spring night. There was a long silence in the front seat.

"I'm sure you've got work to do," said our Iz helpfully. "And I'm sure we will be seeing you again. Maybe at Larry Blake's."

"Right you are!" said the saint. "Let me off right here," and as they were pulling over, he said:

"Take this for now. You'll need it. Especially, Cookie will need it."

And he handed them his halo.

AND THAT IS how our traveling band came to head toward San Francisco Bay with the reckless air of those who carry the dagger of Achilles, the halo of Saint Francis, and from Homer a piece of wood heavy with secrets.

Maria-Elena was unmoved by all the commotion.

"Francis used to come through Gerlach all the time. He likes the desert, and Pyramid Lake, and he always looked a little bedraggled. You'd think, being immortal, he'd have a lot more time: but no, he's got to run with the sun and moon, spin the desert zephyrs, fill up the canyons with voices that speak in the syllables of light and shadow. I'm telling you the guy hardly has time for a margarita."

Renato shook his head. "I'm just a painter. How did I get thrown in with all you down-and-dirty metaphysical types?"

"Didn't you always think that the world within a painting is a real world?" asked his lover Maria-Elena.

"You bet."

"Sounds metaphysical to me."

"Are we going to live by the sea, you and me and our moon-eyed daughter?" he asked shyly.

But Maria-Elena was fed up with his presumption. She turned to him with all the force that comes naturally to a country-bred Daughter of the Moon. "What makes you think that you would make a husband to me? That you would be the father to keep pace with a daughter who has new moons for eyes? It is madness to think that because a man is a devoted lover, he will make a strong husband. Do you think that, by some magic, you will take on the tenderness of fatherhood? Do you think I would give my life and my baby into the care of a man who is merely a lover? It is not to be."

Maria-Elena turned away from Renato, and he was ashamed.

Coming over a rise, just where the Sacramento River flows into the Carquinez Straits, our vagabonds had their first look at San Francisco Bay. It curved around to the north, and then to the west. The wind lifted the water; the afternoon light did some sugar-dusting.

Cookie had out a map.

"Let's head for the Berkeley Hills, overlooking the whole Bay. I've got some orientation to do."

"No harm in seeing the stage before we go into action," said Muscovado.

At the end of Golden Gate Park in San Francisco, on the beach, a woman was singing. She had a clear, affectionate voice, and all others on the beach were silent, listening to her. It was as though the sky listened to her.

Tabby and Grimes and Dorothy were sitting in their Sierra meadow in the morning light. Tabby was full of energy.

"What's next, huh? What's next? I want to get to work. You know who we are. It's what we've been waiting for."

"Goodness is a force. When people see goodness and power working in unison, then they feel protected," mused the meditative Grimes.

Dorothy was wondering where she'd take this story. So far, it was too good to be true. But there had to be more action. If there was no action, there'd be no airtime.

"You got to understand," she said, "this is about markets. The kids from a tough background, facing up to abuse and pain and humiliation; two boys who decided to fight back—that's the story for the networks. The response has been incredible. Especially when you went on to give away all that money, what a stroke! You're humble and generous; but dangerous. It gives the public a frisson."

"A what?" asked Tabby.

"A sharp thrill."

"What about the guns? What about action?" demanded Grimes.

"We want the smallest touch of them, just the right proportion. I want everyone to cheer for you, to respect you; and to feel just a little bit afraid. When we get to making videos for military groups, or gun clubs and self-defense groups, maybe the police associations and evangelical militias, that's when you can really let fire. In the meantime, we've got to keep you on-screen; we've got to keep them feeding."

"How about Berkeley?" asked Tabby.

In the Berkeley Hills, atop Grizzly Peak, in the late afternoon, the Hurricane Troupe watched the fog with stealthy acrobatics come in through the Golden Gate.

Cookie checked it out. "I've heard of fog but never seen it. Looks like the fuzz under a duck's wing. Like the foam on a strong beer. Like smoke out and about for the night, jes' tryin' to find some fire."

"It reminds me of every woman I've ever loved," said Muscovado with sudden sadness and bitterness. Every one of the Hurricane Troupe was stunned. "The same thing happens every time," he explained. "I live with a woman, one day I wake up, and instead of the happiness of a morning with another chance to love her—I wake alone. It's as though they were made of mist and float off from my life. Always I have been strangely left. You, Iz, loved one—you of the sass and beauties. Don't do that to me."

There atop Grizzly Peak, there was a long silence.

"Well, it does kind of give me that misty feeling, Musco," said Izzy brightly.

But Muscovado, for once, didn't think Iz was so funny.

"The sun, the sea, the stars, all of them stay with us. But one lover, to stay with me, even one—that's too much to ask," said Muscovado miserably.

"Damned if I can understand why they go," opined Cookie, "not when you cook such a helluva jambalaya."

"Don't worry about it, Musco," said Izzy. "I wouldn't leave you except for one reason: because a sixteen-year-old girl couldn't stay with anyone, even Jesus, even if he was playing slide guitar late into the night at those little clubs with blue lights and sweet smoke."

Chiara shook her head. Was this a daughter, or what? And she chimed in:

"Muscovado! There's no liberty for a woman quite like leaving a man. It's good practice, this moving on. A woman should learn fidelity to love, so that she can come to love fidelity—don't you think?"

Muscovado looked at this professor, and then at the shining Izzy. Because of the low sun, her opalescent shadow simmered long and bright in the golden grass.

"To hear you talk, damn near everything is some kind of favor," he sighed.

"That's one of the proverbs of God, you big dummy," said the peacock in his irritating way. And he stalked around, whistling and shrieking. And as though this were some kind of obscure signal, Tupelo the cat went over to Muscovado, flopped down at his feet, and gave him a number of winsome looks. He knelt down to pet her. Winsome looks worked on Musco like gravity.

The coyote passed among all of them, putting her head in their hands, looking at them closely with her pale eyes.

The fog dove, tumbled, spun under the Golden Gate Bridge and advanced on the bay, and as it did, the sun, going low over the ocean, laid with its usual courtly manner a rose-and-ashes mantle upon the movement of the mist. The whole Hurricane Troupe watched the show, and as the darkness came on, the lights of San Francisco spread their pastels, the fog swung to shore along the East Bay and came with its colors up the hills, toward them.

All of them stood becalmed by that cool swirling, as the spiritous motions enveloped them. And who, in all those hills, did not that night feel, bone marrow to fingertip, what they felt? That is, which of us, where sea and land live together, is not astonished at our strange, condign, demanding good luck? Even Musco felt a little better.

They camped out on Grizzly Peak that night and so in the clear morning were able to see all the way across the Central Valley, where the sun rose over the watching Sierra; and then, turn and look into the Pacific Ocean, still in its white blankets.

In a dormitory on the campus of the University of California in Berkeley, a young woman was watching the lilac bush she kept on her balcony. She had been gone most of the summer, and the plant had gone mostly without water. Now, under her touch, it covered itself with fragrant blooms.

In a bar in the Haight-Ashbury district of San Francisco, near Golden Gate Park, Homer and Saint Francis talked late into the night about the Hurricane Troupe, the Lost Coast, and about the way people tell stories where love and hatred have to slow-dance.

The sun rose, the white layers were thrown off one by one, the naked Bay stretched its limbs. Muscovado and Izzy had run the pickup down the hill and come back with coffee for everyone, and they stood there with the hot brew.

They stood, our travelers, watching the Bay towns where their next adventures awaited them. California was looking just as happy and perilous and uncanny as Nevada.

It was time to debate their next move. As usual, Ananda and Chiara stood up and did their striding and flung around their ideas and bemusements.

"First of all," said Ananda incisively, "what are the facts?"

"Good question," approved Iz. "I've got no idea, except that I'm sure that Musco here will always waft allspice. Way to go, Musco!" And everyone applauded Musco's vapors.

"It's always good to have a list of facts," agreed Chiara.

"Oh, God," complained Iz, "you got a professor, you get a list."

"You damned book people," said Cookie gruffly. "If it ain't in order, it don't exist."

"Well, you're right: to hell with the facts. We've got a riddle to solve, but most of all"—Chiara had her biggest smile—"Ananda and I want to do the obvious thing: get pregnant, raise the children, and live happily ever after."

"What!" the entire Hurricane Troupe chorused. "You two! You want children? Now?"

"Why not?" asked Ananda. "We're having more than enough fun to go around." Everyone had to admit it was sound reasoning.

"These kids will think of me as an old fossil of a sibling," complained Izzy.

"You'll be a charming fossil," said Chiara, grinning, "a conservative, nurturing, mature older sister."

"Okay, so you two are looking around for the right father,"

noted Muscovado, who thought this news might cause riots among the men of Berkeley and San Francisco. "What are the rest of us going to do?" Musco, being a journalist, liked always to get the whole story.

"You all know why I'm here," said Cookie. "And it ain't jes' lovin' this roadtime we all have together, or lovin' all of you. It's that Antelope on the Moon, he was there when the soul of my Juha was taken up into the rocky hands of the North Yuba Canyon, he was there watchin'. He knowed the way Juha was taken to the Land of the Dead, an' he told me how to read the light on water, there on the river and now on the Bay, so as to follow the way my Juha went. An' now here I am, and I know that somewhere near, along the coast or out on the water, the Land of the Dead touches the earth. An' that's the place I have to find. I have to find it. I'm not leavin' my Juha, not ever. I'm lovin' my Juha, I am lovin' him. What is this dyin' business, any-way? Does it mean we have to give up? I ain't givin' nothin' up. If lovin' cain't undo dyin', then what happens to our days? What about all our days together, rambling around and listenin' to the stories of the high-hearted, strange-livin', far-seein' bunch we've found: Antelope and the Indians and the angels and the rest of them, our friends, our friends, we're lovin' along with them, ain't we? What about all our days? I ain't givin' up Juha. The story of me and Juha is not done. I figure mebbe the Land of the Dead needs to see jes' what kinda fierce lovin' a cowgirl can do."

Everybody was quiet, thinking how they might help Cookie, thinking that she was taking on an impossible task. As though things weren't strange enough.

"Well," observed Renato, "this is easy work. So far we've got two women planning a family and solving a riddle; and a cow-girl going to bring her husband back from the dead." Renato looked at his lover Maria-Elena, mother of his child.

"What about you, Renato?" asked Maria-Elena.

"I'm going to learn about light. Even simpler!"

"Light?" said everyone quizzically.

"This whole bunch has gone loco," observed Muscovado Taine.

"Why can't you do somethin' practical, like teaching horses to fart?" Cookie wanted to know.

"I've got to learn. It's my only hope. This woman I want for my wife, a Daughter of the Moon, is full of hidden light. Our little girl, she also carries the radiance. I want to learn about light, so then to offer myself as a husband to Maria-Elena," Renato reasoned, rather desperately, some thought.

"So how are you going to do that, crazy man?" asked Izzy.

"Well, there's supposed to be a university down there in Berkeley. I'll start there."

Maria-Elena was shaking her head.

But Renato was not done: "And then I'll need to show her what I've learned and all I want for our daughter, and so I . . . I'll do something, I don't know what, but some painting, so true that my lover will come to me. She'll want me to stay. She'll know for sure."

Maria-Elena walked off by herself.

"Go for it, Renato," urged Chiara. "Anything's possible in Berkeley." All of them looked at Renato; he stood with crazy hope.

Chiara turned to Musco and her beloved daughter, Izzy. "So what about you two?" she asked, knowing the answer.

"I'm going to go right on courting this wise young wild fragrant beauty," confirmed Musco.

"Nah, I think you've used up all your courtship routines. Maybe even your allspice smell is going to give out. You'll start to smell like a plastic factory, or something," teased Izzy.

And her lover replied evenly, "The rambling around and reading, the animals and saints and poets, the way your eyes turn gold in your pleasures—all we have done is just the beginning of the beginning of the foreplay of my courtship."

Everybody gave low whistles.

They were ready to roll.

Chiara put into Cookie's hands the piece of wood that Homer said was meant for her. And then Izzy gave her, just to complete things, the halo of Saint Francis. No one could say the cowgirl didn't have any gear.

"What am I supposed to do with these?" she demanded.

"That's what you're supposed to figure out," said Chiara.

And then she handed Muscovado the knife of Achilles. He took it wordlessly.

Station KICU, from San Jose, California—Our News Is *the* News:

"And that's sports, way to go, Nate, so what if we've got only losers to report tonight, huh?"

"To close our newscast tonight, we want to return to the Sierra Nevada to take up again the story of Tabby and Grimes, the abused boys who have generated so much public comment.

"As we reported last night, these two teenagers had been forced to flee San Jose, after being assaulted by a preacher now charged with embezzlement, extortion, fraud, and statutory rape. The preacher's son, Tabby, and school friend Grimes took some of the ill-got gains and in northern California gave them to people that needed help.

"Something here has struck a chord with all of us, tired of crime and greed, discouraged by violence.

"We've assigned our reporter Dorothy Gallagher, who tracked the young men to a mountain meadow near Downieville, to stay with them and tell us their incredible story: their new strength, their hopes and dreams.

"It turns out that Tabby and Grimes have plans. Dorothy, what do you have for us tonight?"

And Dorothy stepped forward in her khakis and flannel shirt with a kerchief. She was wearing boots, and her hair, usually bound up for the newscasts, now hung loosely along her face. She wanted to convey a more serious, rugged mood. This was rough country. The story was here; she would get as rough as she needed to.

"Kitty, I've stayed up here in the Sierra interviewing these two boys, who are lucky just to be alive. This morning I asked them what they wanted to do now, and this is what they told me."

Tabby comes onto the screen, in a string T-shirt, hair trimmed. "Well, ma'am, me and Grimes have been thinking. Let me tell you about our dream. We've tried"—Tabby hangs his head— "we've tried to do good, as much as we could. That's how we want to live. As soldiers for goodness. We know what has to be done. I know what evil is." Tabby bites his lip. "No one should have to suffer like we did."

Grimes comes on camera. He's at the edge of the meadow, by the side of a big ponderosa pine. "We're going to start over. Everybody knows how bad it is; how beaten down we all are. But a beating can make a man tougher. It can make him understand what the world is like. I guess you could say we've been in training all our lives."

Tabby steps up again. "We're coming down from the mountains and into the valley. If you need protection, we can help. I'll be . . . be"—Tabby breaks down a little—"the volunteer who stands for trust. The man you can turn to when you're afraid. The man you can count on. Around us, nobody will get away with anything. I'll be the son who came home cleansed. Came home to bring my father's church, cleansed, back to life."

Grimes comes on camera. "We have to band together; no more being helpless. No more being alone and getting hit again and again. Beaten down. Held in contempt. We have a dream of strong men in a good church. Men who keep promises. Fierce men who don't let women get hurt. Ever."

Tabby looks at Dorothy, who steps before the camera. "From the Sierra Nevada, this is Dorothy Gallagher, for station KICU."

Early the next morning, the Downieville sheriff, having heard all the brouhaha about Tabby and Grimes, came up to question the two about the murder of Juha. He had put it together after hearing that the truck the townsfolk remembered Juha driving had been seen with two boys in the cab.

Dorothy had already left for town when Tabby and Grimes saw

the sheriff coming laboriously across the meadow in his uniform. Both of the boys could see the shiny badge.

"Finally," said Tabby with relief, "some reinforcements. He must have heard our story from Dorothy, and he's coming as a show of respect."

Riding along the Grizzly Peak Road, along the ridge of the Berkeley Hills, the Hurricane Troupe hit the road leading down into the back of the UC Berkeley campus. And not too far down along the jigs and curves, beguiled by the midday glittering and lapis proclamations of San Francisco Bay, they really thought they should get out of the cars and do some theater. How long had it been? Were they not the Hurricane Troupe? They had to keep in practice.

"Go for it," urged the peacock. "I'll let fly with some more ding-danged proverbs of God."

"I could go for a little entertainment myself," piped up the coyote. "I mean, c'mon. You go all over Nevada, meet the wild ones. You learn ax-throwing. With Nattie you're allowed to go dance for dance with space and time. You zigzag down the road with Homer and Saint Francis, and you get to the Bay and what do you do? Camp out like a goddamned pack of Eagle Scouts. Did you intend to saunter around and say gee whiz for all eternity? Or what?" Such was the comment of the coyote.

"Who asked you?" Cookie wanted to know.

"You had the air of inquiry," said the coyote.

Cookie promptly pulled over into the parking lot of the Berkeley Botanical Garden. She rolled down the window and asked a student going by, "Is there a theater around here? We've got a show to put on."

"Right across the street." The student pointed. "There's a little one in the redwoods."

They parked and walked over.

It was a small amphitheater in the grove. The big redwoods

winnowed the light, so that only the finest bright particles illuminated the stage. The silence flowed evenly over the theater and eddied in the shadows. There was a rough odor of dust, mint, and resin. The big trees seemed bemused and attentive.

"Well, now, I think it will be just dandy. Open air. And plenty of room for everybody to spit, in case we got any deep hackers in the audience." So did Cookie pass judgment. "But what are we going to put on? What's the goddam script?"

There was a long silence: a band of travelers plunged head-first in the pool of their own bafflement.

"Yep, this is inspiration at work all right. Why, I can just hear ideas going off like firecrackers," gibed the coyote.

"Firecrackers in a cesspool," added the peacock.

Chiara turned on them. "Now we've had about enough of your cracks. Here we've just pulled in and you two expect us to hit the stage and start spewing lines!"

"Yeah!" chimed in Cookie, who loved to cut loose with a good snarler. "And I got to go to the Land of the Dead, and if you think in the meantime I'm goin' to slave day and night on some theater chain gang, then you're a cackle-brained fool. Listen, coyote, can't you go off and hump a pet somewhere and leave us alone for a while? And as for you, peacock, I'm about ready to make a hat outa you."

"Goddam hothead cowgirl! Who could not love you?" commented the coyote.

Cookie barked at her.

"Well, there's a better idea, anyway," said Izzy brightly.

They all turned to the lustrous Iz.

"We've found the theater. But where's the party?" she asked sagely.

Just then a student ambled by. They fell on him like a pack of wolves.

"Wait a minute! Just a minute!" he cried. "The party's on Telegraph Avenue. Everybody knows that."

And they all bolted for the pickup and wagon.

5

the Hurricane Troupe with relief and gratitude strode into the crowd. The street was blocked to traffic and filled with the booths of the Berkeley shopkeepers. Cookie was accosted by a young man who offered a "turning of the tarot cards that give a picture, I mean just as good as a god-dam video, of the future."

"Thanks," Cookie told him, "I already know my future. And what's a video, anyway?"

The carnival of commerce closed around them. Crystals were displayed that would cause the gremlin that we all hold hidden, the veritable child within, to leap out, dart into the kitchen, eat a cookie and make a mess. One stand sold bumper stickers with slogans to support the reduction of the oppressive four seasons to a harmonious and dialectical three. Another, rival campaign proposed to establish by fiat that the seven-day week had, in fact, eight days, and then credit the extras to everyone's account, so as to increase the human life span and delight the body politic. There were herbal creams for sale that, rubbed lovingly into the temples, had, according to the testimonials displayed right there in the booth, transformed the lives of three people: a funda-mentalist Christian, roly-poly with bigotry, had become a jazz saxophonist; a statistician, with terrible insomniac anxieties that the world was by two or three standard deviations seriously off trend, had gone off to bet the horses and make a fortune; and an aged accountant whose debits had irretrievably lost track of his credits, had become a family therapist—reveling in a realm where nothing added up anyhow.

The next booth was devoted to body piercing and tattoos. Could our bodies be wholly given over to our creative zest? Sure! Was not our skin the canvas that, punctured appropriately and slathered upon with colors, would once and for all free us from centuries of tyranny to our own body images? You betcha. Ears, nose, nipples, foreskin, buttock, even the Achilles tendon and the temporal lobe, they could all be pierced for the strategic placement of rings, bangles, sticks, feathers, or little flags of many nations. For a small extra charge one could walk away with a complete set of the stigmata and a beatific look.

"I think I get the idea," said Renato, "the rest of California is too serious. This show keeps the state in balance."

"No," corrected Maria-Elena, "the whole rest of the country is too serious."

A juggler walked up to them. "That's exactly right," he said, "and Berkeley is going to be here until everybody gets the joke."

They could buy hats festooned with the faces of characters from thirty-year-old comic books that nonetheless were bright as beacons in many a middle-aged memory. They could try on special jackets that, incredibly, had been pissed on by every member of the famous motorcycle gang the Shrinking Violets. The gang, when drained of fluids, roared off to Ensenada to get some beers and prepare a new line of products for market.

They could try on T-shirts that bore quantum-mechanical notations describing the creation of the universe. Another shirt had chemical formulas describing the mutation of DNA caused by watching television, in which the genes instruct the cells to turn the brain into a potato dumpling.

And was commerce to be stilled? No! For there were lurid paintings on black velvet that depicted secret Aztec narratives handed down by shamans from the time of Cortés to a spiritual elite who had a fancy handshake, communicated in pictographs, and smoked a big hookah.

The world was for sale. They could buy Aristotle and moon rocks and butterscotch sundaes, necklaces and aphrodisiac dust collected from the wings of tropical moths, rutabaga pies and blueprints of paradise, chocolate and key chains and photographs of the fourth dimension; trips to the Himalayas. They could even buy a walking tour of a Los Angeles suburb. Here the tourist trekked across a lawn to a tiny concrete porch, there to pet upon the head a member of an American Nuclear Family—a group recently featured in a grim pictorial in *National Geographic*.

They could buy chocolate handcuffs for use in the so-called "bondage of sugar," from a couple who sold a whole range of edible equipment, including two chastity belts made respectively of peanut brittle and of tofu-based cotton candy, so as to accommodate the aggressive toothy buyer as well as the dentally challenged; and these two products contrasted remarkably with the single-model rock-candy jockstrap.

The Hurricane Troupe was scattered from one end of Telegraph to the other. And what items had attracted our misfits?

Ananda and Chiara were walking hand in hand, each of them eating an ice cream cone.

Izzy had bought a blue-and-green headband that glittered in the sun and was still barely visible in the opalescence of her excitement.

Musco, in his courting mood, remembered the open-air Caribbean markets as he strode about with Izzy. Here was a market, this was a city, and cities take young lovers and cook them up for the delectation of the world and each other. They walked about bantering and considered joining a trip to Kashmir to a temple visited by the souls of women yet to be born, or a trip to the rain forests of Ecuador to ride jaguars of the imagination become material by means of a magic chant. Maybe they should move to Africa. Maybe they should learn a hundred languages. Maybe they should sail out under the Golden Gate and seek the spiced harbors meant for them.

Maybe they should discuss all this in bed.

"Iz, you know that wherever we go it's going to be like a brand-new gig. We can make up the tunes. What say we live in Berkeley for a couple of years, then maybe roll on south, Guadalajara maybe for a year. I've got a buddy there who could set us up with jobs in a restaurant he's got in the Plaza Remedios. We'll learn all the chilies in Mexico and serve up sauces boiled so long you find the recipes only in geology textbooks. Let's do it, look what happened in Gerlach, there are peppers there that raise the temperature of the soul, Iz! Let's go for it."

Izzy was standing in the hubbub of the street, just across from the flower stand in front of Cody's books.

"Come with me, Muscovado Taine," she said, taking him by the hand across the street to a stand where she bought blue and yellow flowers. She led him over to a table in a cafe, loosened the bouquets, and began to play with the flowers. She put some in her hair, she dropped some down Musco's shirt; they bought iced coffee with rich cream and she looked at her lover. In her ebony hair the yellow petals were like pieces of dawn light, the blue petals like lustrous cutouts of the sky at dusk, and with shining eyes and the certainty of a loved woman she looked again at her Muscovado Taine and said, "So where exactly would we go after Guadalajara?"

"Costa Rica, Iz, my Izzy. I've got some friends that set up a little inn on the Atlantic Coast. I know they would give us work there, we could tend bar, we could go around and fix things up, we could take people into the forest. My friends decided that they wanted to go where there are parrots, where the sound of the forest at night is sometimes like chamber music, sometimes like brass bands, sometimes like music made for a world yet to be created. And this is what the music of the rain forest says, Iz: 'All things are possible, this is the world, here is our chance'—come to Costa Rica with me, Iz, my love, that's the place for us, you are the one I love. We'll sweat rum; late in the day we'll watch the light off the sea; I want to see you there, Izzy, I want to love you there, I'll bring in flowers every morning and braid them into your hair, Iz, my love. Marry me, Izzy."

And Izzy put some flowers down his pants.

* * *

Maria-Elena, the pregnant Daughter of the Moon, and her lover Renato walked along Telegraph, ducking in here and there for a cool one, spinning along the street like two characters in a novel.

They fended off a man trying to sign them up for a class in pretzel-folding, and a woman who wanted their membership in the Goodness Society, a group of people dedicated to "the mass murder of the collectivity of social injustices in all their myriad institutional forms in this historical moment in the multidimensional evolution of being-in-time of society."

"Hard to resist," admitted Renato to the recruiter. But they moved on. And it was important they do so, for they were near to receiving an official request from their voluble unborn infant.

"I must say, with this pregnancy you are coming into your own," Renato said. "For instance, all I have to do is spin you in a circle"—which he did in his gentle painterly way—"and I see in your profile the movement from first crescent, then gradually to half, then so on to the gibbous moon. Two more months and you'll be full."

"I feel pretty full just as I am," said Maria-Elena.

"Don't be callin' for an early out," commented the infant from the womb. "I'm happy just where I am."

They both shook their heads.

"Besides, I plan to be born in extraordinary circumstances on the Lost Coast," continued the baby.

Izzy was still gazing at her many-petaled lover.

"Well, since we're making plans," she said in a voice that laced Muscovado Taine's spine with cinnamon, "I say this: if I want to live in Berkeley and Guadalajara and Costa Rica with you in my arms, then I must promise myself to you. And there is only one place in the world I might think about doing such a thing."

Musco waited.

"Lost Coast," she said. "A good place to give promises. And a good place to kiss someone good-bye. We need to get there before I'll know."

And she put another flower down his pants.

Renato said, "One more thing about this trip that's strange: so many men in love."

"Strange!" snorted Maria-Elena. "It's about fucking time."

"You scared us," said Tabby matter-of-factly.

"You really did," agreed Grimes.

"And we're tired of this kind of treatment. We just won't take it, the disrespect," added Tabby.

"You have no idea what a strain it is," said Grimes, "but we have tried to get people to understand. Didn't you want to be admired? Don't you know how much this hurts us?"

"This whole thing makes me feel really really sorry," observed Tabby. "Here we are, known to the whole television audience as protectors, as lifesavers, as defenders of women. We bring hope to the beaten down, the disappointed. We told you all this. It's the story everybody knows, the true story. The real one. And what do you do? What do you do? You try to arrest us! Pathetic!"

"How could you, after we said how we needed you?" asked Grimes. "We've worked with cops, been out on the beat with them, done favors for them, and now just like them we're people who count. Who can get the dirty job done. We thought you'd understand. We really wanted you to. The forces of love and protection need more power, everybody knows that. Everybody except you, I guess. It's such a pity."

"Really really sad," said Tabby.

"A bad mistake," agreed Grimes.

"This is a new world, a better world," mused Tabby.

"Now, when you make a mistake, you have to pay," explained Grimes.

"No waiting," said Tabby. "Actions have consequences. It's real justice. Somebody has to do it."

For the last three hours the sheriff had been staked out on the ground. He did not mind so much that he was naked to the midday sun and that the two boys had tied him to stakes, stretched so tautly that it felt as if his legs would snap apart at the knees, his arms burst from his shoulders. What he did mind was the big fire built between his spread-eagled legs and in that fire, heating as it was held in big iron tongs, his sheriff's badge. He minded his mouth filling with blood when Tabby had cut off the tip of his tongue and roasted it in the fire very happily as though at a family cookout. He minded the stinking imprints all over his body where in the past two hours the boys had pressed down the badge, scarlet from the fire, the star sighing into his flesh and held there until his blood simmered up around the edges of the metal.

It had been so slow to get started; the boys had been so reluctant, so admiring of him; and so incredulous he couldn't see his chance. The first few burns, Grimes had given up on it and gone off to puke. Tabby had pleaded with him, reminded him that nothing in this world was possible without brotherly love; and finally he had come back. And they both knew now that they had to follow through and be responsible.

Tabby withdrew the tongs from the flames.

"Hot enough, Grimes?"

Grimes cocked his head. "I would say not just yet. Too pink. It has to be the color of lipstick, that dark ruby lipstick. Just like Angelica's."

Tabby contemplated the problem. "I think you're right, lipstick is right. Hot kisses."

And he lowered the star back into the heat.

The sheriff, whose senses had been erased by the pain, woke up just then because he was suffocating on his own vomit. He turned his head and coughed and spit; he felt his burns like so many demon stars.

"Looky that. He's awake."

"The law awakes."

"He's doing his job."

"There when you need him."

"Always vigilant."

"Where the action is."

"Law of the land."

"Just think what he could have been. He could have been starting a new life."

"But no, he's dying in his own slobber."

"A sad story. Sad."

"A tragedy."

"He shouldn't have hurt our feelings. Can he still yelp?"

And Tabby took the bright red star and set it in the palm of the sheriff's hand, and they were both very distressed by the howling.

"That was only the palm of your hand!" yelled Tabby.

"This really is so distasteful," said Grimes. "Let's get it over with."

"We'll never do this again. We didn't even mean to, not at all. Do you understand?" Tabby looked longingly at the sheriff.

"We'll coordinate our efforts!" suggested Grimes. "While you give him a few more star marks, I'll watch his face, until he begs me to cut his throat like he did before—except this time *really* begs me. Besides, I want him to say that he sees how good we are. How we loved him and wanted to work with him. Everyone should have a last chance to see the truth."

"Let's get to work, old buddy."

It only took another ten minutes.

They wrapped the body, then carried him three hours through the pines and buried him on a ridgetop. They liked the view, and Grimes, because he felt so guilty and sad, even cut a cross into the chest of the corpse before they filled in the grave. So were their activities taking on more and more of a religious cast.

They washed in a stream and, dead tired, headed back to the camp, talking the whole way.

"There's just some way I don't feel . . . don't feel brave," said Tabby in a discouraged voice. "We've got to get people to understand that we only want them to feel safe."

Grimes was so weary. Just when Dorothy had showed up, and things were going the way they should, this happens. It just didn't seem heroic, somehow. "Let's not ever do that again. It's just not right."

"There has to be punishment. We both know that," pointed out Tabby.

"After this, when we have to punish, let's do it in public. Where everybody can see. Where we'll have some support. Where everyone can see that it's loving."

Tabby brightened at this, and in relief and gratitude put his hand out to Grimes. "It's a deal! In public only."

The next day, Dorothy Gallagher came back up the hill. She had been in Downieville posting a long article for the KICU *Sunday Afternoon Magazine*, talking with her station head, plotting strategy to keep the story going.

She adored the air up here. Growing up in San Francisco, college in Santa Clara, she hadn't much left the Bay Area. Though it was hard to stay neat, she loved this story. It was all an accident, her interviewing Angelica and finding out about the trafficking in corpses, the embezzlement, even the nice long blow the good pastor liked to get during his sermon. And now it had led her here. She even liked sweating as she climbed up the trail to the landing where Tabby and Grimes were waiting for her. The views up and down the canyon got better and better. It was as if the canyon were a choir and she was rising with its song.

The television reports she had filed had been a sensation in the Bay Area. She had been serving as an agent for Tabby and Grimes and Angelica and got a commission off any payment by the out-of-state newspapers and other media who wanted the story. She got a piece of all the interviews in northern California; the boys talked about the charities and community groups they had given money to.

Dorothy expected a bid from one of the national news shows. It was a story that had the heat it needed to go national.

Tabby and Grimes were waiting for her.

"I've called about the interviews in San Francisco," she said briskly. "We should head down the road in three days or so. In the meantime, I've got a job for you."

Tabby had his thumbs stuck in his belt. "Just let us know."

"The sheriff in town is missing. He told the deputy that he had an idea he wanted to check out, he didn't say what, something about that big lunk named Juha who was killed near Downieville. But the sheriff hasn't come back. The whole town's scared shitless. They think there's a murderer on the loose."

"Sounds like a job for us boys," said Grimes with a big smile. Redemption! he thought. They could get back in action, so everyone could see what they were really like.

Dorothy could see how excited they were, how ecstatically eager.

Cookie was stopped in front of a booth that sold tapes of the songs of humpback whales. Something held her there. Maybe it was the photographs of the Pacific, whose blue was the only thing she'd ever seen that looked as big as the high desert of the Great Basin. Maybe it was the songs that had to speak for the whole ocean.

It was the same with meadowlarks and coyotes in the Basin. Was the desert a sea? Cookie stood there for a long time looking at the pictures of the whales, and she would have walked off if the Miwok Indian sitting there had not said:

"Antelope on the Moon mentioned that you'd come by."

Cookie whirled around.

"He said you'd want to come down to the harbor with me, see

my sailboat, and talk to me about where a woman might go if she set out across the waters. Besides, I know a place to get some good salmon jerky." And the Miwok smiled.

Cookie looked him over: broad, tough face, big rough hands, balanced square build—as though he were carved into the air.

"And you've got some fancy goddam name, right?" asked Cookie.

"Gus," he said, extending his hand. "Ready?"

He led Cookie off through the crowd. And right there on Telegraph, in the middle of the crowd and following a stranger, in a city far from the Great Basin and the Sierra—even right there she could smell the mixed odors of sawdust, sweat, sage, and grass, of whiskey, pine, and sweet green river water, of wood varnish and soil: she could smell Juha.

Ananda and Chiara were at the beach, in twilight, and in a story-making mood.

They pitched ideas around, they set their ideas out in the air and played with them like cats.

They decanted ideas, then held them up to the light and examined their color.

They set their ideas out like so many facets, in hopes of fitting them all together into a jewel.

"But to hell with all these ideas," said Chiara. "We can do anything we want. Isn't there some inclination that you've always had, like an imp, that now can just jump out and take action?"

"Come to my embraces," suggested Ananda.

"Why on earth would you love me?" asked Chiara, who settled into Ananda's arms.

"It's in the nature of things."

And our Ananda bestowed numerous prolonged kisses upon the face and neck and lips of her lover. Then, their affection and their conversation being so easily united, she went on, "We have to be wise, my love; so much is at stake. We have to see if this is the time when we should think only of safeguarding each other." Ananda kissed Chiara some more, her temples and neck.

6 3

"This is a love we can live within, my sweet one. We could settle into the world together."

Chiara had, in Ananda's recent quietness, heard this coming. "Tell me everything you have thought," she said, brushing back with her hand Ananda's radiant blond hair. "This has been such a strange ride."

Ananda ran her fingers along Chiara's face. "I know that all the way back in Eureka when we all fell in together, we set out, come what may, for Lost Coast. But look at what *has* come! This loving of ours, Musco and Izzy cartwheeling together through the days, Renato and his lunar lover; Cookie . . . all our newfound storytellers. We need to count our blessings and guard this loving. We know so much now; we have each other now."

Chiara considered. "But everything started when we decided to set out for Lost Coast. What if we break the spell?"

"What if we're broken by the trip? I'm afraid of losing you."

"I'm not sure," said Chiara with her cheek against Ananda's, "that we can stop. Because we need to finish, even with the risk. Because we've learned this loving on the move. Because of Juha."

Ananda looked away. "You may be right. But if you're not, then we'll squander everything."

Chiara wanted suddenly to walk off by herself. Ananda was so troubled that they needed, she thought, to be apart for a little time, just so they could each have their thoughts run straight, rather than bent by the force field of their affection.

The light was fading but the waves were still bright.

"Why don't I walk up to the Conservatory," Chiara said, referring to the ornate glass greenhouse in the upper part of Golden Gate Park. "You can meet me there later on."

Ananda was glad for the time. "I will come to you." And Chiara, leaving her with a long embrace and seven kisses, went off into the twilight.

On a street corner in Oakland, a young woman named Laila was singing. She liked to sing there because the street ran to the west, and she could see the whole of the twilight in its beautiful deep

6 4

blue. Big clouds were bunched along the horizon. She sang, and just as she thought, after a time she saw a movement in the sky measured to her voice.

Ananda waited by the waves for a time, thinking and hoping. She didn't notice that around her the sky was going dark as a cave. Finally she stood up and went toward the park in search of her lover. And so began the events that would one day be told as

THE STORY OF HOW ANANDA AND CHIARA LEARNED THAT THEY LEAVE BRIGHT MARKS ON DARKNESS

Ananda knew the general direction, but she had not reckoned on the unlit rambling park, with its long sections of dark forest. And it was not long before she had fallen over a root and sprawled headlong among eucalyptus leaves that littered the damp soil. Astringent vapors from the leaves circulated around her. She had been sure that she could go right to Chiara. But right then in the darkness of Golden Gate Park, with her fingernails full of dirt from her fall, she felt unexpectedly desperate. The ominous asides and outright warnings of Nattie and Antelope on the Moon rose up in her memory.

Maybe the spell had been broken. All she could think of was the body of Juha by the side of North Yuba River, Juha fresh from the slaughter, a man so close to the world, and so at home with Cookie in their unsought rough perfect love. Why on earth— and who? She thought she knew the basics. Whoever murdered Juha, he had his reason, his way of life, his own complexities of deliberation. And the world that person lived in? It was a world she knew, purposeful, wonderful, inflammatory—a mix of sought-for, persuasive training, leading to achievements of violent happiness, by means of happy violence. It was a world Ananda recognized, that she had taken for granted in the days before she had left for Eureka. And now, in Golden Gate Park, at night, wanting to bring to her love affair with Chiara the light of another story, she thought for the first time in many months that the world of high emotion, of victories and miseries, of our striving and our measuring of ourselves against one another, was the only world that counted. It was the only world that would ever count.

Everything about this dark night confirmed it: her being so cold, the ocean wind clattering in the eucalyptus, their greasy leaves underfoot, the oily shadows that brushed by her, in which the only thing that distinguished one moment from another was the degree of darkness. There was a thrill of familiarity in it, as though some bedeviled and suppressed reality had come round, energetically, to claim her.

Ananda saw it now: she and Chiara were going to have to come to their senses and get back to work. She would go shouting through the park and find her lover; and they would get back to the business of living.

Ananda was sore and cold and, turning in the darkness of the trees, lost.

"All that may be true," said our Izzy, who stepped out of the shadows just at that moment, "except that you and Chiara, when you look for each other, leave bright marks on darkness." And Izzy gazed with amusement at her.

"That's a lot of nonsense," said Ananda intemperately, "and what are you doing here, anyway?"

"Musco and I were sporting around on Telegraph when the coyote came to find me. She led me over here," Izzy explained simply.

Ananda sighed. The last thing she needed right now was a timely appearance by the adventurous Izzy. Ananda looked at her. "I don't even know how to find my way to Chiara across this park."

"I'm here to help you. I can see where you want to go."

"You can see in the dark?" asked Ananda, her curiosity getting the better of her.

"You remember when, in the Nevada desert, the coyote took me off in a canyon and gave me the gold of her eyes? Because of that gold, I can see in the night."

"What good is such a thing, unless you're an owl, or you're rescuing a confused blonde?" said Ananda wearily.

Iz went to her fellow traveler and put her young arms around her. "Ananda! Let's find your lover."

Ananda took her hand and let herself be led by the girl. As they went, Izzy said, "I can not only see in the night, I can see the marks left by love on darkness: those bright marks."

"Is it kind of like those emergency flares everybody carries in their cars?" The winds off the sea chuffed through the trees.

"I didn't really understand it until Francis explained it to me and Musco over coffee on Telegraph Avenue. He said it was simple: love and light can become one another; this is why love makes us shine within. It's a light I can see." So Izzy patiently explained.

Ananda and Izzy would always remember the walk, Ananda for the irresistibly growing hopefulness, and Izzy because she never thought she would have such a happy chance: to lead to her mother through the darkness the woman her mother loved. Daughters, she thought, should be good for something.

They would stop whenever Izzy saw the sparkling in the air, the misting of light. They would stay there until Ananda could see it too. So it was that Ananda learned how Chiara, loving her so much, had, as she went her way, left a trail of light for her.

At the blackest part of the trees, Izzy stood aside, and Ananda walked straight on alone to take the bright-souled Chiara in her arms.

On the Berkeley campus, a young woman stood among some redwoods. When she moved her hand, the big trees, with a creaking of wood and rustle of branches, leaned to one side or the other.

Renato set up his easel on the Berkeley campus. It was the first of many canvases he would do of his pregnant lover.

"Do you have to paint me?" asked Maria-Elena.

"I'm just following the instructions of the child in your womb. At night when I have my head on you as you sleep, she whispers to me, 'How 'bout a few portraits, say, of Mom lounging around under the oaks?' "

"It's bad enough to have them yakking when they're toddlers," grumbled Maria-Elena.

"Sit there by the oak, and while I paint you, I want you to help me figure some things out."

"I will answer all your questions."

Renato kept painting. "Since you can see things that no one else can see—why could you not see that Juha was to be killed? Why didn't you warn us? He was building a cabin. He was in love. He was our Juha."

But Maria-Elena looked at Renato sadly and shook her head and said nothing.

6

SAN FRANCISCO BAY, a late-summer afternoon: salt breeze banking through the Golden Gate, canter of light along the water.

Cookie stood on the dock of Berkeley Harbor and looked out toward the Gate.

"Fussin' around on the water—it looks slippery and wet and messy to me," she said.

"If you can ride a horse, you can ride a boat," replied Gus with finality.

"Horses go on solid ground, like any smart animal."

"Going across solid ground, you can't get where you're goin', cowgirl. You need to learn to ride all over again."

"Let's go then. No use waiting one more goddam minute. If we're goin' to chew our gums, let's make it count. Where's your boat?"

Gus turned and headed toward the end of the dock.

"Ya know, Gus, it jes' goes to show: every time you mount up, anything can happen. One day, it's morning on a ranch in Eureka, and I'm climbing onto Juha. Now you're tellin' me there's another ride ahead, I got to watch the wind, and I ain't seen nothin' yet. Is that about the shape of things?"

Gus motioned ahead, and Cookie saw moored in the last berth a thirty-foot oak yawl with a Sitka-spruce mast. All the wood was varnished to the color of brandy. The brightwork of the boat joined its flashing to that of the blue and gray water.

The boat had arcs like the crescent moon, as though calling those curves out of the sky. . . .

"That's the shape of things," said Gus.

A professor of art on the faculty at UC Berkeley happened across the campus just as Renato was finishing up his portrait of Maria-Elena by the oak. The professor stopped and, swept up by the painter's devotional study of his lover, recognized that Renato was an old-fashioned sure-stroking genius.

"Would you come and lecture to my class this afternoon?" the professor wanted to know. Renato, of course, was ready to try anything at this point, on the theory that a man trying to court the mother of his child should explore every possible persuasion.

"Sure. On what?"

"On why anyone should bother to paint."

"No sweat, though I'd want to introduce a few related issues."

"What did you have in mind?"

"Oh, you know, light, color, marriage—the usual things."

The professor looked at Renato curiously. "Fine, come right along."

Renato was nervous. The problem was that, in teaching, a man became more visible to everyone. Would Maria-Elena see a man she could want as a husband? What chance did a painter from central Nevada have to convince a Daughter of the Moon of anything?

The professor walked Renato and Maria-Elena across campus to his class, a survey course with an enrollment of three hundred. This at first daunted Renato, since in his life he had generally not, excepting the dear ones of the Hurricane Troupe, talked to more than one person at a time. It was a lot easier for him to talk with a brush in his hands; or, best of all, with his beloved in his arms. This, however, was impractical with an audience of three hundred.

Maria-Elena and her baby found all this very funny.

"Okay, Renato, go! Educate them!"

"And speak up! So I can hear you in here!" demanded the baby.

"Where's the coyote when you really need her?" groused Renato.

But damned if he didn't notice some golden eyes near the back of the hall. Then the peacock strutted straight on into the classroom, brushing students with his tail and squawking at Renato. As if this animal accompaniment were not enough, at the head of the classroom, stretched out on the podium, he found Tupelo, gray and attentive. Tupelo looked inquiringly at him with her big yellow eyes.

Once behind the podium, he gave Tupelo a few pets, shushed the peacock, who was shrieking encouragement, and then looked out at all the undergraduates. They were like a herd of mustang in a valley—still and poised with their wilderness of energies. And he gave them a lecture on

PAINTING FROM THE HIDING PLACE OF LIGHT; OR, WHY THE WORLD HAS ITS CLOTHES ON

"You may wonder," began Renato, "at the strange title of my talk. But that is what a painter must do: give himself to air, there is a glittering in the middle of the air, the hiding place of light is there. You have to find it.

"So, how do you paint? As though in an embrace: there are only a limited number of ways you can move your arms.

"Let me explain by concentrating on two paintings, the first by Paul Cézanne, and the second by zany Douanier Rousseau. First, what to do about this Cézanne, anyway? Slide please!

"*Pommes et Biscuits*, 1880. Now it may be objected, they don't look like apples. It doesn't even look like a chest. But this painting, which is so beautiful it would make a coyote faint, is not about what the world looks like. It's about the world as it is.

7 1

"Let us look at it closely. The rough chalky reds, oranges, yellows; the blues and violets in the borders of the plate, in the wallpaper and the painted flower on the front of the chest, the discolored, uneven lines and surface of the chest and the dark, bent metal latch; pink and yellow cookies, even.

"Now, apples rot and plates break; chests decay and the gentle light streaming from the left of the painter will not be seen again. Yet through all change, all the losses, there is a blessing that the moments bear. It is to be found in the ordinary, the near, the everyday, the familiar. It is always present.

"It is the blessing found within what we see. It comes forth to meet a grace of vision and an amorous constancy of soul. This is the match that must be made; this world will marry souls only.

"And that is the marriage we see here: the apples take on rough full raw colors, we feel on our fingertips the chipped and faded varnish on the chest, the shining golden edge of the plate leads our eyes to its arc of light. The scene approaches us. What is this directness, this sensuous aggression? Why does this picture come for us so softly, yet with a movement so bold and sure and learned? Why do we want so much to give ourselves up to it? Why do we take on a mood of cherishing and luckiness?

"Because this is the world with her clothes off.

"Look at what Cézanne has painted: not the world we see. He painted, within this world, a paradise that desires us.

"This is what Cézanne, brush in hand, meant; a solitary, ignored old man, painting in the south of France. A man who worked with slow hopefulness and rough, unreserved dedications.

"He meant: love undresses the world."

Renato paused. The auditorium was silent, and in that silence as the students gazed upon the painting, he said a little prayer that the world in its own sweet time would come around to each of these young people.

Then he heard the voice of his unborn child: "Where does he *get* these ideas, anyway?"

But Maria-Elena, her mother, had been listening carefully

and thought that Renato wasn't such an idiot for a guy who didn't have any obvious celestial ancestors.

As for Renato, he decided to zip right along to Douanier Rousseau.

"Rousseau shows us another secret. Next slide please! Look at this ball game! What do we notice? Well, we don't notice much, because we have to grin. Then, the grin lengthens out into a smirk, the smirk turns to a smile, we move on to the chortle, the chuckles, the guffaw, until we boom out an old-fashioned belly laugh.

"Rousseau: the only modern painter who managed always to be funny. He was another eccentric, a custom inspector most of his life. He had a ritual: on cloudy mornings he would drink red wine; on clear mornings, white. He loved to lounge around, to saunter the streets. He could not live without a woman. He played a tiny violin and hysterically crooned popular songs. He loved courtship, rather more, we must admit, than many of the women he courted.

"He saw our world as a place of love and bemusement; and for this, he was thought to be a naïf.

"Look at those ballplayers! Look at those outfits! Their bodies twisted up like pastries, suspended in air as though they all were having antigravity fits, playing by their own rules, so serious. Having their game. Like most of us.

"They twist, they gambol, they know exactly their purposes. They have no idea how funny they really look.

"They have no relation that counts to anything else in the world. Just themselves in the tedium of their game. They are crazed and distorted by what they do.

"They are content, concentrated, equipped, committed. They know what they are doing. But it is knowledge that fixes them forever in their own intentions."

Renato paused. He liked this. The good thing about students is that some of them are still alive. It wasn't like talking to, say, a petrified forest.

He pointed at a student in the back row.

"What does it make you think of?"

"It makes me think of rap music."

"Fine! Then please improvise some lyrics about the artist."
And Renato thought how much Rousseau would like this.

"Sure!" she said, and she came up and joined Renato at the podium.

Another student, down in the front row, just happened to have his drum set with him. He quickly set up. Seating himself, he did a few beats, jangles, and runs.

"What's your name, anyway?" asked Renato of the female rapper.

"Jamalia Sweets," she replied with a smile.

"Go for it!" said Renato. And the drums sounded off, heavy on the bass to give her an underbeat. She let it go like this:

Sippin' on the red wine, sippin' on the white
Brushin' down the daylight, brushin' all night
He's a strong man strong man, and he's fuckin'
With our heads our heads an'
He been laughin' at Paris Paris—

Le DouaniER RousSEAU!
Le DouaniER RousSEAU!

Take him to the cafe, take him straight to bed,
He's foolish foolish, an' he's showin' us
Laughter laid back happy on canvas
Paintin' big jokes into the light—
Tease you all day tease you all night

Le DouaniER RousSEAU!
Le DouaniER RousSEAU!

Some of the students were dancing in the aisles. The drummer did a swoon and dive, there was clapping in rhythm, a number of students shouted out opening lines for the improvisation of new lyrics, there were students sketching and some taking notes, three couples headed out the door laughing and with the mellifluous step of the young going to strip one another.

I've got a goddam academic as the father of my child, thought Maria-Elena with alarm.

These are close quarters for dancing, thought her baby.

This is art history, thought Renato.

"Are we going to rap or are we going to nap?" asked Jamalia Sweets.

"If you could intone another stanza, please!" said Renato professorially.

Ananda and Chiara walked in, eating ice cream cones.

"What is going on? I thought I was the teacher in this group," said Chiara.

"We're all changing professions, remember?" reminded her lover.

> *He's stocky stocky, an' he brush you brush you*
> *Frontside backside brush you real slow*
> *Let's see which colors pretty filly you will show*
> *Laugh you into bed, fuck you till you glow*
>
> *Le DouaniER RousSEAU!*
> *Le DouaniER RousSEAU!*

"I find myself more interested in the progress of aesthetics in Western civilization," noted one student.

"It makes me think maybe I don't have to be a *zhlub*," commented another.

I'm getting lonely, thought Maria-Elena.

I've got a father who's a grandstander, sighed the baby.

Ananda and Chiara were eating each other's ice cream.

"That's enough, that's enough!" shouted the original stunned art prof. Though even he had forgotten himself for a moment and jived in the aisles.

> *Le DouaniER RousSEAU!*
> *Le DouaniER RousSEAU!*

Students streamed in from other classes. Somebody plugged in a guitar. A young girl in a yellow dress who had been selling ice cream out by Sather Gate wheeled her cart straight into the lecture hall, to the relief of the multitudes—the room was getting hot.

Renato rejoined Maria-Elena.

"How do you think it went? Did I strike the right balance between dignity and engagement?"

"Even I will admit it—he really *is* adorable," said the baby. "Way to go, Dad!"

Renato smiled a smile big as the crescent moon.

"Where did you come up with all that?" asked Maria-Elena.

"All that time painting out in the desert. On my breaks I used to hike to the top of a little hill and give lectures to the hawks and coyotes on different painters. I mean, I could belt it out. I would sing it out. I did feel somewhat crazed, but, hey, what's new? Anyway, animals, especially the burrowing owls, they used to line up. They were especially keen on Giotto."

Ananda and Chiara came up.

"So!" said Chiara. "A closet professor!"

"You'll turn out to have been practicing law in secret, I suppose," suggested Ananda.

"Not me," said Renato modestly, "though I did once have to be an expert witness in a case involving a barroom painting ruined by being continually spat upon by one patron."

"A masterpiece, no doubt."

"One of mine, actually."

Tabby and Grimes were fresh from sleep when Dorothy held the first of what she called get-smart conferences.

Dorothy had made sure their clothes were laundered, and now the lanky Tabby was stretched out in some pressed khakis and a tight T-shirt, with the stocky Grimes in some rugged corduroys and a flannel shirt. She checked them out, looking ahead to the Bay Area; she wanted to communicate toughness and style, command and ease.

"Look, this is the way I see it," Dorothy Gallagher was saying. "We have got to define you guys. I mean, the stuff with the whore and Tabby's dad, handing out all your blessed money, the camp you made here to hide, it's good enough for a start."

"Once you're a hero, it just doesn't go away. It's like a tattoo," protested Tabby.

"Not so. It's a fire. You've got to feed it stories."

"We understand fires," said Grimes.

"So what about this sheriff?" asked Tabby. His hands still ached from frying the uncomprehending officer of the law. But he and Grimes, even a day later, still felt sorry. They wanted to make up for it. A hero can make a mistake. But he finds a way to make it a triumph.

"He's just what we need. You've got to get involved. You're good in these mountains. I'm sure he's dead. His family is worried sick, the news of his disappearance has already hit the Sacramento papers. If you could do something, we could *build*. We've got to hit them again, keep it new. Build this fire higher."

Both Tabby and Grimes laughed out loud.

"We know what you mean!"

And they all exchanged high fives.

"And one more thing. We've got to do something about you, Grimes."

"What's the matter with me? What's the matter with me?" Grimes felt ashamed all of a sudden.

"You're not well enough defined as a character in this story. A sidekick, okay, somebody who's good with guns, we can use that for the specialty news markets. But you've got to have more general appeal. Tabby's the one with the ass-happy body-snatcher fundamentalist dad; you just don't measure up. Sorry, but that's the way it is. We've got to get your stock higher. You've got to bring more value to this deal."

"So what's the plan?" asked the chastened Grimes.

She looked at the roughcast boy. She loved this. She took out the books: *Words Are Muscles: Pump Up Your Vocab* and *Spit and Polish: How to Shine as a Speaker.*

"You study these books. I'll get you more. I want you to be the thoughtful one, the one who reads. The young man who wants a better life and is willing to work hard for it. I'll get you other books to have around for the interviews, you know, good self-development stuff—setting goals, using positive emotional energy, staying focused, visualizing success. Be an example to the young people all over the Bay Area, all over California, and then all over the nation."

Dorothy went to Grimes and took him by the shoulders. She felt the smooth sheets of muscles; she could see that he needed encouragement.

"Grimes, you can be the hero you always wanted to be. Do this for me."

She went to Tabby and held him the same way.

"Tabby, you're the man of action. Raw, dependable. You've faced the past and the pain, the abuse, the shame—and transcended it. You can't even sleep if you know there's someone out there to help. Even though you've given away every penny, even though you're in the Sierra far away from home, you want action. You have that contagious self-confidence. You can deliver."

Dorothy paused, looked directly at Tabby. "I need you to find that missing sheriff."

Tabby, full of emotion, looked at Grimes; then back at Dorothy. In a determined, passionate voice he said, "We'll get it done. You have my promise."

On the fire trails that lead out to the end of the bluffs in the Berkeley Hills, Laila, resident of Oakland with a singing voice now lusty, now soft, walked slowly. She watched the sunlight on the Bay, the fog under the Golden Gate. But most of all she watched the sky.

She was alone. Who would believe her, anyway?

Muscovado Taine and Izzy, right there on Telegraph Avenue, were not a pair to refuse the intoxications of possibility.

So they both went immediately to get jobs at Larry Blake's Rhythm and Blues Club. Iz lied her way into a bartending job— who could compete with a résumé that included the Jalisco Club in Gerlach, Nevada? And Musco landed a position as cook. The menu was soon adorned with dishes no one had ever heard of, such as saltfish and akee fruit, gungu soup, various goat curries that bubbled in their bowls like lava, jerked chicken that made the tongue curl like paper in a stove, and of course the famous jambalaya. With all of these preparations he would insist that the customer drink rum on ice with fresh lime. In fact, he often brought the drink himself and sat down and caroused with the diners, until someone yelled at him to get back to work.

Right there behind the grill, dreadlocks askew with his enthusiastic cooking, he crooned Caribbean dance tunes, digging songs, songs about pigs, crows, sisters, hopes, bammy, and the blue sea. He danced, he speculated aloud on the distinction between the fuck capriccioso, the reggae, the *maravilloso*, and the rococo. These speculations he incorporated into the flyers for the menu that described his specials:

GOAT CURRY: a Jamaican goat sautéed in butter and oils, and then along with the cooking juices let simmer in a sauce of curry that darkens to deep gold. Served with peppers green, red, and yellow, steaming rice. Butter-fried bammy on the side. A carnal meal. My best wishes for that old-fashioned tumbling among the stars that follows.

It was a job.

As for Iz: there were two bars at Larry Blake's, and she worked them both. The peacock loved the upstairs bar, and he would roister around and shriek when he was teased. The bar was tucked away on the mezzanine and was the gathering place for all the astrophysicists in the Bay Area. As for the downstairs bar, in the room where the music was, she regarded it as a kind of exotic one-room schoolhouse. For one thing, the astrophysicists, seeing her upstairs, followed her downstairs. They were joined by other professors, and poets and directors, savants, ornithologists and Sanskrit scholars. And there by shadows thick with the accumulated blues, in the parti-colored, velvety neon of the bar signs, the soft rose light from the backlit shelves of spirits—right there in the depths of Larry Blake's Izzy completed her high school education and started college. She made lists of books, got ideas on Dante and Hallaj, gained a sense of whether the hubbub about quantum mechanics was worthwhile; she considered becoming an astronomer, a carpenter, a linguist, a software engineer; a drummer, a particle physicist, a saxophonist; a butcher, a baker, a candlestick maker.

She was buoyed up, in any case, by her certainty that she was a pretty damned good bartender.

The professors would start showing up at the bar at around four in the afternoon; they would come and go for hours, ideas whizzing across the room. They decided that out of the whole series of 154 of Shakespeare's sonnets, maybe only two dozen were really *that* good; and that the invention of jazz marked one of those doors in history that we had to walk through to get to the future. They decided that Plato and Rumi were best taught together, as were sex and metaphysics.

"Have you been to the Jalisco Club?" asked Izzy suspiciously of the teacher who had proposed this last pairing.

"No, and where the hell is that, anyway?"

"I'd say midway between."

"And one more question: what is all this singsong about Douanier Rousseau? I mean, it's orgiastic."

"It's Renato."

"I heard his lecture. Is he the one with the pregnant wife?"

"That's him. She's going to give birth to the thirteenth Daughter of the Moon; all of them have new moons for eyes. They don't need electric lights at night. These women shine. It's terrif."

"Why is he doing all this lecturing?"

"He's courting the mother of his child."

"Oh, for heaven's sake—" began the teacher.

"That's right!" And Iz went off to serve a drink.

In Nevada City, lounging in the courtyard of the Blue Dream Cafe, Nattie and the old mechanic Antelope on the Moon knew that the whole story of their dear travelers was moving forward, gathering speed.

"I jes' didn't think I'd be worryin' so damned much about the lot of them," said Antelope on the Moon grumpily. "It's like we're parents, or somethin'."

"They're going to need more help," admitted Nattie.

"Well, until then, I'm goin' to get back to work. I'll be in the shop in Austin. Give me a call." And the Antelope shuffled out.

Nattie watched him go. She sighed and wondered why, when Tabby and Grimes came through Nevada City on their way to Berkeley, she couldn't just put them to sleep or something. But it would be like putting a whole country to sleep.

In the Smoke Creek Desert, Beulah stood in a canyon to the west of her ranch house. There were low clouds. Beulah, the mother of a lightning bolt, had come to watch her boy play along the rim-rock and in the wet meadows. He struck and struck again, and rock cracked and slid down canyon walls, and the water in the meadows turned to bright steam.

In Larry Blake's, Izzy was looking long into the coyote's eyes. What was this animal doing here? she wondered. And then she knew: meeting Homer and Saint Francis. They were bound to turn up here, Izzy reasoned. Homer would like the blues lyrics, and the saint would like to remember playing here in his salad days.

And sure enough, Izzy looked around and saw the two of them coming down the stairs; the one stocky with a boisterous walk, the other lithe and graceful.

"You're looking really rather judgmental today," gibed Iz at Francis.

And he winked at her.

"A pitcher of ale!" boomed Homer.

And, the pitcher in the big rough hand of the poet, the duo went off with the coyote to a dark table in the corner.

And before her stood Muscovado Taine: sweaty from standing over the grill, with a tropical lilt in his voice and a spicery of shadows in his eyes, he stood.

"I wonder if I might have your company tonight for a late-night bowl of goat curry and glass of rum on ice with some lime and nutmeg?" he asked.

"Muscovado, I never intended to love you so much. I mean, every bit of me. Even my hair loves you."

Cookie got it right away. Gus, of course, had expected no less, since he had gotten the lowdown on Cookie from the Paiutes and Shoshone in Nevada. So he knew that Cookie was the kind of cowgirl who could ride down a shooting star, if she was in the mood. And she was always in the mood.

They were out in the Bay, headed for the Golden Gate.

"Lessee, now if I've reckoned this up right—it is jes' like a horse. Boats are horses. You an' the boat, it's jes' like you got one body, so you can ride this crazy beast right on out wherever you damn well please."

They were going close-reached, the spray full on the deck and the blue water ahead throwing off light like firecrackers. Cookie had helped Gus haul up the mainsail, then set the foresail; the little yawl had picked up the wind and they rode west on the animate waters.

This was Cookie's kind of work. Always something to do with your hands, always time to do it in. They sailed around for hours, bucking on a close reach, going smooth with the wind abeam, then turning one more time and with the wind at their backs running before the swift breeze.

"Let's turn back toward the wind. We're headed out the Golden Gate," said Gus.

"We don't ever have to sail back to the harbor, do we now?"

"You're every bit the woman that Beulah said you are," said Gus, smiling. The winds dashed spray over them.

"Yep, I think I'd like to sail that big sea and find out where the wind and water are going. You got to teach me, Gus."

A dolphin surged out of the water at their bow.

THE HURRICANE TROUPE stayed in Berkeley and San Francisco for a while, even though the coastline was calling; even though along Lost Coast the gulls and the cormorants, the murres and the sandpipers, were wanting to see our travelers.

But were they to be lured away from their solemn and professional responsibilities in the big city? Not our bunch.

After their tumult of love, all of them wanted, just for a time, to stay put. For anyone can fall in love; it was staying in love, as a search for beauties to give away—this constancy, so much less studied and celebrated, they sought to make their daily practice.

After Iz got off bartending and the restaurant up above stopped serving, it was late and the band in the basement had got past their early simmering and came on to storm—it was then Musco and Izzy headed through the crowd toward the dance floor.

Music like the sea: sometimes running through them giving a sharp salt sting to the heart, sometimes like whitecaps rocking under them, sometimes falling over them, so that they had to dance drenched in a heaven of rhythm and blues.

Afterward they walked out onto Telegraph Avenue, into the

cool autumn fog. In the darkness the streetlights set halos in the air down the avenues as far as they could see. They walked together, Muscovado Taine and Isabella Boccaccio Acappella Mandragora Palmieri, lovers from the desert and the mountains, the spring and the summer; and now lovers in a city of their own.

Ananda and Chiara, having made several visits to colleagues in law firms and universities, firmed up some old contacts and partied their way to some new, now once again turned their attention to the beach. In San Francisco, they decided once again for the sands at the far end of Golden Gate Park.

Their close conversations about letting the others go on to Lost Coast could wait. They had a riddle to solve.

" 'Flowers and forests move with her beauty / Do tall trees watch her? Does Nature see?': I think that's the one we should take first. What's your guess?" fired off Ananda. These were two women who liked the taste of problems; it was all those years in the professional trenches. A couple dozen problems for breakfast, another couple for lunch, was about right.

"Maybe we should assign all the letters of the riddle a number, according to its place in the alphabet, and do a numerological analysis," said Chiara, laughing. She had once spent a summer decoding Arabic poems by this technique.

"My understanding," noted Ananda, "is that such an approach is suitable only with a Semitic language."

"Well, of course it is. So we have to take another tack. Now, what did old Nattie mean by 'move with her beauty.' I've got a sense there's some trick there. Especially because Nattie seems to hang around with that wily Antelope on the Moon. You just know they think they can put one over on us."

Ananda mused a minute. "Well, they've given us a line of poetry. What's the last thing you'd expect about so figurative a line?"

Chiara watched with affection her golden-haired lover. "You're the last thing I'd expect from the world, my lover," she said, throwing both their ideas off the track for a minute as she kissed Ananda into a fever.

After a pause to let the heat disperse, Chiara ventured, "The very last thing I'd expect from a line given us by Nattie and the Antelope, is that it be literally true."

Ananda looked hard at this outlandish idea. "If it were literally true, then trees would actually move. The beauties of the woman we are seeking would move them."

"That's totally crazy. Completely wacko. Out of bounds."

"I know. You can't help but like it."

Two dolphins, three, then four, were riding the bow wave, and Cookie and Gus glided on, watching the bolt and shine of the animals. It was late afternoon, and the light slanted through the Golden Gate, so that all the waves in the Bay were spools of light, their spray sewing the air with bright threads. Coming from the water the flesh of the dolphins was suited in light, and diving, they left on the surface of the water a tattered fabric of sparkling.

"Where are they taking us?" asked Cookie.

Gus pointed out through the Gate, but looking into the low sun she could not make anything out.

Gus kept pointing.

They had found the sheriff's body, the town was in an uproar, there were television crews from Sacramento. Tabby strode into the sheriff's office and looked around; everybody knew him because of the newscasts. But he was even bigger and stronger than he looked on the tube.

"Let's go find 'em!" he said.

The evening news that night carried shots of Tabby being made a deputy sheriff. He loved the uniform, the badge. But they gave him a little tyke of a gun, a little toy .38, the kind of thing a six-year-old would laugh at. It made Tabby mad.

                                *   *   *

Journalism, like any work, is not easy. Confronted always with
the obligation to give a clear, objective description of events, a
reporter, even a gifted one such as Dorothy Gallagher, can get
irritable. It was hot. She was sweating. She hadn't heard from
Tabby. Grimes kept stuttering and faltering. Her makeup was
running.

"Say that again, goddammit! This is serious. I want you to
practice! Do you think I'm spending my time up here on this story
so that you can lie around and fry your lazy ass in the sun? Say
it again!"

Dorothy was sitting on a chair in front of Grimes, who had just
stuttered his way through a little speech he had made up for her.

"Remember you've got to *look* smart! Get a new expression. It
looks as though if you opened your mouth, insects would fly out."

Didn't these kids realize the opportunity?

"I wanted to go with Tabby and find out who got that sheriff.
You should have let me go."

Dorothy knew she had to discipline him. She said quietly but
seriously, "Grimes, I got news for you. You follow my goddam instructions. And you know why? I made you. Want to be on television? Want to be rich? Want to be a hero? I'm your best shot.
Without me you got no chance. You can go back to San Jose and
be a thug."

Grimes looked at her, and he knew she was right. With discipline, you could get anything done. You had to make the sacrifice. If you learned from people, then you could leave them
behind.

"Now let's hear it!" Dorothy yelled.

Chiara and Ananda were in the geography department of the
University of California at Berkeley, looking over aerial maps of
the whole Bay Area.

"This is absolutely crazy," said Chiara. "I've never done anything so literal-minded in my whole life."

"It is ridiculous. But I think we're on to something. Besides, it's good to do some old-fashioned nitty-gritty practical work. I think we're going to surprise that old Nattie," said Ananda as she aligned a series of base maps and some overlays.

"You think we're going to find groves of trees that have changed position?"

"There's not that many places to check in the Bay Area. The list I've got so far is Golden Gate Park; Mount Tamalpais; Muir Woods; Tilden Park at the top of the Berkeley Hills; and the Santa Cruz Mountains on the Peninsula. I've got the base maps from five years ago—detailed layouts of the older trees, done for a biodiversity project by the forestry department here; and some recent shots of the same areas that I can overlay. It should be simple to align them and see if there's any significant change among the older groves."

Tabby was still mad when seven hours later he was walking the banks of the Downie River, just below where they had found the body of the sheriff, and came across two men who had just finished putting away their fishing gear. They were lounging around on the riverbank and smoking a joint. Both of them were packing pistols—they belonged to a gun club in Sacramento and had brought some targets with them in their truck, for when the fishing was slow. Both of them had knives in cases strapped to their belts. And one of them had a little silver cross on his lapel; his wife always put it on when he went fishing, for luck. Tabby couldn't help but remember the cross on the corpse of the dead sheriff. It made him furious. Who did they think they were?

Everything works out for the best, Tabby thought. And he had that rush: good luck again. It was fate—the killers turn up right in front of him. What a story! But it would take strategy. Maybe he could get them mad, and they'd show their true character. So many people are killers; they had to be identified and rooted out.

"I see those knives! I see them! Think you can cut my throat? Think you can get me too? C'mon, motherfuckers, goddam dope-smoking faggot killers! Did you think you can get away with another one? Creeps! You killed him and then fucked each other, didn't you? Goddam perverts! C'mon! I know it was you. I'm taking you in."

"And who the fuck do you think *you* are?" said the younger man, wide-eyed. He had an earring. "I mean, can't you go take a pill or something? Just leave us alone." And he turned to walk farther upstream.

Tabby drew the .38.

"You're both under arrest for the murder of the county sheriff. He had three kids, young kids, did you know that? Did you know that, motherfuckers? Or were you in a goddam dope haze? Goddam blind with dope? I'm taking you in."

Ananda and Chiara spent hours with the maps. The geography department had a beautiful old building on campus, with high ceilings and tall windows. The dusk set the light slanting across the room, sweeping the table with pale rose. Chiara had checked and rechecked quadrant after quadrant of forest, comparing the maps against the recent photos. Where there was a question, she had transparencies made, which she set over the maps. The aerial photography was so sharp; most of the images of the trees matched up exactly, save those spots where there had been some logging, or a landslide or wind damage. But not all. She checked a last time. Then she looked up at Ananda: "I can't believe it!"

Ananda had her own astonishments. "How many do you have?"

"Two."

"I've got three. Three places. She's at work."

*   *   *

Even Renato himself had forgotten just what a repertoire he had. All that time on hilltops talking to the coyotes and sagebrush had really tuned him up.

The show went on. Such was the popular enthusiasm for the painter's interpretations that, with some deft university politicking by Chiara, he was invited to give twelve lectures on campus, entitled "Art History: One Long Courtship of Light." He was paid handsomely, wined, dined, feted, plunged into a brawl of concepts over innumerable dinners; he was dismissed as a charlatan, hissed at by rival faculty members, who saw him as a threat to the law and order of the academy.

He covered Duccio and Simone Martini, Carpaccio and Giovanni Bellini, Titian and Delacroix; he tossed off Dürer and Vermeer, Fra Angelico and Matisse, Cézanne and Rembrandt.

As the lectures went on, the university had to keep moving the site to larger and larger halls, until finally he was speaking at Zellerbach, an auditorium reserved customarily for Nobel Prize winners and symphonies and Indonesian gamelan music with its sweaty rainbowed dancers.

The rappers always sat toward the front, and Renato always insisted that the food stands be let into the hall, so that his audiences could not only sing, stamp their feet, and generally whoop it up; they could snack.

Maria-Elena and the baby, who by this time spent hours chatting it up, were both amused to have a celebrity in the family. Various of the faculty members gave little parties for Renato, and she would sometimes go; but whereas Renato had a real taste for the long joke and so made his way through the brouhaha with aplomb, Maria-Elena sought other interlocutors. Especially, she sought water, which she had seen so little of in the Great Basin, and which is a substance of particular interest to the lunar among us. She followed University Avenue all the way to the Bay, in fact to the very harbor where Gus had taken Cookie for her first sail. And there our Daughter of the Moon from Gerlach waited for night. She waited for the arcing down of the moon into the Pacific, so as to be attentive to that flashing on the waters. And that is how she heard

"Maria-Elena my daughter! Ready to bear into this world the thirteenth Daughter of the Moon—the one we've been waiting for!" said the moon, a first crescent. First crescents are known to be especially eloquent and helpful.

"That's me all right," commented the baby.

"But *I'm* her mother. How many mothers can a girl have?" inquired Maria-Elena.

"I'm going to work it just the way I did with you and your sisters. You are the mother of the girl; I am the mother of her eyes," explained the moon.

"She will have new moons for eyes?"

"Just like her mother. It's the only way a woman can have eyes that are black, but hold a brightness. Very effective. What, do you think that Renato is wild about you only because of your witty repartee?"

"And my witty repartee?" inquired the baby.

"Now that's going a little far! Renato and I *conceived* you, remember? You weren't around for the romance. So don't be taking credit!" Thus Maria-Elena reprimanded her baby.

"Maybe I had foreknowledge," said the baby sulkily.

And the crescent moon said, "So tell me, Maria-Elena, my beloved, how I might help you, I who am the mother of your eyes."

"What can I do with this mad Renato? Still he pursues me; I cannot get him to understand."

"He must come to know that a woman with new moons for eyes is not wholly of earth. You know darkness, and a world beyond darkness. You can see what other men and women cannot see."

"Still he wants to marry me."

"Nothing more dangerous for the fully human."

"And for me?"

The moon paused and looked silently across the waters at her daughter. "Among all the Daughters of the Moon on earth, few have ever married. This is, my dear one, because they can marry once only: for this world and every other, once only. Is there such love in any man?"

"To hell with the whole business! Tell me a story." And Maria-Elena settled back with her hands upon the outlines of her child.

The moon murmured right on. "Once upon a time when destiny was better known, the light of the moon fell in love with water. It was natural that we should meet. We love longest those with whom we can best play. And such is the playfulness of light and water, that all other kinds of play are derived from it.

"The light of the moon and the waters of the earth fell in love, there for all to see, every night. And in the days when men and women could learn together, they understood that in our play there was a beauty they could bring to their own loves.

"But the wheel of fortune turned, as it must. Men and women drifted apart, as though heaven is not the home meant for us; not the place that we are meant, by how we live, to give away to one another."

"And they're lousy in the sack too," threw in Maria-Elena.

"What would you expect, with such ideas?" asked the moon in her rhetorical way.

"So what are you going to do about it?"

"No, no, no. What are *you* going to do about it? I am, as I believe you can see, busy."

"Well, what's wrong with just telling them the facts?"

"They'll think you're crazy as batshit."

"So let's just get back to this so-called time in the once upon a time," retorted Maria-Elena, "when everybody knew that moonlight and water were hot and heavy, and lovers of those days could look at light and water and understand it was loveplay. What was so special about people then? Huh?"

"They could read what was before them."

"This is sheer lunacy," said the baby, interrupting.

"You'd think this would be obvious, to read the world, rather than to stare out at it dumbstruck, like so many pork chops."

"In Gerlach, all of us used to go out and read the sunlight when it would lay down a mirage on the Black Rock desert," remembered Maria-Elena.

"This is the difference. Reading! You have to teach the ancient skill of reading the world, so others may learn what is meant by what they witness."

"So I'm a worker in a celestial elementary school."

"Exactly. It's a job."

"And then?"

The moon looked around the sky some, then turned back to her daughter. "I've got to talk fast now; remember I'm a first crescent tonight, and so I'm going to set before long. But if you make it to Lost Coast, set right to work. You will find students there. Take them down to the shore, I'll meet you there. Wild country is where they can learn. Teach them to read the pattern of the moonlight upon the water, the quicksilver statements. Teach them, for heaven's sake! The world we are given is a message bearer and a storyteller. And when the book of light is laid open upon the water, your students will have their chance to follow a treasure map of understanding across the earth.

"They must learn what is given them on trust. Teach them!"

And then the moon set.

Ananda and Chiara taped the maps together to make a composite of the whole area. They sat close and looked at the groves each of them had marked. There was no denying it—on Mount Tam, in the Muir Woods, in the Berkeley Hills, the Santa Cruz Mountains, in Golden Gate Park—in each place there was a grove of redwoods or eucalyptus whose trees in the last five years had taken up new positions. There was a harmony to it; it was as though the trees in each grove had taken steps in an elaborate dance.

"Where can we find her?" asked Chiara. "We can't go everywhere."

"There has to be a clue. One of the groves has to be her favorite."

Tabby had made the fishermen walk ahead of him the whole way. This was going to be easy, he thought. He could feel how his long legs, with their spindled muscles, supported him as he strode gracefully, following them with the gun. He thought, It has to be like ballet. Sure and stunning.

"You're going to be sorry for this," said the older man. "But it'll make a good story for my kids." He was confident. He had seen this kind of nut before out here in these little Sierra communities. This one looked a little more whacked-out than most, but he had worked with delinquents, and he knew how silly and incompetent they were.

"A moron like you shouldn't have kids," said Tabby. And he could see the older one starting to get a little mad.

It had taken some time, but the country was easy once you hit the trail alongside the river. Tabby waited until he was within sight of the town, just at the right spot—distant, but within range of the cameras, close enough so that with editing everyone would be able to see what had happened. He'd made sure they filmed him headed up the Downie.

Tabby struck his pose. He fired a shot in the air.

"Everyone is going to see how pathetic the two of you are. You shouldn't have looked so guilty, it was a dead giveaway."

"You're goddam crazy, mister, we ain't done nothing. Let's get to town and get this over with! You'll see you've got the wrong people." The elder fisherman, looking at Tabby, was in a rage now. What a stupid punk! All he had to do was pick the right moment to stand up to him. He'd bet that overmuscled kid couldn't even use the gun. He just needed some sense slapped into him.

"Just stay right where you are," said Tabby. "I'm going to

count to ten, and then if you're too scared to fight, if you're cowards, not even men at all, I'm going to blow both your faces in. Too bad, huh? You're too stupid to defend yourselves, aren't you? You're just two goddam faggot cowards, two pussies waiting to take the hit, mouths full of scum, you scum-fucking pig of a father, turns my guts just to look at you, smoking a lot of shit."

God, he loved this. It was just like the Republican Convention.

Both of the fishermen were red in the face. Tabby could see them getting ready to take a shot at him. Each of them had moved a hand slowly closer to his gun. Maybe they would both draw at once, wouldn't that be a kick?

The younger fisherman thought, Won't it be fun to pistol-whip this obnoxious prick? It can't happen too soon.

The father said under his breath, "I may have to pop him one. It'll bring him to his senses. Don't worry."

Tabby moved slowly toward them, counting, counting. "One! Even though you're killers, I love you. I really love you. And you shouldn't be sad, because this is going to make so many people happy. Really happy! You have no idea! Two! You won't be missed too long by your families, don't worry. Lots of people hate their families, but everybody loves justice. Three! After you're dead I'll feel bad, but I'll make it up by all the good I do. You can absolutely count on it. You've got to believe me. It's a vow. Four! At least this is death with dignity! You've got an important part in this story!" And then at "Five!" the father smiled and reached swiftly to his belt and drew his pistol and fired and Tabby took a bullet in the arm. Tabby watched the younger man taking his gun out clumsily. Pathetic! How did people get so rotten?

Tabby shot them both in the face, twice; but with sincere regret.

A hundred people from the town, all the camera crews, everyone suddenly was there. Tabby, even in his pain, helped them recover the bodies. People came to touch him. He stood tall and silent, very moved.

At twilight, Gus and Cookie were just out from beneath the Golden Gate Bridge when the sun touched a scarlet rim to the western water. That was when she saw the islands.

The dolphins dived and left them.

What is left on earth of a dead lover?

Around the silhouettes of rock the last of the light was rich and thick.

As the sky darkened, the islands seemed to rise off the water, to spread—as though the darkness called them into the sky.

Why did she smell sagebrush there on a wooden boat just at the edge of the Pacific Ocean?

The islands continued to rise, as though they were the night itself.

The salt of Juha, which she had licked off his shoulders, licked off his thighs—was it the same as the salt of the sea?

The sky and the sea went black, and there were only the cries of the birds.

Juha's baritone, which boomed and rumbled in his body as though it were a bass fiddle—did she hear those notes in the low resonance of the wind in the rigging?

The cries of the birds lit the night like flares.

Where to find the lover alive? And the lover dead?

"The Farallon Islands," said Gus.

"Those heaps o' rock stickin' out of the water?"

"More birds breeding there than anywhere in the North Pacific—cormorants, gulls, murres, I reckon a dozen others. There are sea lions, elephant seals; whales and dolphins cruise by—more life there on those islands than anywhere along the North Coast."

Cookie watched the black islands.

"Course, it's a disguise," Gus added.

Cookie turned toward him.

"It's just so lively there, no one would think right off that the Farallon Islands touch the Land of the Dead."

"Leave me here!" demanded Cookie immediately.

"The Land of the Dead will open to you only if you sail here by yourself," he said as he fell away from the wind and headed back toward the Gate. "You have to sail by yourself, in your own boat."

Cookie was in the stern, watching the Farallons.

"Juha!" she cried. "Juha!"

Ananda and Chiara sat so close together their hair mingled. The table lights of the library illumined the mix of blond and black. They bent their heads, looked at the dancing groves from every angle, tried to judge whether there was a pattern. The groves were roughly equidistant from each other, and so they considered them as points on the circumference of a circle and tried to find the center. It turned out to be in San Francisco Bay.

"Great. She's out there treading water," said Ananda resignedly. "We'll go out and sit there in a rowboat. Then, after baking in the sun and freezing in the fog, we'll come onshore and have to spend the rest of our days camping out, just to find this woman."

"What if it's not a circle?"

Up in the meadow Grimes was sweating and stuttering. But Dorothy thought he was coming along.

"There is no need for violence. But there is need for defense. We need to protect ourselves. We need people to take responsibility. If a man can protect himself, he can protect other people. It's what will save us—a dialectic of self-defense."

"Good! Repeat that!" commanded Dorothy.

"A dialectic of self-defense."

"Repeat!"

"A dialectic of self-defense!"

"Good. Try another one."

Grimes hemmed and coughed.

"Another one!"

Grimes looked at the notes Dorothy had written for him. "I've done enough."

"Just run through the words."

"Melancholy, sentient, kaleidoscopic, euphonious."

"Got those?"

"I've got 'em."

"Good. Then remember! Practice! When you've got them down, then we'll go to the next word list." Dorothy felt a little better. "That's enough for today. Let's go check on Tabby."

A waiter in Larry Blake's had given his loft to Muscovado and Izzy. It was down in the warehouse district toward the freeway. The waiter was spending his time in the Himalayas, counting yaks. Having this austere biological task made it imperative that he find someone to house-sit and, as it were, keep the home fires burning. In this case, of course, it was more of a conflagration; but so much the better.

It was just like the cabin they had had near Sierra City: as soon as they moved in, they put together a simple pattern—that is, they did the same thing every day. It was as though all over the world, each place had its template of love, and Muscovado and Izzy felt a moral responsibility to find that pattern.

The days began with a morning ritual. And the details? What might they do after their waking in one another's arms, the sheets redolent with sweat and allspice?

In the morning, every morning, Muscovado made good on a promise he had given to Izzy when wooing her way back in a barroom in Eureka. It went like this: when the eastern light banked through the high windows of the loft, slanting down onto their bed, Musco, who got up early, would watch Iz roll into the warmth of the light and stretch her way into wakefulness. After some minutes of private languors in which she pieced together her dreams, she would rise, and as she stood in her spare splendors, he would go to her, lead her over to a cushioned bench near the window, and sit her gently down in the middle of the morning light. Muscovado, stepping then around behind her, would move his easy hands into her rich hair and, holding softly the glossy strands, he would take the brush he had waiting on the windowsill and pass it slowly through those warm black shifting ribbons, stroking along her scalp, then all the way down that beautiful darkness to the last of its length in the small of her back. Over and over, from side to side, now and then gathering the dark currents in a big hand for a deep, slow stroke, again and again he ran the brush purring along the length of her back.

When over her skin her hair spread like some distillate of midnight, Muscovado would stop and caress her shoulders, kiss her neck. And then he would stave his hands again into that dark softness and separate out three thick strands; holding them, he'd brush once more. And then working easily, and with a little song, he put in a perfect braid, tying it off at the end with a little piece of blue cloth.

Then he would kiss her neck again.

Izzy, as we might imagine, was now awake.

They would pick out each other's clothes. This was easy, since they had so few. They would dress one another. Tucking in Muscovado's T-shirt was a task that Izzy performed with real care. Slipping on Izzy's silk shirt and buttoning it up with his smooth rhythms, Musco whispered his affections to her.

"I don't think they're really going to be able to match this at the beauty salon," observed Iz.

After such ministrations, they felt ready to go out for their coffees and then come home for their books. All morning they read and talked, and after lunch they went to bed; then over their books all afternoon they laughed and argued and teased. Later they went to work at Larry Blake's, Muscovado cooking and Iz bartending, and then their sweaty dancing until they sallied off into the cool fog.

It was so happy the end of that autumn that you could almost say it looked like a life.

Just at the moment, however, since this was their day off, they were invited for a drink in San Francisco with Homer and Saint Francis.

"What do they want with us?" Iz wondered.

"What do we want with them?" Musco wondered.

GUS THE MIWOK had sailed all the way back into the Bay, Cookie striding expertly now around the boat. She changed fore-sails, she reefed the main, she sailed up and anchored near Belvedere; and there he gave her the lowdown on the pumps and engine, a big marine diesel. He pointed out backup equipment and showed her how to use the sextant; he even pointed out the lead sheets he stowed below, for nailing over any breach in the hull.

"All this is easy as suckin' on plug," commented Cookie. "All you're doing is goin' on a long pack trip, where you stow as much of the ranch as you can on yer horse. There's jes' more room for stowin' here. Simple. I can handle everythin' on this damn thing. And so take me back in and let me get to searchin' for a boat of my own. I'm ready."

Gus looked her over skeptically. "Mebbe so. Mebbe not. You ain't settin' out to do no simple thing here."

"I'm goin' to sail to the Farallons tomorrow, that's what I'm goin' to do. I'm goin' to find me my boat and then I'm sailin' to the Farallons. Juha!"

"Only a handful of people know about the Land of the Dead.

And those that do, don't necessarily want to ramble straight out there; often as not, they just head in the other direction."

"Let's go."

"There's danger, even for a tough cowgirl. Sure you're ready?"

"Time to go."

"A woman could lose her only chance. You only get one damned chance."

"I'm ready to go."

"Think you could haul up that main?"

And when they were headed back toward Berkeley harbor, Gus said, "Of course, you can't sail to the Land of the Dead in just any boat."

"So why didn't you tell me before, asshole?"

"Don't be spittin' names at the guy who knows where you can find this partic'lar boat."

"You mean there's only one?"

"Only one. In the whole world."

"How do you know which one?"

"Well, it's the only one that's been there before."

"And you know where she is?"

Gus was silent for a while as they cruised in and tied up at the dock.

"Lemme put it this way: it reminds me of a very old story," he said.

Chiara had traced the five groves on a blank page; she filled in the lines and put it in front of Ananda. "It's a perfect pentagon."

Ananda looked at the figure. "How does that help us?"

All the way to town, Tabby had let the blood run down his arm; he wiped the arm across his face to paint himself with it. Some of the deputies and the townspeople stayed close to him.

Tabby ripped his shirt to make a compress for his arm wound. It left the shirt in tatters, but you could see the taut rib cage and the washboard abdominals. He stood tall, stopping as he walked, wincing with pain. He made sure that the cameras caught good profiles. He wiped his face again. Good definition there in the muscles of his forearm; gripping the torn shirt he could give them the roll and play of those strands.

The crowd watched him.

"It was them!" he cried out hoarsely. "I was bringing them in when they drew on me."

"I saw them shoot," said someone in the crowd.

"We all saw them!"

"You had to do what you did."

"Lucky they didn't get you!"

The bodies of the blasted fishermen had been dragged along the shore. The townspeople were outraged, they kicked and spit on them. Everyone had known the dead sheriff.

Tabby looked around at all of them. He could see the awe. All at once he felt how he wanted to take care of them all.

It put him in a manly rage.

"Dopers! They were dopers," he yelled in disgust.

"Drives them crazy!"

"Perverts."

From down by the bodies someone hollered, "Here's the drugs. The boy had his stash right in his pocket. They'd smoked most of it. Right in his pocket."

"Right in his pocket. Shit."

"Get those bodies to the undertaker before I puke," said one of the deputies.

Someone had brought a video camera.

"Now listen all of you!" said Tabby. "Listen up!"

Tabby's heart was beating fast, and he would remember these minutes as the time when life was perfect.

The sun shone on him. There were tears in his eyes. One of his big arms went across his body to hold the compress on his wound. His face was streaked with dust and blood. He felt the gun at his hip. The children in the crowd looked at him with fear and adoration.

"Listen to me. Now's the time for respect. These two addicts—we have to forgive." Tabby hung his head. "I forgive them for taking that shot. Now they go to God. But we're here together. Safe. Knowing your families are safe. Vowing to keep them safe. But we have to act! We have to get justice!" He spun and pointed and stared. "We have to get justice by the throat!"

He was quiet for a minute, trying to get his bearings.

"No more being afraid," he said quietly.

He looked at them all, in a circle around him. His eyes were wet.

"You can count on me!" he said huskily. He could see they believed in him. He loved these people.

Another silence.

"Let's get that wound of yours taken care of," said one of the deputies.

"Not yet," Tabby replied with determination. "I want to go to the family of the murdered sheriff. I want to pay my respects. I want them to know they're not alone. I want to hold in my arms that poor widow and tell her I did my best for her. Then we can find a doctor."

"I'll take you up there," said the deputy.

The crowd gathered closer, they were smiling. They touched him lightly and patted him and led him off.

For another hour Ananda and Chiara studied each of the groves. They both saw it at the same time: the westernmost grove, nearest the ocean, at the end of Golden Gate Park, had five big eucalyptus in the center of it; another perfect pentagon, this one reproducing in miniature the enormous figure that covered the whole Bay Area.

"Near the beach. We were right next to her," said Ananda.

"Let's go," said Chiara. "Let's go find her."
They strode from the library.

Dorothy and Grimes had come down out of the meadow just as Tabby went off to the widow. Dorothy went among the towns-people. As soon as she found out there was somebody with a video camera, she went and found the woman.

"Have you got the tape of the gunfire and of Tabby's speech?"

"It's right here," said the woman proudly, holding up the cam-era. "I just learned how to use one of these blinking things. He's so cute, that Tabby. I want to go right home and play it."

"Go right home and play it, that's sweet. Really sweet. But you should give that camera to a pro. I could shoot the rest of the day with it."

"It's mine!" protested the woman.

"For chrissakes just give me the fucking thing!" said Dorothy as she wrenched the camera out of the woman's hands, then brushed by her, going to look for Tabby.

Grimes lingered behind.

"Don't be melancholy," he said to the woman. "You're a part of history."

"Who the hell are you?"

"I'm Grimes." He put his foot up on a bench and spoke with confidence. "Working with my friend Tabby, I am seeking to break the dialectic of violence."

Dorothy found Tabby at the house of the sheriff's widow. The boy and the woman were sitting together at the kitchen table, and the woman was sobbing.

Dorothy looked him over—the torn shirt, the blood and dust, the soiled clothes. He looked exhausted and dedicated and happy. She could see the curve of chest, the abdominals.

"Perfect! Way to go!"

Tabby smiled at her.

The woman drew a sleeve across her face.

"Have you hugged her yet?" asked Dorothy.

Tabby looked at the woman. "Of course I have. I told her about the perverts that got her husband. And how they tried to get me. And I told her that justice is done. Isn't that right, now, ma'am?"

The woman nodded her tear-scarred face.

"Hug her again," said Dorothy. "I need the shot."

Tabby yanked the woman out of her chair.

It was a moonlit night. But even from the beach Ananda and Chiara could see the trees moving. As the two women approached, they saw a campfire in the middle of a clearing and, standing alone and close to the flames, a young woman. She lifted her arms, the trees bent and moved to her gestures. It was as though she were conducting them, as though the big trees could see her.

There was no sound but the moaning of the tree trunks, the clamor of leaves, and the soft, constant wrestling of the fire with the wood.

The woman turned to them. "What are you doing here?" she asked in the voice of one who had never been disturbed during her secret work.

"My dear woman," said Chiara, "we are here, I think, to tell you a story; and to hear yours."

Gus the Miwok and Cookie sat on the open land just on the north side of the Berkeley harbor. Cookie was so impatient she wanted to brand the slow-talking Gus. Gus, for his part, thought that she should have been able to figure out that about the last thing you want to do is rush a meeting with another world.

"So where's my boat?" said Cookie in her continuing subtle way.

"You have to find it yourself."

"Right, Gus. Like mebbe it's in my pocket or somethin'."

"It's as good a place as any to look," teased Gus.

Cookie, indignant, rummaged around in the capacious pocket of her windbreaker and withdrew from it the gnarly stick of wood that Chiara had given to her.

"Yep, looks like a real sleek-hulled racer here. Looks like it's been chewed on, whittled at, splintered down, and slathered over."

An old dog nosed around Cookie and sniffed at the wood.

"At least somebody's interested," observed Gus, looking at the mangy animal.

"You're not goin' to help me, are you, dipshit?" snarled Cookie.

"Just 'cause you're a desert-bred rock-solid capable bitch don't mean I can't just leave you to figure this story out all by yourself," observed Gus affably.

"Just 'cause you can sail a boat like somebody who's an old sidekick of the wind, and you know this coastline like maybe it was the body of your old-time wife, don't mean that I'm goin' to stand still whiles you dillydally. What are we doin'? I'm stuck here with a molasses ass. I've had it! Get out of here! Go ahead and leave! I'll find my boat on my own."

Gus gave her a long look, then stood up and walked slowly away. And she was alone by the Bay.

A silence from off the waters surrounded Cookie. And memories of Juha rose up within her. How could she seek him so outrageously? What did she have to go on? Nothing but the rightness of loving him; it was within life. That was the bedrock she knew; it was where she stood now.

Still, her Juha, built like a mountain. Not to have the taste and smell of that shy and boisterous man: every thought of him pressed on her like hot iron. He had given himself to her so innocently and completely. It was as though, unknown to himself, he had been waiting for years just to be a husband. Married, everything had made sense to him: in his work and laughter, his walk and play and hopes, Cookie was his rejoicing.

Her longing for him was with her constantly, an absence, a terrible error. It was as though nature had been corrupted: as though the earth were paper beneath her feet, and midday sunlight made her colder, and wind passed like coarse sand over her skin. It exhausted her.

She was used to being in company with her fellow travelers; now, alone, she hardly noticed her sobbing; nor did she notice how her tears fell on the rough piece of wood she held in her hands. The salt tears swelled the wood; there was a sudden shining along the shoreline, but she did not notice.

Cookie stood and walked toward the water. The dog that had come round earlier followed her, barking and barking.

"Maybe *he* can use this damned stick," she said in a low and hopeless voice, and she hurled it as far as she could into San Francisco Bay. It was a stick that had been waiting for three thousand years for such a throw from such a woman on such a mission.

The wood was the gift Cookie had received from Homer, and it was all that was left of the ship that Odysseus had sailed to the Land of the Dead.

As soon as it hit the water there was a rushing of air and light. As she watched, trying to keep her feet in the roaring of winds from an ancient world, there was a cracking and a moaning of wood and a shout as though from all the coastline, a shout that fell away to the whisper of centuries. She could hear a singing off the sea; the wood grew and set and shaped itself, with rough, irresistible power came forth and took form because it held within itself the high-hearted songs, the salt, the ease, the splendor of one of the oldest stories in the world.

Cookie saw her suddenly, settled into shapely lines, just offshore, the boat conjured for her: a strong-timbered dark-stained full-bodied beautiful ketch, anchored and silent on the black and silver water.

*   *   *

Her name was Festina, and she had hair like a rain of fire. Chiara and Ananda walked all of Golden Gate Park with her; now they were back at the sandy beach at the end of the park. They had heard from the quiet girl how flowers blossomed under her touch, no matter what the season. How trees somehow followed in her footsteps, if she wasn't looking. How in wild country deep in the Sierra Nevada when she moved her hand, the wind would rush through the pines on a ridgetop.

It was the end of the day. There was a comely and offbeat collection of people that every evening turned up at this very beach to cheer the sun as she got in bed with the sea.

The three women walked together along the shoreline, barefoot so that the sand could give their prints to the onrushing saltwater.

The women moved in delight at one another. The seasoned Ananda and Chiara had studied the strangely gifted Festina, they had questioned and marveled quietly—and now a kinship bound them smoothly together.

Ananda and Chiara were ready to give her the only gift they had.

As for Renato, his lecture series was coming to a tumultuous end, with a daylong improvisation on all the painters under study, gigs by a collective of twenty-seven bands, salsa and reggae, rap and jazz, R&B, plus a choir, and three tuxedoed groups playing chamber music, all accompanied by a food fair.

Ananda and Chiara had even come by one afternoon and put on an ax-throwing exhibition. This art, which Beulah had so brusquely and lovingly taught them out in the Smoke Creek Desert, wowed the peace-loving Berkeleyites and gave them a freshened sense of the possibilities out there for professional women.

Ananda even played some jazz for a spell, just to keep her trumpet warm.

Still, even with all the hoopla, Renato was desperate. Maria-Elena had taken him to bed the night before and told him even as she made love to him that the time in Berkeley was coming to an end. The time had come to leave him and go on to Lost Coast and have her baby. She told him she loved the joy in him; but she could not believe that it was a joy that led to the devotions of marriage. And even if it was, he was a man of one life, not like her, a woman with another way of living, who had a role beyond his vision, beyond his understanding; it would always be so. How could she describe the work of a Daughter of the Moon—the work of a woman who can read the lines of moonlight on the Pacific waters; who must teach her own daughter the working of the sky in the stories of the earth. She was a woman no man could ever possess fully. And no man, once he understood that, could want to marry her.

Renato had seen in her dark, shining eyes how serious she was. And so, his hopes at an end, he wanted at least to show her, with a painting, everything he wanted for her and their daughter. He wanted something no one else could ever paint, that no one could have expected: amusing, impious, outrageous. He had nothing, any longer, to lose.

But what would be his subject? To collect his thoughts, he went to Larry Blake's and had Izzy serve him up a certain concoction of light and dark rums, fruit juice, lime, cinnamon, and nutmeg, all let to sit and soak together in a big bottle: the drink was called the Mahatma Gandhi. And, having talked with the Mahatma, it came to Renato: a giant solemn religious mural. There were buildings all over campus that begged for a mural. But what subject?

He wanted a subject that was neglected, improbable, so that the painting would be not only the portrayal of beauty, but a discovery of beauty. What is it to have a daughter if not to live in continuous discovery of her beauties?

Renato thought of beloved Juha, who back in Nevada had brought sonorously to life the cries and calls, the bellows and coos of many an animal not commonly heard from in the barroom. Such was the full-voiced Juha.

What could Renato do? Not with voice, but with paint.

After yet another colloquy with the Mahatma, he had it: he

would take up a commonly forgotten scene from the Old Testament—when Noah, stocking the ark, having gotten two of every animal on board, had then, to finish the job, to get two of every insect on board. Poor Noah was frantic, thinking, How am I ever going to sort out all these dung beetles? And the stinkbugs? The numerous sucking lice? Would there be enough time? And the unforgettable jeweled snout beetle, maybe I should take four of those babies? All the same, I have to attend to the honeydew cicadas, rosy aphids and sapphire flies, punkies and painted ladies, lightning bugs, fairy moths, potato bugs! And what about the larvae, the pupae, did he have to take two of every damned thing? Surely no one would ever mind if he simply passed over the rat-tailed maggots?

But when after the flood he came to dry land, all of them flew from the ark, and he saw their beautiful wings.

It was old-time religion! Renato sought out a suitable wall on campus and set to work. Maria-Elena, curious, came out and set up an umbrella and a blanket on the grass, spread some books around, and planned out her lunar studies for Lost Coast.

9

WHERE DO YOU meet a saint and a poet? And who would want to, anyway?

Muscovado Taine and Izzy set out across the Bay Bridge toward San Francisco, following directions dashed off by Homer right on the bar at Larry Blake's. They turned here and there, ascended the hills and then dropped off the face of the earth, they zipped, they wheeled around, finally to end up at the ZamZam Bar smack in the middle of Haight-Ashbury.

The ZamZam was a dark room lit only with pink light of remarkable sleaziness. The bar was set in a horseshoe, and the walls hung with papier-mâché imitations of arabesques deriving from the mosques and public buildings in Iran. The bartender was an eccentric who rejected with contempt all orders for drinks, barking at the customers, until each of them figured out they had to order a martini. This drink he prepared with alacrity and served up with grace and courtesy.

And so it was that Musco and Izzy, hanging over the ZamZam bar, came naturally to chat with Homer and Francis, as all of them sucked at their martinis.

"That Cookie, I love her, now there is a capable woman!" boomed Homer. "But stubborn! Here I give her wood from the boat of Odysseus, and she does nothing with it for weeks! I'm lucky she didn't whittle it down and use it as a toothpick."

"I'll bet she figured it out," said Iz, who, though charmed by the robust, exuberant poet, would not stand for any rebukes of the dear Cookie. "She could fix a river if it were broken."

"I had to send her the dog Argos so she'd get the hint," added Homer. "Argos is looking pretty good for a three-thousand-year-old dog."

"You ain't so bad yourself," said Iz. "What do you say we find a place on the coast, and you come and teach me to improvise an epic?"

Homer looked smilingly at the simmering girl. "There are many rhythms to master, many techniques of metaphor and pleasure, of metaphysics and amusement. It would take a long time," he answered in a voice like the wind off the sea.

"Yikes," said Muscovado.

"That reminds me of a story," said Saint Francis as he swiveled on his barstool and told them

The Story of the Saint and the Woman He Loved

"Now just about everybody knows the standard-edition story on me," he said. "Heard the voice of God in a ruined church, fixed the place up, talked with animals and founded the Franciscans, got zapped with the stigmata, blah blah blah. But stories are like facets on a gem: just one way to look inside something. And so here in the ZamZam I would like to turn that gem to look through another facet; to follow the light into another of the stories that lived inside my days among the hill towns of northern Italy."

"I think I'd like another martini," said Izzy.

"Make that four!" boomed Homer. "I love to see Francis with a buzz!" he whispered to Izzy. "Sometimes he'll go out and have long smoochy talks with the alley cats."

Francis cocked an eyebrow at Homer. "You pagans!" he exclaimed. And then he went on:

"Well, it's true that God spoke to me in the ruined church,

but he was answering my prayer. I had prayed to him to help me earn the love of a woman, a young Tuscan beauty in Assisi. Now, I couldn't see what a part-time construction job might have to do with it, but I went ahead anyway. I did the work as best I could. God promised me: if I could do what He asked, I would win to my side the woman I loved.

"When, later, I learned the language of animals, I thought, I will tell them about my beloved, so that the birds and the foxes will know of her graces. When I heeded the call to a simple life in the open air, I thought, Give me, for her, the light of the stars—let my words go before her like starlight sewn in the air, so that wherever she walks she sees that glistening.

"And I heard the call to start an assembly of men to live in peace, dedicated to the beauties dwelling within the darkness of this human world. I thought, If in a dark time I can do a work of love, then, seeing what I do, she will know that in this world I can love her.

"And it took so many years, so many years. I did my work, I watched her, slowly we came together and we were able to work in common. She came to understand my labors and commenced a work of her own, the founding of a subtle and remarkable sisterhood that took up a trust of secret goodness. And, through all our labors, I would pray for the chance to touch her hand, a chance to walk with her in springtime in the open air.

"The months and years passed; my prayer was not granted me. The work we had begun took up all our lives. We had responsibilities to honor. Many of them took us away from each other; the decades passed and I cried out for hope—even just to touch the shadow of her hand; even just to walk in a garden where she had once walked.

"She was, to me, what sunlight meant. She was, with all I did, the one I praised.

"And when I was about to die, I went to her in my last sickness. In sorrow I took my leave of her. And as I was nearing my death, the Divine Voice said to me:

" 'Francis, how was I to know you saw in her all sunlight? How was I to know she was the centerpoint of all your praises?'

"And I thought of our bitter death in darkness, and the Divine Voice said:

" 'I could not know these things unless in this world you would renounce all other lives but that one lived, daily and secretly, for love of her. That is what I have given you, this chance. And since you have held nothing back from her, so now love will hold nothing back from you.

" 'Know one of the secrets inside the inside of your story: any true marriage of souls crosses the boundary between worlds. And know how destiny is prepared: when you leave your aged flesh, you will take on your body just as it was when you first loved her. And, when she crosses that same boundary, she will come to you in her youth, as she was when she first loved you. And so will your lives together begin.

" 'You will roam the centuries together, the two of you, as the lovers you were meant to be. With your touch you will call from one another the graces of pleasure. The long curve of seasons will be the arc of your embraces. History will be the home you have together. All the places of this earth will be yours; forests and faraway islands, coastline and mountaintop and fields of flowers, all yours, for a wandering of lovers. And your work together will make a story that will move like a music of rejoicing.' "

Francis paused, remembering. And then he went on:

"Now as you might well imagine, this gave a certain jauntiness to my death. And I was, from the next world, able to assist the work on earth of the woman I left behind. And one day she came across the worlds and passed into the place of my cherishing.

"That is the telling of one man's love—a life lived, to the view of others and to the view of the centuries, for the purposes of religion. But here in my city, someone should know the truth. And you are the ones chosen, you two lovers."

Francis grinned at them.

"I've got some questions," said Izzy brightly. "First of all, where is she?"

"I am going to meet her in an hour for a burger and fries. Then maybe a movie, then maybe we'll go turn to mist and tumble with the fog."

"Her name, the things you do now when you go among us, the kind of tricks you play, the people you seek out, the places you've been, the songs you sing, the bars you visit, the hopes you have?" So pressed our delectable Iz.

"Her name is Clare; but for the rest, that is another story."

Muscovado Taine had listened with tropical rapture to the account of Francis.

"Could I talk with you privately, sir?" he asked, and Francis nodded, and he and Musco walked out the door together, leaving Iz and Homer together in the bar.

A special feature news report from KICU, San Jose—Our News Is *the* News!

"All of California has turned its attention to the little town of Downieville, where just last week we reported on the gruesome slaying of the sheriff. We remember that the young Tabby, a fugitive from his abusive father, took up the search for the killers.

"Now, in a new turn of events, Tabby, deputized to look for the killers, found and cornered them in a river canyon near the town. In an exchange of gunfire, the young man was forced to kill in self-defense both of the murderers in full sight of some of the townspeople. Yesterday you saw the extraordinary film of that encounter. Today we bring you exclusive interviews with Tabby and Grimes.

"Let's go now to our reporter Dorothy Gallagher in Downieville. Dorothy, show us what you've got."

"Thanks, Kitty, I can't tell you what it's been like to be up here in this tragic, exciting time. I'll let these young men speak for themselves."

Tabby comes on-screen—the dirt, blood, torn shirt, gun still at his side.

"It was them or me. I hated it, I hated it. I just wanted to bring them to justice, so they could confess before their God." Tabby weeps a little. "They told me they done it. They said I'd never bring them in alive. I almost did it, I almost had them in. That's what I wanted.

"I want the people of Downieville to know that I had to kill because of love. Love for all of them, who have taken us in. I just wanted to protect them."

Grimes comes on to comfort Tabby, then looks into the camera.

"I've been thinking about all we've learned since we were driven out of San Jose. We're tired of all the cheating and lying; nothing's fair anymore. We need hope. We need a dialectic of self-defense. We're taking action. We've given our money away, but we still have our courage. There's no use being melancholy. It's time to fight back. It's time to be men and keep promises and look out for each other. It's time."

Kitty breaks in: "Dorothy, does this mean we'll be seeing you and these boys before long?"

"That's right, Kitty. We're leaving the Sierra tonight. I see a big drop in the crime rate in the Bay Area." Dorothy laughs.

"I hope you're right. Come on home, Dorothy!"

"And that's our bulletin—this is KICU, San Jose—Our News Is *the* News."

"Way to go, kids," said Dorothy. "Let's get ready to go."

Grimes was grumbling. "Why do we have to go back so soon? Everybody loves us here."

Dorothy was exhausted and proud. "Because I said you have to go back. Because everything's going perfectly."

Tabby liked this. "What do we call ourselves? That's what I want to know."

An old woman walked by just then, recognized them, and said to Dorothy, "They're just what we need! At last! At long last! They're like the police of Jesus!"

"That's it! The Police of Jesus!" enthused Dorothy.

"That's not right," Tabby broke in, "that's too harsh! I don't want anyone to be afraid of us. I want everyone to know we understand mercy, that we have a soft side, gentle, just like a saint." Tabby looked at Dorothy, at Grimes, and knew he had it.

"The Police of Gentle Jesus!" Tabby stalked around, he pounded his fist in a palm. "The Police of Gentle Jesus! The Police of Gentle Jesus!" Fantastic! Loving!

And Tabby went over to the woman and put a big hand around the back of her head and laid a big hard kiss on her face that later that night the woman would notice had left a crimson bruise.

"You're a smart one," he said. "A bony old broad, but smart."

Tabby was exultant. The Police of Gentle Jesus! It was full of hope.

Cookie knew she didn't look any different from any other sailor getting ready to cast off. But just as a woman painting her house may be, in the rhythm of her brushstrokes, teaching her thoughts a bright new music; as a child climbing a tree may be learning how she might rise, once she has roots; so Cookie, as she stowed gear and rigged line and readied sail, there on the deck of a boat whose wood had known the pace and touch of Odysseus, prepared to sail to the Land of the Dead.

"Juha," she whispered.

Cookie, like any cowgirl, had wondered at the unreality of death. Juha had many times visited her in dreams; she always knew when he was going to turn up. Even in a dream the air changed in anticipation of the great bulk of his innocence. But these dream visits always were brief—a blast of Juha, without comfort or solace for her; some animal calls and cries that faded as she woke; though sometimes she saw his shadow and she knew he was lingering, waiting before he went back to his work in the next world.

Yet there was one comfort: Juha's shadow carried his smell, of pine resin and sunlit grass and sage; and so from these waftings in the night, Cookie was given the one thing that kept her from grinding her teeth to a powder: she was given to know that Juha was safe.

"Juha, for heaven's sake!" she exclaimed as she thought of his juggling four big framing hammers out in the meadow in front of the cabin they had built in the Sierra. And the way he would take time, in the middle of the day, to come over and kiss every one of her calluses, a habit to which she often reciprocated, in one of the classic traditions of carpentry, by taking off his pants. In this way, by such exchanges, they had built a cabin with the proper blend of craft and affection and left it full of a muskiness that hung like fog among the beams.

Cookie looked around her boat: this was, she thought, a working ketch, broad-beamed and tough, plenty of stowage below, the wood dark with age and sealed tight. She had rigged enough line so that she could sail it single-handed, but it wasn't really meant for that. It was meant for cruising, for following the wind as it turns over a sea that is turquoise in the morning and lapis in the afternoon.

Cookie finished up and got ready to haul anchor.

She felt as if she were saddling up out in Eureka and heading out for a long ride in the Great Basin. The Basin was there, meant to be ridden, until the motion of her horse matched the current of beauty that ran in the high desert. Here, headed into the Pacific, she would balance on the deck of her boat until the motion of the sea opened passages that led to the Land of the Dead.

Cookie got the mainsail up, the boat slanted out toward San Francisco; she set the mizzen and jib; a fresh breeze was riding through the Golden Gate. The day was clear.

In the Smoke Creek Desert of northern Nevada, Beulah saw speeding up the dirt road toward her ranch house a pickup she knew belonged to Antelope on the Moon. The Antelope came straight in to her.

"She's headed for the Farallons," he said.

*   *   *

Ananda and Chiara knew it was right: they were there to begin a story for the young woman they had in hand. They had conferred; but how could they have known they were setting in motion

THE STORY OF FESTINA, WHO, LOOKING FOR ORDINARY JOBS, FOUND HERSELF IN A ROMANCE WITH FORTUNE; OR, IF THE SOUL GOT TO WING IT, WHAT IN BLAZES WOULD IT DO?

Festina, a senior at UC Berkeley, in biology, had set out to Ananda and Chiara in full and strange detail her uncanny affinity with the plant kingdom. Sometimes the Sierra forest, proving to be really rather more mobile than she had been taught, gathered round her and tried to prevent her from leaving. Her departure thus required some fancy broken-field running. Occasionally a section of the forest followed her right down into the Central Valley, which was not good for the crops. Festina was, however, in superb physical condition.

To try to escape the Sierra forests but maintain her fitness, she had taken off with her lover for the Mojave Desert. There, she studied roadrunners, which of course entailed a good deal of sprinting through the mesquite. In addition, she noticed that mesquite was growing more luxuriantly around their field cabin. And, in that cabin, when she took her man, another strange biologist, to bed, and as their delectations took on the sweaty variety natural to candlelit little cabins far out in the Mojave, then it was that the floorboards of the cabin came alive and burst forth with shiny green leaves and flowers of new yucca and desert acacia and ocotillo.

It was a new approach to houseplants.

It was as though, around her, the vegetable and the animal became one.

Maybe I need to get a regular job, she thought.

When Ananda and Chiara asked her what she wanted to do

about these difficulties, she replied, "Good and bad fortune are both still fortune, and nothing so distracts the demon of difficulty as planting a big smacker on his forehead."

The two older woman had a simple plan: they would send this splendid youngster to Rome, to an old lover of Chiara's, Lorenzo, who happened to be the best-known botanist in Italy. There, he would take her out and share with her a bottle of Barbaresco and see whether, influenced by so excellent a wine, she burst into song right there in the restaurant. If she did, he would become her patron and mentor.

And what happened to Festina? What was the fate of this young woman helped forward by two women who were themselves remaking their own days?

Having sung with Lorenzo, he took her all over Italy, to the forests and the plains, and recounted to her the evolution of plant life in the country from ancient times. Festina made her powers known to Lorenzo by leading some conifers down a hillside and making artichokes emerge in midwinter.

Settled in Rome, Festina began work on a program of research that demonstrated by appeal to sources classical and modern, and by study of various menus and a survey of vegetation, how the possibilities for the evolution of cuisine in Italy bore a direct relation to its primeval forest cover. She proved all this by pointing out that where the forest was broad and wild, singing and dangerous, the food and wine were unmistakably superior.

The Italian nation was won over. An extensive reforestation program was carried out. Every wild thing was celebrated. The birds cooed and roistered and soared; wolves dashed and howled. The sky dressed up in a softly glittering blue cape and swept through the trees on midmorning walks. The stars reappeared. The nation, having made room for the forests and animals and for its own genius, knew what to do next: parents began singing to their babies the country's rediscovered songs, specially made and newly beautiful songs—the ones that come from the future.

And what babies they were! One hundred and fifty years after the arrival of Festina in Rome, there was born a woman whose paintings would rank with Giotto and Fra Angelico, and a man whose paintings would be hung alongside the canvases of Canaletto and Titian. And a poet: she who was destined to walk the avenues of Italian history with Dante at her right hand and Ovid on her left. And they both were smiling, even when she left them behind.

And not only that, but the angels that once were so common in that country came back and moved in and did some good cooking. There sometimes were visitors from faraway places, such as Fallon, Nevada.

When Festina died, they rang every church bell in Italy. And, as that woman was made permanent, the wind in the trees joined its song to the calls of the animals, in wonderment at her life, and in farewell to her.

Such was the legend of Festina. Of course, Ananda and Chiara could not know what narrative they were setting in motion. But they knew a prophecy was at work; and they loved Festina and her strange gift.

Festina's trip to Italy had been set, and as the three women talked and joked and confided, a wave washed the cool water over their feet.

They all stopped to listen to the Pacific.

The big sea was blue-gray and bursting with waves. Spray arced into the wind, as though teasing the sun to color the sparkling it lifted into the low light.

"And so when are you going to have these babies?" inquired Festina, who was fascinated by the couple's maternal plans.

"We've chosen our man. But we still have to ask him," said Chiara. "Surely he will want to come to the bed of our longing."

"It won't be long now," replied Ananda as she and Chiara stripped and both of them ran into surf so cold that you could almost believe that the hope of the ocean is to wake up the soul.

Festina watched the two women swim far out.

It was midafternoon when Cookie cleared the Golden Gate. The ketch sailed smartly, Cookie tacked her way into the open sea, the gulls swirled in and out of her rigging, the other boats gradually fell away until she was all alone on the water.

"A girl starts kissin' on someone in a bar, and this is what happens!" she said aloud as the waves dressed with light and undressed.

"Was it my damned fault? He was jes' sittin' there like a tree trunk. I had never seen no shy tree trunk. Arms like branches, hands big enough to get lost in, now that was a neck worth kissin'! Like settling down in a pasture to graze, it was, kissin' that neck. And all them animal calls! It was like you had open country inside you, Juha, and all those animals moved right in. It's as if you and the blessed animals all knew each other, an' they were singin' in you." So Cookie went on.

She could see the backs of dolphins in the distance, and cormorants floated around her, angular and curved like black question marks.

"And that was some kinda marriage, Juha! You jes' left everything you knew behind and made a brand-new start inside o' me, didn't ya, Juha? Do you remember that dancin' we did? And all those stars comin' down outa the sky right into that little bar in Gerlach? Do you remember the lovin'?"

Rough and abandoned, with cries and calls of mating birds and bellows of breeding sea lions, with a glistening as though the stone were threaded with lit sparklers—before her the storm-marked rocks of the Farallon Islands rose from the sea.

"And all that roamin' around with our buddies, Chiara and Izzy an' the rest of that weird-ass bunch, all the stories, Juha, now wasn't it jes' like the whole desert came to see us? If I hadn't a-loved that desert so much, how could I ever have loved you, Juha? It was jes' like one o' them desert ranges got up and it was you. Juha, you were so shy you had no idea a woman could love you so much she'd take that shyness and cook it up and eat it for breakfast. That's what I had to do, Juha, before I could eat you for breakfast on a reg'lar basis."

She steered for the largest island, whose contours were hidden in clouds of birds. Their calls were louder, and she could hear the surf cuff the rocks, crackle across the stone beaches, then purr back into the blue depths. The male sea lions, in glossy coats of slick gold, with arched backs guarded the shore. Elephant seals roared. Seals barked. There were nests everywhere, cormorants and gulls, murres and puffins, over every inch of the island, a litany of bells and chimes, hooting and whistling, caws, screeches, skirling. Over the stone rocketed the shadows of the flying birds.

"And our cabin, Juha, there in the mountain meadow, we were giving it to each other, weren't we now? Weren't we jes' thinkin' about gettin' it done an' handin' it over to each other when you went an' got yourself killed? Well, I want you to know I finished it, Juha, I finished our cabin up. It was looking mighty fine; did anyone think that dyin' was going to stop our cabin gettin' done? Did anybody think that dyin' was goin' to stop us, Juha? Juha? Now I am come to the Land of the Dead, Juha, and I am going to find you, if I have to sail this boat by myself to the ends of the earth, I will find you. If I have to sail this boat into the sky, I will find you. If I have to—"

Cookie saw a bird spread its wings and rise straight up off the island.

Ananda and Chiara had one more riddle to solve; and they were on a roll. For this last riddle, they needed help. So, at the suggestion of Festina, they rode together over to the East Bay and set up a booth on Telegraph.

" '. . . calls with her music / Children of the sky to her fingertip.' It can't be just any kind of music," speculated Ananda. "I don't think you could call a child from the sky with, say, a tuba. Or a nose harp."

"It's right in front of us, as usual," rejoined Chiara. "Whoever she is, she 'calls' something from the sky. Therefore she must not be using any instrument at all—except her own voice."

"There you go being literal-minded again."

"I learned it from you on the first go-round."

"So she is singing . . . and she has to be singing in a place where she can see the sky. She has to be singing outdoors."

"Bizarre behavior."

"The Berkeley Hills would be perfect: she could see the big sky over the Bay, have some privacy, and do . . . do whatever it is she does."

"It's time to search."

The booth was done: a table, a chair, and a sign. The sign read:

VOLUNTEERS NEEDED TO SOLVE RIDDLE AND
CONFIRM PROPHECY

It was perfect. Festina, of course, turned up with a dozen friends, and twenty of the members of Renato's art classes swarmed around, and some young women who remembered the ax-throwing exhibition that Ananda and Chiara had put on outside of Zellerbach Hall. A long line formed, and the two older women and Festina gave everyone their assignments, dividing up the Berkeley Hills among the volunteers. They were searching for a woman singing to the sky.

The group fanned out.

Ananda and Chiara, though, didn't join them. They wanted to talk to a man about sex; and so they headed back for San Francisco.

It was on Haight Street, back down near the park, that they had their rendezvous. They went straight for the ZamZam; and there, the two of them found Izzy in a rather affectionate conversation with Homer. The muscular poet was no longer booming when he talked; he was in fact standing rather close to Izzy, murmuring and cooing long-weathered phrases—as he talked, it felt to Izzy as if her face and neck were being touched by his rough hands.

"Does your mother always show up when you are being romanced by one of the poets of antiquity?" inquired Homer.

"It's nothing I wouldn't do for her," shot back Iz. And she and Chiara embraced because the days were, even for this mother and daughter, moving rather fast.

"Where's Muscovado?"

"He had a few private questions for Saint Francis; and I've got a few questions for you."

"I'm *stunned* you don't have all the answers," said Chiara, laughing.

"Men! I want to stay with Musco; and I want to run from him. Look, for example, at this sonorous beauty," said Iz, nodding her head toward Homer, who, true to form, was besieging Ananda.

"I have looked at him," Chiara informed her.

"Every man, I bet, has his own way of loving."

"A woman can't get in two beds at the same time."

"Is that Heracleitus?"

"A new translation."

"The better Muscovado gets, the more I think that I have to go."

"A filly is born to run."

"Why is it that I'm confused?"

"Must be the rhythm and blues."

"Don't start that again!" remonstrated Izzy, and they both laughed at the memory of the drive across the Midwest, where to relieve the monotony of the plains they had spoken in rhyme for 750 miles.

They did another round of mother-daughter hugs.

"I'd love to sail you around the Bay, but the only boat I have is being used just now," Homer was saying to Ananda.

"Couldn't you just cut loose with some dactylic hexameter?" asked Ananda.

"Not in English. Hell, the poets here are scared to stray too far from their stupid iambs."

"But if he loves me and he's long and strong and mischievous in bed, why do I want to go?"

"It's a good thing, I say," Chiara said to beloved Izzy. "Otherwise you'll make the big flub: thinking, if he's this good, it means our life will be good."

"I need a few years to look around. You know, fresh from the bedroom maybe, but on my own. If I had some time to rummage around, I could have some surprises ready for Muscovado Taine."

"It's just like Socrates said, 'The unexamined come is not worth having.' "

"I think that's close."

"How about 'Come onto others as they would come onto you'?"

"Ask not if you come for your country . . ."

"A come in time leads to nine."

"The course of true comes always runs wild."

"To come or not to come—there's the rub."

"She'll be comin' around the mountain when she comes!"

"You don't need any damned maternal advice. You're too funny to need advice."

"I know. I like talking to you, though."

"I didn't come out here for these adventures. I thought we'd just hit the beach and find a lounge chair and read Aristotle," claimed Chiara.

"Bullshit. You *knew*! You could have *told* me that we were driving off into some wilderness of enamored men. I thought we'd just cruise around the country and stop for some ice cream now and then, maybe score a root beer float, who knows?"

"You're not the only one surprised."

Izzy laughed. "You and Ananda will have exotic children. They'll have black-and-white-striped hair, like zebras."

"Two babies, for a start. They're not even conceived yet, and already we're loving them." But before Izzy could get the facts on this splendid prospect, through the door walked the glistening Muscovado Taine, and by his side the lithe form of Saint Francis.

Musco came straight over to Iz.

"Have I got news for you," he said, and he took her by the shoulders and with his dark, tropical eyes gazed and gazed at her.

WHAT IS THIS world? Weary bearer of our histories, mute witness to our purposes and turmoil, celestial accident burdened with our accidental hearts?

Are stars merely stars, the ocean merely an ocean, islands no more than islands?

Do we count days, then let our deaths make a sum, so that the calculation is finished and the world takes up other quantities?

Do stories visit us for a time, then abandon us forever?

Is what we see what there is?

Is love an idea, hope a trick, work a calisthenics to keep us useful?

Is the world no more than the world?

At twilight in the Pacific Ocean by the side of the Farallon Islands, a woman in love saw the movement the sky makes toward the sea, for their rendezvous in darkness.

She saw darkening waters at play with the crescent moon; saw how the sea safeguarded that brightness.

Cookie had talked with Gus before she set out; and now she took out all her anchors. She had a heavy yachtsman's anchor with enormous flukes, three grapnels and a big mushroom anchor, a stock anchor and two huge plow anchors. All of them had thick leader chains; her deck was so full of iron she was lucky to be afloat at all. But she was taking no chances.

One by one she cast and set the eight anchors, so that there was chain everywhere leading into the water, surrounding the boat and keeping her upright and still, except for the rise and fall of the hull as the waves passed underneath. A cowgirl at sea had fastened herself to the earth; she rode the waves and watched and waited.

Cookie stood before the mast on a boat whose wood once sailed though an ocean of stories; and the Farallons stood high to protect her.

Suddenly she saw it: the turn of wings toward her; as though burst from a secret vault of air, a parti-colored bird flew straight toward her boat. Beneath the flight of that bird came a riptide of waters, an explosive movement of shadows, the sea fallen apart with sparkling.

The worlds broke open.

A sound deep, as though from the center of the earth; darkness so thick, the whole twilight sky fell into it; the far horizon was undone, its light and waters and sky surged toward the Farallons. Cookie was knocked down, her boat slammed toward a darkness that drew everything visible into it, the bass note of death sounding and sounding, all the chains that held her boat straining, she could hear them grinding on the wood of the hull, she heard a timber snap from the force, then one chain explode, then another, another, another, the boat was starting to turn, she stood up in desperation, another chain snapped and she was thrown to the deck as the boat turned on its side. . . .

When the side of the hull hit the water, Cookie grabbed for the mast, and she hung on as the ancient storied wood bucked once, another chain snapped, the mast bucked again; and then the whole boat rolled upright and suddenly it was quiet, nothing could be heard but the bass note echoing among the islands.

Cookie stood at the bow of her boat and looked everywhere,

everywhere; but she knew she could ask nothing from the Land of the Dead. There was nothing to see, except, against the darkness, the parti-colored bird; and still in the water a riptide of sparkling that moved closer and closer to her hull. Cookie braced herself. The rigging was in tatters around her. The boat would not survive another knockdown. The bass note echoed still. The darkness was thick as oil.

Who is it among the Dead who keep their voices? None, save those whose sentences, like so many shooting stars, cannot pass through the air without the shining of affection.

And just as there landed on the rigging of Cookie's sailboat a strange and beautiful bird of the Farallons, the tufted puffin; just as at the beam of her boat surged the biggest dolphin she had ever seen, and then behind him, around him, a whole school driving up out of the sea and pounding into a wave, soaking her with cold fans of saltwater—just then the deep voice of Juha lit the darkness:

"Husbands! A gal gets one, she can't get rid of him!" And Juha cut loose with his bass-drum laughter.

But Cookie in her confusion and joy could not find him.

"Juha, you come right here to me! Juha!" she cried.

The dolphins breached again, now in pairs, now in threes, now in unison, and the spray fell in tumult across the deck.

Cookie would have frozen, except that this region of souls held the warmth of hearts. And so she didn't even get a chill. Knowing this, Juha splashed her five more times.

The spray even reached the puffin, who sat elegant and bemused in the rigging. His plumage shined. His body was black, his thick beak orange at the base, striped with scarlet toward the tip, and shaped to make a wacky smile. In his snow-white face was set a stunning pale gold eye, from which a delicate crease led to a shaggy tuft of feather at the top of his head, giving the bird the air of a maestro.

The bird gazed with golden eyes on our Cookie. He flew off the rigging as the dolphins crashed around the boat. He went swooping down, then lifted himself high; and curving down with beating wings, he came to light on her shoulder.

"I love you!" boomed Juha in his baritone. "Juha loves you!"

Juha was in a jaunty mood, which just goes to show that occasionally a guy gets to take his swagger all the way to the next world.

"But what on earth is he? Is he a puffin?" teased Juha.

"Juha, don't you be goin' off on me again, you stick right by me this time, don't you be strayin'!" shouted Cookie.

"Is he a dolphin? A school of dolphins?"

"Juha!"

"We'll ride the bow wave and then run ahead. I am every one of them, every single dolphin. I am all of them together, held here in this world by you, Cookie. You will see: I'll watch over this boat while you sleep on the high seas. My love, my wife, we'll play with hours and days, dive in a promised land of peaceful waters. I have ventured far, and know that all my joy is loving you; my peace, is loving you."

Cookie could feel the soft feathers of the puffin against her neck and cheek.

"And even to be dolphins was not enough for my return to you. I needed wings." The puffin brushed a soft wing along the cowgirl's cheek. "I will perch here on your shoulder. With my tuft and golden eyes and painted beak I will make you laugh; even in the next world I needed your laugh. I will call to you; even in the next world I needed your name. I will perch here on your shoulder with my feathers brushing your neck; even in the next world I needed to touch you, Cookie, my love. Cookie the one I love."

"Juha . . ."

In his raucous, deep whisper he said, "Your Juha is this far returned to you."

In the waters of the Pacific, for hours, rode a wooden boat surrounded by stories and dolphins. On deck a woman held a soft, comical puffin; with her rough hands she stroked him.

The sky and ocean were close and alive.

Riding down Highway 49 from Downieville along the North Yuba, driving fast and laughing, Dorothy Gallagher and Tabby and Grimes blasted through Nevada City and Grass Valley and hit Interstate 80 and headed for San Francisco. An evangelical group in the Sunset, over by the beach in the city, had gotten in touch with Dorothy and promised to meet them on the way with uniforms they had made as a church project.

Uniforms!

"The Police of Gentle Jesus! They're on the way. They'll have their say. They're headed to the Bay. The Police of Gentle Jesus!" sang Grimes out the window.

Dorothy was pleased with the name. It was just the thing to ensure church support, but it wasn't too offensive to the network audience. She had been getting good reports from the office. The boys had been attracting a lot of support from the evangelicals, but they weren't identified with any one group, and so they looked independent. It was honest faith, honest effort. Of course, the boys didn't understand these subtleties.

"I don't care if you rhyme now and then. Just don't forget to use the goddam vocab," intoned Dorothy, hot and impatient. They were getting so vulgar. The things a reporter had to put up with!

"Don't be persnickety!" sassed Grimes. "Or Tabby and I will just have to strip you. It'll be euphonious, I promise!" Grimes was in a good mood.

"We'll make you sing, pretty one," said Tabby, feeling strong and courtly. "But do you think you could wait until we get our uniforms? It would kind of make it official."

"Now I know you two are feeling good, living out this story I've made for you. Just remember that if you touch me, you won't be a story anymore. You'll just be white trash." And Dorothy smiled at them.

"You think we believe that?" asked Tabby.

"You're a story I've got on the boil. I'll just turn off the heat and let you float like scum. I know you understand. Even you two. And so why don't you kiss my hand?"

She held her hand out.

Tabby looked at her for a long minute; then he kissed it. Dorothy swung her arm over the backseat and dangled her hand in front of Grimes.

"You too. Right now!" she said.

It was wonderful. She'd write a book about it someday.

They pulled into the parking lot of the Church of Jesus Christ Our Lord and Savior in San Francisco and stepped out of the car into the sunlight and into the waiting crowd, all dressed up, excited, sweaty. Over to the side there was a packed squadron of teenage girls, each with red-and-white ribbons in her hair. The minister was at the head of the whole lot of them.

"Welcome! My welcome to you!" he cried. "Two young men doing the work of God, men who bring peace to bear on evil! The peacemakers are come! Which one of you is Tabby?"

And Tabby stepped forward, close to the man. The minister was an impressive figure, with white hair and bright blue eyes and an upright bearing. He took Tabby by the shoulders and looked at him with dignity and gratitude, everyone could see it. Both of them were standing very straight. And the minister said in a gravelly voice, full of tenderness:

"I know how it must have hurt you to have your father betray the church. We all know. Yet through him, God was working in you. And as you are magnificently redeemed, so may he be redeemed through you!"

In the background the congregation gave a murmurous "Amen."

"Let us go into the church and have the presentation," said the minister, and he led them into the big concrete building.

"This is goodness the world cries out for. Let no one be deceived: goodness may be harsh. When a good man must be harsh, it is only the prelude to his gentleness," declaimed the minister as he passed with the two strong boys through the congregation.

When they were all assembled, with everyone watching breathlessly, Tabby and Grimes stood at the front by the pulpit. The minister gestured to one of the teenage girls, a blond seventeen-year-old in a white dress. Her face was pale as cream; she felt nervous to be the one to give the two heroes their present. Both so strong and dreamy! Where had they come from? It was as if they were delivered from the future, from some better world.

She came forward with a box. Her breath was short.

"It's okay, sweetheart," Grimes said considerately.

Now that's really blond! Probably blond everywhere! thought Tabby. And he felt a hot tenderness for her. This was the world he wanted, full of girls like this one. She'd probably never even been hit by a man, not even once. This world could be so good! To be sensitive with women, and respect them: this was at the center of everything.

"Tell us what you've got there," said Tabby kindly.

"We've been working on your uniforms," she began in a wavering voice. "We wanted everyone to recognize you. And so here they are."

And she opened up the box and drew out two stretch-nylon workout shirts the girls had shopped for together.

The shirts were folded so that both Tabby and Grimes could see the lettering on the breast. Grimes knew what to do.

"Sir," he said, addressing the minister, "if you could give us a place to change, so that we could show our appreciation for this sentient gift . . ."

Minutes later they strutted out. Both of the tops were a little small, which was good, since they were tighter; and of course more likely to tear.

They faced the congregation. The girls stood more tightly together and gasped; the rest of the congregation was quiet for a minute. Then they burst into applause. So brave! And they were right here with them. They weren't so bigheaded that they wouldn't visit a simple church of hopeful people.

The nylon was snow-white. The material caught the light wherever it stretched around the contour of a muscle. This it did often, because after the murder of Juha, all during the camping out in the meadow, they had invented workouts—with stones, logs, wrestling each other, swinging a pick they found—whatever. Hell, if you did it right, you could even build bulk when you crapped.

They still remembered all their routines from the muscle shows.

Tabby and Grimes stood still, they strode around, they stopped and posed, figures taut. They spun and snapped to attention at opposite sides of the room. They posed, they bent and flexed, they looked fierce. It was rhythmic, Tabby with his lithe long graceful form, and Grimes so broad and solid. As they moved, you could almost hear music. They saluted each other smartly. There were more cheers and clapping. Some of the girls were crying. Tabby and Grimes, straight as steel beams, marched toward each other, met, turned again and marched toward the congregation, then suddenly came to attention, stock-still and shoulder to shoulder they stood. The girls stared and hugged each other. Even some of the men were wet at the eyes.

On the breast of each outfit was the legend THE POLICE OF GENTLE JESUS.

The minister intoned, "What counts is bravery in our daily lives, in the struggle for goodness. There is a military to protect our freedom here in this country. But who protects the common people? Who protects all of us? Where are the soldiers of virtue?"

The whole congregation burst again into applause and cheers, louder and louder. It rocked the church.

Dorothy, at the back of the room, lowered her camera and shook her head and she thought, Can I choreograph, or what? Now she just needed to shoot some tape with Grimes, who could talk about how gentleness can overcome any obstacle. And how they would never, ever use a gun, except to save a life. It was an important angle, an important line. With the public, it had— what did her station chief call it?—resonance.

She motioned to Tabby that she was getting the car.

When they drove away, everyone from the church stood in the parking lot and waved and cheered.

Going down the road, Tabby turned to her. "My dark-haired

girl hasn't turned up. You know that. So why couldn't we take one of the blond pies? We could keep her safe."

"When it fits the story." Dorothy was smiling. They needed a guide, otherwise they'd make a bad mistake. Whom did they have in the world besides her? Just as they protected the public, so she needed to protect them.

She felt a rush of goodwill for them; she felt as if she had the best job in the world. The important thing about the energy and excitement of these boys was that they make just the right match with the public. In this way, they could be used for the good. It was what a top reporter must do as she shaped a story—find what the public needed, what they coveted, and give them detailed and prolonged satisfactions.

"And in the meantime," she went on, "head downtown to the Bank of America building on California Street. I've got to see an agent there, and an attorney."

Tabby stared at the road. "Okay, but then you and me and Grimes will head for Berkeley and Telegraph Avenue. I'll bet we can find some classical music on campus. And then there's the young ones everywhere. No offense, but not one of 'em is a thirty-year-old mummy like you."

Renato was not a man who, back in Eureka, had meditated a lot about destiny. He did not, chin in hand, sit in the barroom and squint into the misty canyons of the future. All the same, if he had done so, it is not likely that he would have seen himself on the campus of the University of California in Berkeley, painting an enormous mural meant as a hymn of praise to tiny flying creatures. It was bizarre. But it was Berkeley.

Once word of his project had gotten out, the entomologists on the faculty had (rather *like* insects) come out of the woodwork. They regaled Renato with their tales of the life cycle of obscure tropical moths, they drilled him on the details of the metamorphosis of water bugs.

Renato began writing down the advice:

"Remember a single cicada female can produce 500 million offspring! This mural of yours must be fecund! Remember that! Fecund!"

"Sex among the dragonflies! They mate on the wing, the two of them go wing-on-wing together down the river. Loop-de-loops. Dips, swerves, glides, and figure eights. You have *got* to get them in."

"The four-eyed whirligig beetles!"

Yet, could any of this be painted?

He had lights mounted and he painted at night, runners were called to bring him this or that special color, he put up a little tent right on the campus at the base of the mural so that he could study his work at all hours; he slept lightly and mused awake to take up his brushes again and mount the scaffold and go back stiff and grinning to his labors.

Renato covered one enormous wall of Zellerbach Hall with exactly rendered wings—moth wings and butterfly wings and beautiful wings of beetles—to their last resilient detail, so that the collective work on this subject, conducted over hundreds of millions of years by these dear animals, could there be displayed all at once.

It was a picture of what happens when the living fall in love with air.

It was his prayer for Maria-Elena and her child.

It was true that there among his paints and brushes, Renato was often overcome with a craving for chicken mole with long-simmered beans and a big sheaf of flour tortillas. But his numerous assistants learned to listen as he labored, and when the growling of his stomach began to echo across the square, they went to fetch him his foods.

What happened to these apprentices? Is it true that one of them earned the chance to paint light on rivers, and another to paint cirrus at the top of the sky over the Sierra Nevada?

Did one of them become a painter of history, actually painting events into existence?

From the ZamZam Bar the whole lot trouped: Chiara and Ananda, Homer and Saint Francis; and Musco and Izzy, with their arms around each other, and Musco whispering urgently to her.

"Ya take one walk with Francis and come back full of metaphysical propositions—does this mean you'll want to undress me forever?" questioned Izzy.

"Forever doesn't cover it," said Musco.

"So you have been solving your riddles!" expostulated Homer, who walked with Ananda at his right hand and Chiara on his left. "A good thing. Let's celebrate! How about a sacrifice! You know, cut the throat of an ox, make burnt offerings to the gods of thighbones wrapped in fat, hymn and rumpus and in general live it up."

"How about, say, a bottle of red wine, instead? With some cheese, maybe?" offered Ananda.

"When?" asked Homer.

"Late at night," answered Chiara.

"Where?" followed up the poet, who was beginning to feel very happily the strong grip each of the two women had on his arms.

"Overlooking the Pacific," said Ananda. "After all, you said you'd visit."

"Think of me and I will come to you," responded Homer, who, from the close movement of the two women, really did feel in a rather poetic mood.

"So tell us . . ." began Chiara.

"Anything, my lovely ones, radiant ones, blessed and bold-stepping women! Anything!"

"You're a poet, right?"

"Not just a lot of fluffy musings, but a poet?"

"A student of poetry I am," agreed Homer.

"Soul and sinew of the world, right?"

"Not just breath, but the meaning of the flesh?"

"I would love to tell you stories," began the poet.

"Then tell us—have you ever been in bed with two women at once?" asked Chiara.

"And if you were taken to bed by two women, could you father a child with each of them?" followed up Ananda.

Homer stopped and looked at them in astonishment.

"We hear you poets are very excitable," said Chiara, she of the hair like midnight.

"You will need the wind off the sea to cool you down," followed up Ananda, she of the hair like sunlight. And the two women, as they walked, ringed the poet round with their propositions.

"Come with us up the coast."

"Into the care of this love of ours, children should be given," said Chiara.

"On this very coast, come with a love of your own."

"We will gather light off the ocean and with it make a warm, bright blanket to wrap those babies, and there will be not one cherishing withheld them."

"Come and bed us both."

Ye Gods! thought Homer. A man would *have* to live three thousand years to get this chance.

THE SUN ROSE over the Sierra Nevada, the light filled up the canyons and flowed down to San Francisco Bay, through the Golden Gate to the Farallon Islands, there to swirl round a wooden boat with a woman at its bow. She had a tufted puffin on her shoulder.

I must look like a damned pirate, she thought.

The puffin nestled against her.

"You'd make a good pirate," rumbled Juha.

The dolphins moved through the glistening sea.

"So where to, Juha?" she asked, looking out into the Pacific, which looked as big as the embrace of a husband.

"Now once a husband and wife get back together, they should do something about it. What could a woman and her man do, if they had the ship of Odysseus and an open ocean?"

"Your sentences have gotten snappier since you died."

But Juha was undaunted. "If a woman finds an opening to the Land of the Dead and calls her husband forth; if, by her love, that man learns to move between the worlds; if lovers have a chance to learn their love over again and make a marriage not bound by this one life—then they give themselves to that blessing."

"And so you are a puffin and a school of dolphins because . . . ?"

"Because with all of us and this old boat, we can sail our way into all the stories the big seas and long coastlines hold for us, my tough brave cowgirl. There is a pod of dolphins in the South Pacific that we must visit; I must talk with them, and they will lead us to a little atoll in the Tuamotu Archipelago, where every year there is a gathering of storytelling vagabonds."

"What do they do there?"

"I think it's some kind of chili cook-off," responded Juha promptly.

"So we chow down, and then what?"

"And then we go off to another atoll, this one the most remote of all, where every year all the little hurricanes in the Pacific meet and decide who is going to storm through next season. We'll take a few very tiny ones, and then in Asia we'll give them to shy little girls, who then will have always turning inside their lives strong, sharp salt winds. It will make them bold and happy."

"So . . . what do we do in the meantime?" demanded the practical Cookie.

Juha rumbled, "Try to keep our friends alive. They are in danger, such danger."

The puffin glided around the boat, and she could see how in the morning sun all his colors shone in affection and amusement. The dolphins leapt and dove and were down a long time, then with ragged exuberance shot from the waiting water.

"Juha!" said Cookie suddenly. "Will you be a man again? Can you take the form of a man?"

There was no answer at first, just the waves hitting the side of the old boat.

Then Juha whispered, "Not a man. Not anymore."

Cookie was silent. She looked out to sea.

Ananda and Chiara and Festina and all the searchers assembled on the mezzanine of the Cafe Mediterraneum on Telegraph. They had found nothing, save a few hikers who remembered a woman who late every afternoon used to position herself at the end of the bluffs overlooking the Bay. The hikers had gotten curious and passed by to ask her if she wanted some company. But she had said that she was there to sing, and that these days she could only sing alone. After that, they never saw her again.

"She must be leaving," said Festina immediately.

"Why do you say?" asked Chiara.

"Because when you found me, I was myself getting ready to leave. Women with strange gifts want the open road."

"We have to find her before she goes. Nattie said we needed to find both of you."

"We probably don't have much time," guessed Ananda. "The riddle about the singer is the first riddle. We may have been meant to find her first. If she's leaving, she may well be farther along."

"I think it's time for an old-fashioned desperation move."

"I've got an idea," said Festina.

"Me too," said Ananda and Chiara together.

They all got up at once.

It was Renato's last day on the job. He looked at the finished mural. Across the exterior walls of Zellerbach Hall moved wing after wing, candent and impeccable in the direct California light. Everyone who walked by could hear the movement of the wings, a complex earthly concerto; with an intricate and marvelous speed the insects moved, each of them in a marriage with air.

But was Renato in flight? Nope, he had that lost and wretched sentiment that sometimes comes upon a man who has done something impossible. He had a feeling of abandonment and misery. He was struck down with anomie and despair. He was aggrieved and restless. The world seemed to him full of sinister forces and random malevolence. Such was the state of Renato, and he put away his paints and then trudged over to the grass by the side of the square and sat there in bewilderment.

But then Maria-Elena brought him a fresh-baked flour tortilla, and he felt very jolly.

In the sunlight she lolled by his side, and he reveled in the dark cream of her skin and the black, brilliant hair, the eyes like new moons and in her belly their sassy daughter, who now had that smile that unborn little girls have when they know their mother is in the sunlight.

"You are so funny," said Maria-Elena to the father of her child. "You have sixty seconds of a bad mood, all you get in this life. It's sort of like the mumps—everyone, even you, has to get it once."

"What bad mood?" asked Renato. He was so exhausted there was nothing left of him but loving her.

Festina and Ananda and Chiara walked along Telegraph. Festina, so raucous with the energies of her newly storied future, listened to the two women talk about their own future.

"If we're going to be desperate, it's good to be unanimous," said Chiara.

"It makes sense: look at all the labor to find our Festina," said Ananda. "When, all the while, she was right near us, in the park near to the spot on the beach where we go to watch the sunset."

The three women passed a wooden telephone pole covered with handbills that read THE POLICE OF GENTLE JESUS.

"Let's say she was ready to say good-bye, and she wanted to do her last singing. Where would she find a sky even bigger than the one she saw from the Berkeley Hills; a sky without any hills or bridges, without cities or trees in her way?" said our Ananda.

"She'd go to the beach," finished Chiara. "Especially at twilight. When there is nothing but sky, and water full of the light of the sky."

"The coast is a good place to say good-bye," said Festina.

Ananda and Chiara looked at each other.

Dorothy Gallagher had interviews lined up in Oakland and in San Francisco. The footage from the church had been sensational. They were still getting coverage, the florid, helpless attention that kept a story going. In San Jose they were putting together a special that had interviews with the policemen who knew Grimes and his family; and churchgoers who remembered Tabby's duteous service in the church—his going with his father to tend the sick; his delivering food to an old woman, staying to cook her a meal.

When he left, he gave me a love pinch on the cheek, recalled one. He grilled a steak for me, recalled another, he was so good with the knife, so strong. He made me a curry! said another. My kitchen smelled like curry for days.

Tabby, laughing, watched part of the show. He had to admit his dad was right about something: so many of them were just fertilizer waiting to happen. But it was wrong to sell them. The things people do for money! thought Tabby, shaking his head. Everyone could do the right thing, once they lived in a world of respect and judgment; of protection and handsome young men.

"Okay, Tabby, enough reverie," said Dorothy, walking up to him with Grimes in tow.

She was happy with her show so far. Grimes was getting so good in the interviews. "Justice will come because gentleness is a force that cannot be resisted!" he had repeated over and over; it made his interviewers swoon.

They had all spent a day in San Francisco shopping, what a treat. The great thing about clothes shops is that they were so clean and official. It was as though everything they wore could be a uniform. They bought lots of new slacks and formfitting shirts, some sport coats for the interviews, some tight full-body suits for workouts. The workout suits were neon bright and looked fabulous with wraparound dark glasses.

Tabby and Grimes had checked out the window displays, to get new ideas. If you want to be a professional, you have to pay attention all the time and have a command of the details. You had to know how to make looking good count for something. If you wanted to be trusted, you had to look trustworthy. If you looked good on television, you could look good anywhere.

Ananda and Chiara and Festina stood on the beach at the end of Golden Gate Park, in the last of the light. The flames from a little fire in the sand heated water for a hot brandy. There was nothing to do but wait and hope that they might still find, at the last moment, their woman of songs.

They talked around the fire. Festina wanted to know what her friends were going to do. She had conceived for the two older women such an unreserved affection; she felt tied to them, whatever happened.

"What if," Ananda was asking, "we have our children here?"

"I am as afraid as you are," said Chiara. "But I keep thinking that not to go on would be to refuse a gift."

A cold wind blew off the ocean. Festina added more wood to the fire, and the three of them stood close around it. The wind blew their hair: the fiery red tresses of Festina, the lucent blond strands of Ananda, the fine ebony fall of Chiara.

Festina said, "I know you are sending me to Italy, who knows why. But I trust you two. Whatever you do, in all this time before I go, I want your company."

"We've told you of our travels," said Ananda. "You are at the beginning of yours. As for us, we may need to set aside our adventures just now."

"Maybe it's the travels ahead that teach us how to go on loving," ventured Chiara.

Down by the water, a woman from Oakland, at the beginning of a long journey, was quiet, because of what she had in her hands. It was what she could tell no one. And though she took life from it, she had never felt so cold and lonely as she did just then. So it was natural to her to look back toward the fire on the beach.

"We can't leave for a while yet, anyway," Ananda was saying. "We've still got some stories to tell here."

And shyly, a young woman stepped forward into the light of the fire. She looked hard and long and curiously at Ananda and Chiara. "My name is Laila," she said. Then, because she was so lonely, and because the company and the women and the heat of the fire were such a blessing, she began to sing softly.

Dorothy had kept the payments from the exclusive interviews and the deposits from the churches that wanted to have the boys come and speak. She cashed some of the checks and now paid the boys in currency.

"We're only ten minutes from Telegraph Avenue," she informed them. "C'mon, I'll ride you over there."

She knew what would happen. They'd be sensational on the street, with their rough, bulky grace, and with so much cash in their pockets. It wouldn't be long before Tabby would hit the booths where everyone needed money. Tabby wouldn't be able to hold back.

Even Dorothy had to admit they looked fabulous, with the new haircuts and trimmed sideburns. They looked healthy and tan.

Tabby was a natural. He helped a guy repair the engine of his old car, even going to buy parts for him; then laying some money on him, to smooth his way when he was ready to roll. He gave some money to the Committee to Defend the Free Press; he loved the press, hadn't they found out the truth about him and Grimes? It goes to show, if you live as though things matter, then people find out the truth.

Tabby handed out money to the Fund for Burn Victims; that one really got to him, innocent people had the most terrible accidents—scattered burns from splattered grease, hands forced onto burners, freeway wrecks that bound their victims tightly in flames.

He handed away money to Computers for Kids, to the Refugee Center, and to the Astronomical Society, who gave him a map with all the stars. He remembered some of them from the drive into the mountains, and from the clear nights sleeping in the meadow. The stars were so calm, clear, beautiful. They were as cities should be. They should sparkle. Not all this dirt and piss and turmoil.

Dorothy watched it all, walking with the two boys down Telegraph. It was a blue sailing day, students from the university everywhere, energetic, amused, adventurous. The bookstores and coffeehouses and little restaurants were loaded, noisy, rollicking. There were the usual beggars, street musicians, fortune-tellers, and vagrants with orange hair. No one even turned a head at the Police of Gentle Jesus uniforms.

For Tabby and Grimes, it was like visiting Uranus and having everyone think they were natives.

They moved ahead of their smiling chaperon.

"I can't believe it," whispered Tabby excitedly, "it's so dirty. Almost like a dump with maggots. Berkeley's a dead body and they're feeding."

"So many freaks! Do you see all the jackets and rings? I even saw a nose ring! Can you believe it?"

"They need our help."

"We come to purify. We come to ameliorate. There's so much to be done," followed up Grimes, who had been reading his books.

Tabby was getting better and better at seeing them from outside, looking down on them whatever they were doing; and he was teaching Grimes the art of it. Tabby had gotten to the point where, anywhere, he could see how he looked in that place. It was incredible. The world was a camera.

"Do you think this Gentle Jesus stuff is too faggoty? I mean, what about something like the Hammers of God?" asked the worried Grimes.

"It's too late," Tabby reminded him. "Dorothy has already put the name out."

"The Cocks of God?" speculated Grimes.

"Those vocab books have made you witty," said Dorothy, walking up and laughing.

"How are we looking?" asked Tabby.

"You both know how to move—it must have been the muscle shows," said Dorothy brightly.

It was true: the boys had an aptitude for posing, for the turning and twisting with just the right tensions and angle, so as to present themselves most advantageously. They had loved it then, and the trophies from the muscle shows had multiplied in the gun shop. The whole shop had been track-lighted to show off the guns, the trophies, the photographs of the oiled bodies of Tabby and Grimes.

Now, for oil, they had the attention of people—of Dorothy, of everyone who saw them on television, of the churches—the oil of attention, rubbed into their bodies.

As they stood there in the sun on Telegraph Avenue in Berkeley, everything was just about perfect.

"So, Dorothy," said Tabby, "I'm fed up. What's the use of a guy being perfect if he doesn't have any romance?"

And around the corner, on her way to work at Larry Blake's, with the spice trails of Muscovado's touch still upon her, with her loose fine black hair and opalescent eyes, came Izzy.

Laila, at the end of a long, low song, said, "When I sing, the sky moves; and they come to me."

She extended her arms and opened her hands to Ananda and Chiara and Festina. They could see, turning there, tiny thunderheads that spun and glittered with little electric storms. All the women watched—in each of Laila's hands, a child of the sky.

All along the beach they walked that night with Laila, talking, talking. They took her back to the fire and then walked some more, learning her story. Then later they went off to a warm bar and then back to Berkeley, where they put her up for that night, and for many nights afterward. And the hour came when they set into motion the events that one day so many years later would be told as

THE STORY OF LAILA FROM OAKLAND, AND WHAT SHE SANG, AND HER HUSBAND AND HER COMPANY AND HER WORK

The scrawny child of an inner-city family in Oakland, twelfth of twelve children, scrapper, singer, hot woman with a steady gaze and a sure hand and a gift for working with machines: such was Laila.

In the beach interview with Ananda and Chiara, the two women found out all about the girl's prophesied gift of singing little clouds straight down into her hands. She would get to know them; she would take within herself, for use in her own life, their spiritous momentum. Then she released them to the sky, where they became big blossoming giants. So did what looked like an ordinary woman's life have a music within and a movement in the heavens. What to do with such a gift?

The women mulled it over. And finally they decided to send Laila to a farm in the Central Valley run by an old client of Ananda's. She learned potatoes, she learned peppers, she learned corn. She learned pumps and horses and tractors, cost control and how to hedge a crop in the futures markets, so as to work off a more predictable cash flow.

What then happened to Laila? It was nothing that Ananda and Chiara could have guessed, for they were not yet the women who could see into the future. But they knew, at least, how to give a woman's story the right beginning.

Laila moved to Des Moines, Iowa, and with some seed capital from Ananda, she bought a farm. Now, every farm woman does not require a husband. But Laila had her eye on a broad-shouldered laconic Iowa-bred farm boy named Jesse. He had a beautiful singing voice but was ashamed about it. His shame vanished when he met Laila at church, and she talked him into joining the choir. He was further encouraged when one night after practice, in a transport of religious and musical enthusiasm, Laila sang him straight into bed.

She was the first black woman he had ever seen.

The two of them farmed together for forty years and figured out on their own that there was a music internal to the world, even though way back in Berkeley neither Ananda nor Chiara even whispered to her about the Music of the Spheres.

There was something about their farm, everybody said so, though the neighbors never could figure it. A harmony was there, as if the place stood in some subtle relation to the sky. The way the fence lines were laid out, as though to write something only the moon could read; the way the weather vane, even on nights of perfect calm, might spin round wildly and then point at a faint but entrancing star; the alignment of the buildings, which led the sight of their visitors to a place of sparkling on the horizon. All this was so because Laila and Jesse had, instructed by the clouds, sung their way around the whole sky, even though they lived on earth. Their journeys taught them so much new music. They knew, for instance, just that soft song that would call the palest starlight into the bedroom of newlyweds. They knew a powerful bass harmony that would mend the broken legs of horses, so that the animals became stronger and more surefooted. They knew a whispered melody that would make eagles come into the yard and give the smallest children rides on their backs.

Of course, none of this was apparent to the neighbors. They all thought Jesse and Laila were strange, but friendly. Many of the neighbors would go over to the couple's farmhouse to sing on the veranda; no one knew where the songs came from, or what effect they had. And when everybody wasn't singing, there was always conversation, tobacco, and late-night hot brandies. Everything was easy. Everything was secure and familiar, but in motion; in creation.

And then there were the odd visitors—big strong Beulah from the Smoke Creek Desert. Beulah taught them the art of heaving double-bladed axes, she cooked them up raspberry pies and swigged their brandy straight out of the bottle. Antelope on the Moon even came on out, though not as a golden eagle. For fun he came as a titmouse. Beulah figured it out right away, though, by the way the little bird perched on her shoulder and peeped at her when she was downing the brandy.

Besides the strange visitors, the Des Moines farm had its own secrets, which Laila and Jesse didn't talk about except to each other. Like the way, just at first light, the couple would sing their special songs and then watch as into the bedroom came the little thunderheads. There they would frolic, spinning around the room and across the ceiling and down through the bedcovers, lending a special element to the couple's early-morning amorous playfulness. And the clouds let the farm couple know where in the sky that afternoon they would be found.

Laila and Jesse, out in the yard after feeding the animals, could always find them; and with a wave of the hand and by the manner of their embracing, they could conduct that billowing in the sky. And so would they bring a black storm in all its boisterous life home to their beckoning.

When Laila and her husband died, everybody noticed the singing of the grasses when the cloudbursts blew in.

Muscovado Taine sauntered along Telegraph, but there was a catch in his step caused by his carrying in his pocket the knife of Achilles. Before leaving San Francisco, Homer had insisted that Musco take the knife to work tonight. Take the knife, he had said, and dress lightly.

"What does dress have to do with it?" Musco had asked.

"Otherwise you won't have the necessary mobility," Homer had said sympathetically.

All this Musco puzzled over as he headed down the street, then ducked into Larry Blake's and headed right into the basement. Izzy would already be at work.

As she was serving up a tequila smasher to a bearded, clear-eyed man, Musco ducked under the bartop and embraced his spice-dusted lover. Everyone was charmed by the way, as he hugged her, she hung on tight to his dreadlocks.

"We'll go to Negrita Bay and see the whales—it's on the way to Guadalajara, it's on the way to Costa Rica, it's on the way to the rest of the world. Say you'll go with me!" So expostulated Muscovado in his palliative way.

"Can't you see I've got a job to do?" asked Iz, pulling gently at the dreads and kissing them.

"I think you should go ahead and run away with him," spouted a man leaning against the bar, one of the coterie of physicists who regularly visited Izzy. "You two are warping the electromagnetic field here in the East Bay. It's starting to affect our instruments."

And down the stairs into the bar came Saint Francis and Homer.

"Speaking of electromagnetic fields," said Iz, laughing.

And then on the stairs stood Tabby and Grimes. They stopped, staring at Iz at the far end.

"It's the same girl! The one we saw up by Downieville, that I told you about," whispered Tabby. "What a dream that we should find her. A dream!"

"A family girl, I remember, very nice," noted Grimes.

Chiara and Ananda, in delight at having discovered their two young students, were back in Berkeley and strode across the campus looking for Renato. He was easy to find, since the women had only to follow the resonant humming to its issuance from the mural—a wall of wings.

"Does this mean the lectures are over?" asked Ananda.

"Renato turned out to be such a ham," replied Maria-Elena, who was by her side.

"A big hambone of a father," piped up the baby from the womb.

Chiara and Ananda looked at Maria-Elena.

"Whatever are you going to name that child?"

"I'll look in the lit waters along the Lost Coast to find her name," said Maria-Elena. "The moon names her own."

"We're ready for the coast ourselves. We have arranged for a devoted male visitor," so Chiara informed Renato.

Everybody, even the baby, cocked an eyebrow at that one.

"Well, I for one am glad to see that your traditions of austerity will be carried on," asserted Renato.

"Does he like Mexican food?" inquired Maria-Elena.

"He'll be too tired to eat," said Ananda.

"So what's the plan in the meantime?" Renato wanted to know.

Chiara had the answer:

"Tomorrow we head out for Lost Coast, after a visit to the little theater in the redwoods up by the Botanical Gardens. I seem to remember we promised to put on a play. We of the Hurricane Troupe will seat the audience, light up some jokes, spin some tales, take a bow, and hit the road."

"And tonight?" followed up Renato.

"How 'bout if you rest up?" said Maria-Elena, astounding her compatriots. Such a thing had never occurred to them. But Maria-Elena was just trying to keep them out of danger. "There's hard traveling ahead," she explained. "Musco and Izzy, of course, will be out dancing their asses off. I'll go check on them, just so you all can have the comfort that they're being properly chaperoned."

With a tufted puffin on her shoulder and the big dolphin riding the bow wave, Cookie sailed back into San Francisco Bay.

"They're at Larry Blake's," said Juha, "and hurry the hell up. I mean, gallop on over there, woman."

Cookie felt the agitation of the bird, who flew around the boat and then settled back down with her; the dolphins leapt and twisted and plowed the water.

"What's the problem?"

"Hurry! You must hurry!"

"I'm going. But what do I do with you?"

"I'll stay and guard the boat, in my dolphin shapes; and I'll go with you to Larry Blake's as a puffin. One of the good things about being dead is that you can be in two places at once."

"There's got to be one good thing," grumped Cookie.

"I might as well be dead, otherwise missing you would kill me."

Tabby and Grimes, tall, muscular, with their arms exposed and their bodies modeled by their tight uniforms, stood at the end of the bar.

Tabby was staring at Izzy.

"It's wonderful," Grimes was saying. "I'll bet it makes you think of starting a family."

"A perfect family!" said Tabby brightly. He could feel the coiling in his limbs of splendid energies as he watched the hands of Muscovado Taine move on Izzy.

"Could we get a drink!" he yelled. "A *drink,* goddammit!"

Musco and Iz both turned and looked at them. Izzy's hair fell to the side to give them a shot of the glittering eyes. Musco swung Izzy around so that he was between her and the boys, and he walked straight to the end of the bar and confronted the two of them.

"The bartender's busy right now. You want a drink, you'll have to ask in a polite way. That way I won't be forced to have security come down and throw you out. It's our way of protecting everybody's good time—you get one warning in this club. The second time, you're history. Now what'll you have?" he said, smiling.

Stupid! thought Tabby.

Grimes could feel Tabby tense up, and he knew that his friend was going to tear this ratty black bastard into bloody rags. Tabby would do anything in the defense of women. But that wouldn't be right at this turn in their story, Grimes reflected. They were, after all, so newly launched in the world, they were held in such exotic respect, that it was important to stay with the program. It really did stand to reason that you can't just smash every moron.

So Grimes reasoned. He understood more now. Dorothy was right—he hadn't been reading all those vocabulary books for nothing. If a person knows more words, he has better thoughts.

"We are very sorry to disturb things, we just wanted some refreshments," said Grimes. "We've had to give a lot of interviews, and so we just needed a quiet place to rest and get sentient."

Tabby was red-faced.

"Two strawberry daiquiris, please, sir," said Grimes politely.

Muscovado looked them over one more time, then went along the bar to give the order to Izzy. "Be back soon as I can get a break," he said, and went upstairs to the kitchen to work his shift.

The problem, thought Tabby, is that people die just once. It really limits punishment. What could he do? She's pure! Pure! She must hate it!

"Tabby," whispered Grimes, "stop hanging on to the bar railing like that, you'll bend the goddamned thing. Take it easy."

"What do you know about love?" Tabby growled at him.

"She's working a shift. She's safe, with you here. Don't be melancholy," remonstrated Grimes confidently.

From the far end of the bar, Izzy approached them, daiquiris in hand.

Grimes had a sudden fear she'd recognize them from their trying to snatch her off the side of the road near Sierra City. But too much had changed—the uniforms, the new haircuts; here in the dark basement of Larry Blake's, she'd never place them.

Iz stood before them. "You boys sip on these sweet drinks real slow, okay?"

Is she taunting us? wondered Tabby. Is she asking for help?

But Izzy was gone off to another order.

Homer and Saint Francis were drinking together as usual.

Homer, packed with lives he had made and lived, had a special way of looking: he stormed a room, he went forth in a kind of raucous habitation of space, the wind of his attention blew through the room.

Francis was more quiet, since he did not need to project his attention. The world came to him. He had given himself up so many centuries ago, cleared himself so magnificently of the contaminations of mere personality, that within his flesh was to be found nothing but wide-open spaces. And, wherever he was, the mass of a place, the nature and placement of the objects in a room, the very air and mood of where he was—it all ran slowly into his perceptions, as rivers run into a broad valley. And it was in him that the imperfect and beguiling things of this earth could begin the return to their own true permanent beauties.

And so did the saint and the poet look down to the end of the bar to the muscled and confident Police of Gentle Jesus. Both of them noted the excited clamor of Tabby's desires, and the bolted-down, informed propriety of Grimes's concentration.

"I hate the way it's set up," said Francis, "especially that we of the permanent world cannot intervene."

Homer had a terrible foreboding that made him grind his teeth and pound the bartop. Izzy came right over.

"Are you trying to order?" she asked with a grin, for she had heard about the amorous plans of Ananda and her mother.

"Maybe we should all leave tonight," pleaded Homer. "How about right now? What do you say? Go now."

"Nah, there's such a good band tonight. Musco and I got some dances planned. Guess you'll just have to be patient!" said Izzy brightly.

"Five Gin Wallopers!" somebody yelled.

And Iz glided off into the mists of hard liquor.

"So we just have to watch!" exclaimed Homer in frustration down along the bar. "I want them to keep traveling," he insisted, with good reason.

"How did I get stuck drinking with a lusty pagan divinity?" wondered Francis.

"I will neglect to mention the time in Amsterdam when I came upon you kissing your wife in the middle of the day. You had her pinned up against a brick wall, as I remember."

"It was our anniversary," said Francis, blushing.

"What, the seven hundredth?"

The band started setting up: shuffling around, plunking microphones, tinking on cymbals, making sure a stash was handy. Each of them wondering whether or not there was time for a quick piece.

The lead singer, a blonde named Magnolia, decided not.

"Let's get started early," she said, "let's play late."

"I'm the one who had it hard, not you!" Tabby was saying to Grimes. "I was hurt. I'm the one who learned about God. Hasn't it come in handy? To be God's children, I mean? It's the future. It means we're meant to be a family. Listen, I can see that girl with me. She's meant for the spotlight. She'll be such a pretty wife, once she's free. Without her, nothing's worth it. Not even being famous." Tabby was hissing at Grimes, his hand on Grimes's big forearm, clamped down as tight as he could. He so much needed Grimes to understand.

Grimes thought, You've only met the bitch once.

"You know our legend is just getting started. You know that, right?"

"I made it happen!"

"So don't kill it. Would you kill a baby in a crib? Don't kill our story."

"It's *my* story. I know this is right."

"Wait until she has a break," said Grimes soothingly. He'd go along, but he wanted to get this over with. "You need to talk to her gentle, without all these people around. She was just nervous before, up in the mountains. She was surprised. She wasn't ready, not for a kaleidoscopic guy like you. She'll know better now. Wait till you can get close to her. She'll feel how sentient you are, and how strong."

Tabby glared at the light-stepping girl as she zipped drinks along the bar, teased Homer, whispered questions to Francis; as she was regaled by the newly arrived Maria-Elena about the antics of Renato on the Berkeley campus.

Tabby thought about how she'd want to rub him with oil.

Up in the restaurant in Larry Blake's, Muscovado swayed in anticipation of his trip down the stairs, to gather up Izzy and head out on the floor and have that long kiss before their first dance of the night.

Cookie was in sight of the Berkeley Marina. The dolphins were going wild, swimming out ahead of the boat, then breaching and diving and coming up at the bow, riding the bow wave until they could not contain themselves and then surging on ahead.

"Don't lower the mainsail until the last minute," said Juha. "Sail into the harbor at full tilt, drop the main at the turn, back the foresail, and ease into the first berth."

"Who's the skipper here, anyway?" Cookie wanted to know.

The puffin on her shoulder rubbed her neck and cheek.

"Hurry! For chrissake hurry!" The baritone of Juha sounded everywhere.

* * *

In Nevada City, in the Blue Dream Cafe, Nattie put her head in her hands.

Tabby was feeling good. He stood closer to his friend.

"Do you get it?" insisted Grimes, who had been explaining.

"I get it!"

"You get it, how we have to have a plan?"

"I get it!"

"She belongs to you. Don't you know she belongs to you?" said Grimes again. He knew how important repetition was in teaching Tabby; in fact, teaching anyone.

"She'll be proud!"

"She'll want to marry you on television."

"A marriage in a church, she'll be so grateful, so grateful, on my arm like a sparrow." Tabby knew. Grimes squeezed his forearm and biceps.

Tabby stood up, staring at Izzy. The sweat was showing through the uniforms.

"This is the day I've been working for."

Grimes surveyed the bar. He was sure it would work.

Tabby's muscles were all puffed out, from his gripping of the bar railing. His back was straight, and he stared straight ahead.

"Ready?" Grimes stroked Tabby some more, as though he were a beautiful racehorse.

"Ready!"

"You picked her out."

"Pretty Girl of Gentle Jesus!"

Muscovado Taine, with waft of allspice, all heat and hope and gentleness, came back down the stairs and walked into the bar.

"Let's move!" said Tabby.

Musco was leading Izzy to the dance floor; then she danced ahead and led him.

Tabby, full of energy, swung around the edge of the bar and began moving toward the dancing Izzy and Muscovado. Grimes walked directly by his side; but they ran directly into Maria-Elena, who with her robust pregnancy blocked their way. She was, she knew, doing a daft, risky thing. But she was, after all, from Nevada.

"You could really blow your reputation by walking right over a pregnant woman," said Maria-Elena.

"Don't you dare!" announced the baby, thirteenth Daughter of the Moon. "An innocent baby!" she smirked.

Maria-Elena rolled her eyes. "She's just like this all the time," she said, continuing the patter. "So demanding!"

"You're friends with the girl bartender, aren't you?" asked Grimes right away.

"What about her?" asked Maria-Elena sharply.

"We're going to help her. Do you want to watch?"

Tabby stepped up and pointed to Izzy as she danced with Musco.

"She's finally going to get the protection she needs. And because I love her, and you're her friend, I'll protect you too," he said as he put a reassuring arm around Maria-Elena.

"Salvation happens every day," intoned Grimes.

Maria-Elena was ready: "You two cocksuckers are going to have to trample me to get to that girl." And she smiled.

"Fat thing!" said Tabby as he reached out and swung around roughly the dark-haired Daughter of the Moon. "Don't you know how lucky you are? I'll show you how lucky, you and that lump in your belly."

Lump? thought the baby. But for once she held her tongue.

Tabby and Grimes very smoothly put Maria-Elena between them and escorted her directly into a little side room off the dance floor that was protected from view by a screen.

Grimes slammed Maria-Elena up against the wall, jarring the infant, making Maria's eyes big with surprise and fear. Tabby raised his steel-tipped boot and put the point of it just at the sweet outermost swell of Maria-Elena's stomach.

"Who do you think you are? Hurting me. Who? I'll tell you. You're someone who's going to shut up, so you can understand," said Tabby. "This boot, this is the world. It's mean. It's a world that hates babies. It's a world that locks up people in schools, then works them like slaves for thirty years, then throws them in the trash bin. Nobody gives a shit. But we know all this, we've been there. We said: no more pain. People need hope and protection. Women, especially, do. They need men who will fight for a new life."

Tabby smiled to see how scared the woman was. It looked as if her mind was clearing a little. Sometimes you just had to explain. Why, he wondered, were people so stubborn?

Inside Maria-Elena, the thirteenth Daughter of the Moon drew protectively around her the glimmering material of the placenta.

And Grimes, thinking he could provide the proper emphasis and comfort Maria-Elena, chimed in, "Look what happened to that young girl out there! The one with black slobber all over her. It's lucky the Police of Gentle Jesus are here, otherwise this is the sort of tragedy you get." Grimes shook his head. There is so much work to do.

And Grimes took Maria-Elena and put her arms behind her and bent her back and with a length of rope tied her wrists to her ankles, tight. The great mound of her pregnancy was exposed beneath her shirt.

"And remember! We won't let anyone hurt you! Count on us!" Grimes reminded her.

But from these ruminations he was distracted by the sight of the eager Tabby muscling his way out onto the dance floor. His friend posed a minute, looking good, even in the filthy smoke. Tabby was tensed up, delts and triceps standing out.

For Tabby: the joy, the sense of command! The room belonged to him. The band was set into their rhythms, the colored lights moved in ribbons and sparkles in and out of the dancers, the room was caught up in the oblivion of the music. Tabby was stronger than everybody.

Grimes felt that Maria-Elena needed more explanation, and he said as he patted the woman's stomach, "In this melancholy world of ours, with the risks to sentient women like yourself, you need someone you can trust. I'll kiss that baby someday. I'll protect it!"

He strode out of the little side room and joined Tabby, and they moved together, more quickly now.

They would have the happiest memories of this moment: the two of them turning toward Muscovado and Izzy, who over on the far side of the dance floor still suspected nothing. Tabby knew how the bar light glinted off their uniforms.

They came up next to Izzy. She was dancing with her back to Muscovado, looking back over her shoulder at him, hands on her hips, her lustrous hair falling like a midnight rain. Muscovado danced his way to the touch of her, he put his hands over hers and pressed her to him, kissing her neck as with eyes closed she tilted her head: it was a look that made Tabby think she might not be salvageable.

As Tabby stood up close to Izzy and took hold of her slim shoulders, Grimes wrapped in his hands three big strands of Musco's dreadlocks, and he yanked the Jamaican's head, almost hard enough to break his neck. But not quite. Justice has to be deliberate.

"Are you trying to cut in?" Izzy asked, opening her eyes, with her head still tilted, still in the dream of the music and of Musco.

"That's just it, sweetheart. Cuttin' in."

The Messenger from Death, he who starts the darkness, strode to the bar and ordered a double shot of bourbon. He nodded at Francis and Homer and stood back to watch.

Tabby and Grimes smoothly and quickly hustled Iz and Musco back into the same little side room. It was darker in there, except for an oily blue neon light that leaked in from the main room.

Iz recognized Tabby from the bar.

"I thought you were asked to leave," she said, and she began to turn around for Muscovado and with horror saw Maria-Elena on the floor bent in a curve by Grimes's knots. There was no use screaming. No one could hear them over the music, anyway.

"No, no, sweetheart, I'm here to ask *you* to leave." And Tabby tightened his grip on her shoulders and led her over to the wall. He had thought about how he'd do this. He'd remembered the encounter in the Sierra; he'd been too rough. This was a class girl, and besides, they were men now. He was more dignified, more sure of himself and his future.

First he touched her face. He watched his hand, strong, as he lifted it to her, as he stood before her tall and gleaming.

Izzy, her back to the wall, looked at him with incredulity. Smiling, he took her chin in his hand and lifted her face so he could look directly into her opal eyes.

"We're a team, sweetheart. You and me, we'll show them."

Tabby moved his red face close to Izzy, to give her a look of love. It was a tender look.

Holding her head fixed against the wall, he pressed his puckered lips against hers and lolled his tongue around in her mouth. Then he fastened his teeth on her lower lip and held on as he pulled away, so she had to lean into him. Good loving! Strong!

Grimes was talking to Muscovado.

"When I break your neck, it's going to be a melancholy accident," he warned. "I'll put my boot high up on your back and just give your head a quick snap. You won't be a criminal anymore. That pretty girl will be safe at last. We'll have a little more decency and respect in this town."

Muscovado was taller than Grimes had thought.

He thought of explaining to Muscovado about the dialectic of good, just as he'd done with the television reporter. But what's the use, he'd never understand. It was just like a soldier in a war; somebody had to lose.

Outside, at the bar, the Messenger stood quietly. Darkness was folded in his hands.

Grimes rehearsed in his mind: break the neck, then step back to Maria-Elena and make sure she was protected.

Tabby, having finished his love fest with Izzy, stood with eyes shining and thrilled. It was everything he'd hoped for.

Iz looked at him steadily. "Do that again and I'll puke on you."

Tabby was stunned. He grabbed her blouse at the neck and slammed her head against the wall; virile, he thought. She obviously didn't understand yet.

"C'mon, girl, I'm taking you out of here. My friend will play a little pop-goes-the-weasel with the nigger, then he'll join us outside."

Tabby took Iz by the wrist and twisted it up behind her back so that if she didn't keep in forward motion, the arm would snap; with a nod at Grimes he got ready to march from the side room. Grimes moved Musco closer to the wall. He tightened up on the stupid dreadlocks. And then two things happened that the Police of Gentle Jesus didn't really think were part of the divine plan.

Grimes howled from the sudden thrust into his leg of the knife of Achilles; Tabby felt on his collar a hand so callused and indomitable that it could only have belonged to a Nevada cowgirl.

Cookie spun Tabby around.

"Hi!" she said, and she punched him so hard that he was lifted off his feet onto his toes, balletlike, where he hung for a remarkable moment before he tilted back and weighty with surprise crumpled to the ground.

Cookie whipped out some line from the boat.

"Haven't tied a critter for months," she commented as she crouched over Tabby and with easy, powerful loops bound his hands and feet together.

"Now, the test is, will the ropes hold?" And she fastened her hand through the loops and picked him up and shook him. "Yes, they do!" she said with satisfaction.

She drew out some more line and handed it off to Musco and Izzy, who went to the wounded and whimpering Grimes.

"Give it a go," and they tied Grimes in the same way.

Musco untied Maria-Elena and helped her to stand.

"Let's get out of here," said Cookie.

But they were not quite done: for the strange bird that through all the commotion had ridden the shoulder of Cookie now spread its wings and descended to land on Tabby's back. It was the first time a puffin had been in Larry Blake's. He walked on his webbed feet onto the top of Tabby's head, there to stand quizzically. Then the puffin jumped down and from the floor looked long and strangely into the face of Tabby; then padded over and stood before Grimes. And they heard the rumbling of the voice of Juha:

"Do you know what happens to the murdered? They come back. They come back. You cannot kill them again. And they show you to everyone. Everyone I loved, every single one of them, knows who you are now."

Cookie and Musco and Izzy and Maria-Elena all stopped dead. In disbelief and fury they looked at the trussed-up Tabby and Grimes.

"We've got to go!" Cookie said in a bitter, strangled voice. "We've got to go!"

12

IZZY AND COOKIE stood together on a ridge in Tilden Park
in the Berkeley Hills; upon Cookie's shoulder still perched the
stocky little puffin.

"When do we leave?" Izzy was saying.

"Oh, no, that ain't the message. No way. No, you should just
stay around and wait for those two good citizens to come for you
again. Think of yourself as girl-bait, that'd be smart." Cookie was
shaking her head.

Whereupon Izzy embraced Cookie, and the puffin gave forth
some little squawks and cries, some chitterings and low clucks.

"You look like a pirate with that bird on your shoulder," observed our Iz.

"It's work I was meant for," said Cookie with a wink.

"Could I pet him?" Iz asked shyly.

"He likes that."

And Izzy took her slim, artful hand and ran her fingertips and
then her whole cupped and gentle touch slowly down along all
the puffin's body.

There was a throaty, low rumble in the air.

"Juha!" whispered Izzy slowly. "This loving you, it's part of our
breathing."

The rumble in the air sounded again, Cookie smiled at the delicious Izzy, and they stood in the sunlight exultant, to have Juha with them at all; in the sunlight full of sorrow, to have seen and touched the murderers of that massive gentle man in love.

Izzy remembered with sadness and repulsion Tabby's kiss. She wanted to be cleansed. She wanted to show that boy the beauty of the man they had taken away. Cookie had retrieved Juha. But he would never again lead her in love through the dry grass to a green river for a swim in the heat of the noon. Knowing his killers, knowing Juha: they had to find a way. Cookie had gone to the Land of the Dead; the rest of them needed, whatever the hazard, to witness his life as a man and show how they had loved him.

Renato and Maria-Elena were talking together and looking at a handbill that Renato had lettered:

• • •

The Hat-Tricks and Hot-Pillows Low-Life Storytelling Dirty-Angel-Plain-Folks Improvisational Hurricane Theater Troupe

PRESENTS

A MORNING OF STORYTELLING

in

THE LITTLE REDWOOD THEATER

Admission: Free. But bring your lover.

The Hurricane Troupe will give their stories into the embrace of the following questions—
1) What does love have to do with chili peppers?

*2) If the immortality of the soul isn't just a lot of
horseshit, then what should we do about it, huh?*
3) Can a machine make paradise?
4) With regard to life as a whole: Why? And why not?
*5) And once again: What is this stuff about a carnal
metaphysics?*
6) Could we laugh heaven home to us?
7) Shouldn't it be easier to avoid being killed?

*SO: SEE YOU THERE: AND REMEMBER,
THERE'S NO SHOW UNTIL YOU SHOW*

•   •   •

"Think that's about right?" asked Renato of his moon-eyed
lover.

"At least it doesn't say anything about insects."

They both waited for some crack from the baby; but the little
girl in the womb had gone curiously silent since the episode with
Tabby and Grimes.

"Well, I guess my daughter is in a sulk," said Maria-Elena.

"Yep, probably in a bad mood. Just in there sucking her gums."

"Just a pouty, sullen little pill. You'd think she didn't have any
parents at all."

"A mute daughter. Great. No more talkative than a little ham."

"All right, all right! I'm not even born yet, and you almost get
me killed! How do you think it feels?" burst out the baby from
the womb.

"Oh-oh, we've hurt her feelings," offered Maria-Elena.

"I wonder if it'll be one of those Big Booming Traumas," said
Renato, chin in hand.

"Maybe she needs prebirth counseling."

"They'll swat at her tiny emotions, zipping around like so
many sand flies."

The baby sighed. It was not as if she could run away from
home.

Ananda and Chiara sat on their beach and rummaged around in the years ahead.

"Are they going to come for Izzy again?" asked Chiara.

"It's what I've been afraid of," said Ananda.

"One smart girl, and the whole world gets mad," sighed Chiara, thinking of her shining daughter.

"If you wanted to kill the future, Izzy is the one to get first."

Chiara knew it was right, and she looked out to sea.

In the redwood grove had assembled the usual Berkeley crowd: Internet sophisticates, street people, polymaths, Tantric Buddhists, investigative journalists, Hare Krishnas in their Kool-Aid–colored robes, several band members from the salsa and reggae circuit, some Cajun guitarists and five complete rhythm-and-blues bands from Larry Blake's, social critics with voices like boiling tar. There were logicians with the angular, beady look of giant stickbugs, Sanskrit masters who were jazz saxophonists on the side, microbiologists who tap-danced, flakes, felons, and four wheelchair-bound workers who had memorized, respectively, the whole of Greek tragedy, the Uniform Commercial Code, the Nag Hammadi Gospels, and Elia's *Encyclopedia of Baseball Statistics*.

"I know someone's trying to kill me, but all the same, I'm going to hate leaving Berkeley," said our Izzy.

"So what *do* we do now, anyway?" wondered Ananda aloud. The assembled crowd was getting raucous, they were throwing Frisbees around, shuffling cards, popping chewing gum in unison and in contrapuntal extravagance, and sashaying around as though in the whole world there were not one single sour thing.

"We get on with the show, that's what!" And Cookie walked down the little slope onto the stage and proved that nothing can so quiet a crowd as the striding into sight of a stocky woman who sails the ship of Odysseus, throws knockout punches at the leaders of civil society, and stands forth with a beautiful puffin perched on her shoulder.

"Goddam!" exclaimed someone in a back row. "She does put me in a hear-and-obey kind of mood."

"Listen up," said Cookie, "the Hurricane Troupe is hittin' the road. But first we need a breather. We need to take some time out and jes' stand around here with you and swap some tales. First up is Isabella Boccaccio Acappella Mandragora Palmieri, with a hot taste for ya."

And our Izzy came onto the stage, her opalescent shadow glittering before her. And she told them

THE STORY OF THE ORIGIN OF CHILI PEPPERS

"This is the story," began Izzy, "of a man and woman who learned how to pack their words with the heat and savor of love; how to make their talk delicious.

"And not just delicious: it was as though their words had more than sound: they had colors. They were glossy yellow, they were firebrand red, suave green, soul-soothing violet. Some were strangely wrought; yet, they did not give away, by how they sounded, their hidden wild heat.

"And as these lovers talked and listened to each other, they understood that their way of speaking gave language a taste. For only in the phrases of lovers do words take on their full flavor and brightness.

"This earth remembers: when this pair died, their words, with their bright colors, wild shapes, and hot variety—to these words the earth gave form and taste and fire. And that is the origin of chili peppers."

The audience got into this story right away.

"Now, stories on what kind of love makes what kind of food, I'll bet you could do a whole book of them, huh?" suggested one hungry young man.

"You betcha," confirmed Izzy.

"An example!" demanded another, even hungrier.

"The touch of fingertips of two lovers just waking up—each of these touches the world makes into a sweet midsummer blackberry. Why else might they taste so good? And why else would there be so many of them?"

The entire audience was now famished.

Izzy glided offstage.

"It's the way the world adds up," said a deep voice from offstage, and with a wafting of allspice Muscovado Taine came slowly forward.

"So it's about time you turned up, you handsome spicy singsong brute," said Cookie. "Want to tell a story?"

And Musco, who had been having a rough week, was silent for a minute. And then he told

THE STORY OF THE BROKEN HEARTS

"Once I knew a moon-eyed sister, and she and her sisters cooked at a little restaurant far out in the desert. One night there came into the restaurant a big unhappy family. Such was their meanness to each other that they had over the years broken each other's hearts.

"There the women were, cooking, and they thought, What is more useless than such a family? And just then they noticed that the room was full of the famous and ominous butcher angels, who roam the earth, cutting out the hearts of those who no longer deserve them. And this is what they did to the family, as they sat stewing in their hatreds.

"The hearts they gave to the sisters, who, following instructions they were given by the angels, cooked them into special tamales for their donkeys.

"None of the family noticed, of course. Why would they notice? They didn't use them anyway. They're out on their ranch right now, a bunch of squabbling carcasses, just like a million other unhappy families.

"And what did it matter? They were already dead, after all. What was a cook to do? Let that muscle go to waste?

"Every now and then I think of this story and remember that

there is a reason for everything—usually, there are many reasons. For example, the existence of such a family is one of the reasons the moon has phases—because there are people on this earth that it cannot bear to look at."

Muscovado Taine was silent again, and he looked a long time at the audience.

No one asked any questions.

And Muscovado left the stage. Full in his mouth was a bitter taste of violence yet to come.

Cookie advanced once more. She looked over the audience of their compatriots. She noted that the coyote and the peacock had come to the edge of the stage. The audience was getting used to this cowgirl pirate, the way she strode around, the way her gestures bespoke the sibylline open spaces of the desert and the strange regions of the sea. Besides, they liked the way the puffin was always nuzzling.

"What is this, anyway?" Cookie demanded loudly. "Don't I get to throw in with some of my own stories? You're goddamned right I do!" And she gave her audience one of her no-nonsense, I-have-sipped-on-the-whiskey-of-wide-open-spaces kind of stares.

Nobody argued, and she told

The Story of the Machine That Makes Paradise

"When I was growin' up in Eureka, now there was another little girl who was even crazier than I was. We were always ridin' horses together, out jumpin' and practicin' shootin' our rifles at full gallop. It got so that she could plug the trunk of a piñon pine no matter how fast she was ridin'.

"This little girl—her name was Clare—now she loved machines. She saw a machine, she couldn't wait to get her hands on it. She took apart can openers, bicycles, radios; when she was older, she went to the mechanic's shop and helped the men overhaul trucks and farm machines.

"Irrigation systems for the big ranches outside of town, control panels of locomotives, heavy diesels of the mining trucks rolling through town—this gal could repair anything. And so it was natural that, when she hit the middle teens, she got to thinkin' about makin' machines of her very own.

"And sure enough: she built a machine to make flat beer fizz. She made a telescope that, when you pointed it at a star, would whisper its name. She made an engine that would run on honey. She made a plate that would clean itself.

"Finally Clare and I was talkin' and I figured, maybe she needed a challenge. So's I told her, how 'bout a machine that makes paradise? I had always heard of paradise, but everybody talked like it was kinda far away. And nothing pissed me off more.

"So she thought about it. Then she built it. Now it took years, all the way into her early twenties, and it was tough because all the cowboys were pestering her, sayin' as how they loved her like sweet loves sugar, like colts love runnin', like springtime loves a mountain meadow. And she did do some runnin' and yippin' with those men; but she built the machine nonetheless. You worked the levers, and it gave you a vision of a promised land you could walk right into.

"There was a problem, though: it jes' didn't get that much use. Only them as could recognize paradise when they saw it could use the machine. So for lots of people, it didn't seem to do nothin'.

"So's we talked about it and changed the design—somethin' that would make it useful to everyone, and at the same time any man or woman livin' in the high-noon-and-midnight sweats of love—that is, folks still interested in paradise—would have that extra bonus.

"So to this day the machine is still operatin', right there in Eureka. And it not only makes paradise. It makes ice cream."

"I always *knew* there was something special about ice cream!" exclaimed a woman in the audience. "Nothing could be that good unless it points on to something else."

"And so what happened to Clare?" asked another.

"She up and moved to San Francisco with some light-steppin' big-eyed soft-whisperin' strange dude."

"Figures."

"Anything a good woman does figures," asserted Cookie.

"Can we join this theater troupe?" asked seven people in the audience simultaneously.

But the coyote was restless.

"Well, now, it would be nice if we had some time to get to that," boomed Cookie. The puffin had been whispering to her. "But you're goin' to have to figure it out for yourselves. We're headed for Lost Coast."

And Cookie, with the puffin riding lightly and looking around, swept offstage and gathered round her the Hurricane Troupe and, talking urgently, shepherded them toward their wagon and the truck.

The audience, inspirited by the stories and the vivid authority of Cookie, scattered through the redwoods and all through Strawberry Canyon.

Which was just as well, for on the road leading from the university up the canyon to the Botanical Gardens and the little theater in the redwoods were coming five silent cars full of new, enthusiastic recruits. And at the head of their body of new soldiers, like a caravan of virtue, rode Tabby and Grimes, leaders of the burgeoning Police of Gentle Jesus.

13

NO ONE WAS left at the little theater when the Police of Gentle Jesus turned up. Tabby and Grimes walked around, kicking debris, shaking their heads, sniffing the air.

"Why can't they just stand still?" Tabby wanted to know.

Grimes looked around at their recruits. "I guess we'll put on a show for the kids," he mused, gesturing to the high schoolers and the other pickups from campus.

The hours after the fight in the basement of Larry Blake's had been a triumph. Dorothy had gotten to the scene just after Tabby and Grimes had been tied up. The music had stopped, the basement was in an uproar at the discovery of the two boys. Grimes was bleeding heavily. Dorothy looked around; no one seemed to know what had happened except that there had been a fight. And then the bleeding Grimes had hollered:

"The girl! Save the girl!"

The room exploded in questions, the police arrived. They had heard about Tabby and Grimes; they untied them and everybody went down to the hospital. Trucks from two television stations followed them the whole way; Grimes was dramatically holding his wound. Then at the police station, Tabby and Grimes shouted that they would meet the press later. They wanted everyone to know the truth.

The police got the story from Tabby:

"We found out about a Rasta, he'd kidnapped a girl and he'd been treating her as a slave. She's only seventeen and she's got this Rasta owning her and he takes everything she earns and keeps it. She's just a girl, he snatched her off a street somewhere. The monster probably keeps her chained up. She'll do anything, say anything, because she's so scared. I couldn't stand it." Tabby took a breath.

"We checked it out, we made a plan. We'd do a rescue. We knew it wouldn't be easy. There was a whole bunch of them, and just as we were saving her, some bitch—she had an animal with her—I'm telling you it's some kind of cult, it's a slave cult that keeps girls and animals—this big woman with a bird comes in and attacks us. It was a she-devil. It's some devil cult—look at the weird old knife they stabbed Grimes with. It's some ritual thing, I'm telling you. This she-devil attacked us and tied us up and they got away. No woman is safe."

It was good to get everything out in the open.

The rest was predictable: the head-shaking, there was so much scum on Telegraph, all the cops had heard about these kids. Tabby was the one who plugged those scum-suckers who had killed the sheriff. How they'd all cheered that one, just to see those motherfuckers go down! Pork them again! Again! And now these boys were back in the city. It was going to be tough for them.

It was true that the story was wild, and that there was no reported crime, and no criminal history of any identifiable cult. They'd go ahead and put out a warrant for the black who did the stabbing; but besides that, it seemed as if the boys had gotten a little overenthusiastic. Best thing to do was just let it go. There was not really much for the police to go on. But they could give moral support—the kids were on to something. There had been a lot of letters to the editor and other public commentary that the police needed to encourage citizen crimefighters. If the public could give the police more assistance, and there was more bravery and vigilance on the streets, that was all to the good. The neighborhood watch programs, the security education classes, the church patrols that were under discussion—every little bit helped.

In the meantime, Tabby and Grimes kept the money flowing to the forces of respect. It was important for all men in uniform to have that vote of confidence from the public; to know they were valued, know that someone understood what a tough job they had now.

The police released Tabby and Grimes without a statement. A press conference for the two boys had been arranged in a church in San Francisco.

Meeting the press was wonderful. Grimes was eloquent; fresh from the hospital where they had dressed his wound, he was flushed and handsome. Sure, maybe what they'd done was impulsive and foolish; but they'd always try to help women, no matter what the risk, whenever they found one in trouble. They were learning.

Tabby was mostly silent. But everybody watched him. There had been so many articles. Here was a guy who took on his own father to protect a whore. And now this. Tabby seemed to get a little taller every day.

Tabby and Grimes had walked from the press conference onto the sidewalk to a car the church had sent, and it was like two rock stars: lots of young girls who had pictures of them, lots of screaming.

And now at the little amphitheater in the redwoods, Tabby and Grimes walked around with their recruits. Even when they were still in the Sierra, they had been getting letters from young men who were tired of taking shit and wanted to join them. There had been more newspaper articles, and some interviews with Grimes in some of the gun magazines. Grimes wowed them with the way he zipped off the specs and the uses of the new guns on the market. Some of the gun companies were calling Dorothy for endorsements; they wanted Tabby and Grimes to try out their new models and write reviews about the need for protection every day of our lives. And about women. If a man loved women, he needed a gun.

"Let's have everybody take a seat!" said Grimes suddenly.

And when the recruits were arrayed and silent in the amphitheater, Grimes teed off:

"How many girls have to suffer? How many of them aren't loved? Don't have a home? Because that's what these people are, people who don't have a home. With their secrets, on the run. People who should settle down and live with their neighbors in peace. Being together. Community. Keeping women safe. No, not them, they have to move on. It's a cult. It's people who have never kept a promise, who have never risked anything, who can't face a fight. It's men who don't know their responsibilities to women. If you can't fight to protect women, how can you learn to be gentle? If you're not strong, how can you learn to be loving like us, just like us, the Police of Gentle Jesus, standing here."

Some of the crowd started to yell with excitement.

Tabby walked onstage, straight and graceful. He stood handsomely before them all. The yelling got louder.

"Look at us!" commanded Grimes. "Look here at us!"

Just off in the redwoods, two Berkeley stoners were passing a joint back and forth, watching the show, and when the recruits surged down onto the stage, surrounding Tabby and Grimes, parting for them as the two led them back to the cars—as all this crashed on before them, one turned to the other and said:

"It's like those old Mayan games, where the team that loses, they all get executed, man. Really cool."

Down at the Berkeley wharf they stood, watching Cookie rig sails and get ready to put to sea. The puffin rode on her shoulder, and in the harbor the school of dolphins moved and sometimes rushed by twos and threes and leapt from the water.

"He always did get a little impatient. Wanted to have me near him, ya know?" explained Cookie.

All of them were there: Maria-Elena and Renato, Muscovado and Izzy, Chiara and Ananda. They were still alive; still had a chance, had they not? This was the Pacific Ocean, was it not?

Besides, Cookie had told them the name of her boat: the *Nostos*.

"You think you can find Lost Coast?" inquired Ananda.

"I'll just sail north until I feel lost. I hope we can make it. Sometimes, looking at all of you, I get that doomed feelin'," said Cookie. She felt exhausted and low.

"You probably just need some more company," suggested Muscovado Taine, who loved the idea of a chance to buck up Cookie, "someone with experience at sea, been in and out of boats his whole life. Now a man like that could come in real handy." And he smiled his tropical smile.

"Probably you're thinking that you'd like a girl aboard, someone you could teach to sail. The girl would be so grateful." And Izzy smiled her pepper-and-mischief smile.

"Will you two shut up and come aboard and help me get this deck shipshape? And who could refuse you two meltdown, long-dancin' lovers anything, anyway?" said Cookie gruffly as the delighted Iz and Musco clambered onto the boat.

"But wait a minute. Don't we get to do something? Are we to be just shunted aside?" protested Renato.

Cookie was starting to blush with all this attention. "A thousand times I have asked myself, how did I get on the road with a bunch that does nothing but yack? It's like a flock of birds. What happened to the old-fashioned hard-livin' strong quiet types?"

And all of the Hurricane Troupe immediately assumed expressions of great sobriety and gravity. They stared down at Cookie. They looked as if they were thinking deep thoughts. Nary a word was uttered. A gray, muggy cloud of seriousness fell down over the dock. Rather than partaking of the open air of the coastline, the dock took on the mood of the catacombs.

"All right I take it back! Fer chrissakes come on board and give me a hand!"

And with a hubbub the Hurricane Troupe scrambled on board

and went about cleaning wood and brightwork, stowing this and that, scouring the galley, rearranging sails, and stepping smartly to Cookie's orders.

And when the craft was shipshape, they gathered in the cockpit and lounged around delightedly, and Izzy asked the obvious question:

"Well, let's say we can get to Lost Coast. What will we do, anyway?"

"Have a wedding!" answered Cookie immediately.

"Who's getting married?" asked Renato.

"*You* should get married, for heaven's sake! Sometimes I think all those paint fumes have got to you over the years. Turned part of your brain to cabbage."

Renato, who had not even allowed himself to hope, looked at Maria-Elena in surprise.

"Before the baby's born," Cookie went on. "It's proper. You're lucky you got me around to make sure everything's done right."

The baby in the womb piped right up. "Well, I should *hope* that I would be born to a couple bound in holy matrimony. Otherwise, forget it. I'm happy where I am."

"I'd love a wedding! I'll cook!" volunteered Muscovado.

"I'll serve!" threw in Izzy.

"I'll handle the guest list," said Chiara reflectively.

"I'll make sure this is a proper civil ceremony," said Ananda in her lawyerly way.

With this talk, Renato was shining inside. But Maria-Elena turned to him and, after a silence, said, "We have traveled so far. And for now we must try to protect each other and finish this one journey. Then we must part. Renato, I have told you: no man may marry a Daughter of the Moon. No man. But we will travel on together, just now. Just for a time."

Renato, worn-out with his lecturing and painting and hoping, was so happy just to have a few more days with her that the shining began to show on him; even his shadow looked brighter.

"Well, I guess we have to sail," said Cookie. "I for one am goddam tired of waitin'. I mean, I know that storytellin' is livin'; but livin' is livin' too, right?"

Cookie strode around the deck, the sunlight polished the sea, the little puffin looked bemused, the whole day was buoyant around the cowgirl's rocking ancient boat. "So I'm headed out. Anybody who wants on board, say now."

"I'm sailing with you just so I can see Musco's dreadlocks slicked back by the wind," asserted Izzy.

"Ananda and I will ramble on the back roads, in the pickup. A long warm ride," said Chiara.

"Well, now, I'm unsteady on my feet enough, with this lunar daughter of mine, so Renato and I will take the wagon up," said Maria-Elena.

The peacock came strutting down the dock. "You'd think that this group has no goddam *use* for beauty! That you see beauty everywhere! Cocky bunch! And furthermore, I don't see us finding out much at all about the Wild Light of God. Which is, after all, what I want," the bird said irritably. "And what about the Proverbs of God? I guess Divinity has been ruled out of order, huh? The way you act you'd think all of you run around with saints, or something!" So continued our irate peacock.

And, sure enough, Saint Francis came sauntering along the shoreline and then, stepping lightly, walked straight out across the top of the water and leapt into the boat.

"Sorry I brought it up," said the peacock quickly.

"I know how you all like to dillydally," said Francis courteously and patiently, "but those two young gentlemen from the bar, along with a devoted company, are coming here to dispose of one or two of you and then take Izzy away. So I think it advisable you move this party up the coast." And the saint smiled his wily smile.

"I'll meet you there," he finished, then turned and did a nice swing-time shuffle-step back across the water to the shore.

They looked across and Homer had pulled the wagon and pickup around and had the doors open and the motors running. Fine! he was thinking. Once an epic poet, and three thousand years later I'm a damned parking attendant! But he did manage to go to the shoreline and salute Ananda and Chiara.

But even the Hurricane Troupe had gotten the message. They rushed ashore and clambered in the pickup and wagon and roared out of the lot. Cookie and Musco and Izzy backed the boat out of its berth and hauled up the mainsail and headed to sea, the dolphins swimming all around the boat.

They didn't need to worry quite so much, though. For Gus, taking charge of diversionary measures, came up with the right scheme. He donned a spiffy blue policeman's uniform, and when Tabby and Grimes and their complement of boys came asking how to get to the wharf, he gave them directions that took them straight to the city dump.

And it was in that dump, stymied and stern and in a hurry to be of service to society, that Tabby yelled out the window for directions. The woman who answered was in a pickup truck that seemed to have a small forest growing out of the bed. It was, of course, the fit and fiery-haired Festina. She told them about a shortcut that would lead them straight to the wharf. Unfortunately, in following her directions they ran into a ditch filled with fetid, enormous ferns that, as they scrambled to the bank to watch, seemed to leap like animals upon their cars. It was as though the plants were growing before their eyes.

Festina, who had followed them, stood there smirking.

But help was near. They were slowly winched out of the ditch by a tough young woman named Laila, she of the melodious voice and beautiful black skin. She said she was glad to help and worked right by their side to make sure their engines were running okay. She wished them well and stood smiling and winking as the boys climbed in their cars and headed again for the harbor. But they found it was hard to see where they were going. It was as though the cab were filled with numerous bustling little clouds. The frustrated Tabby and Grimes had to keep waving the billowing vapors furiously away.

"What the fuck is going on?" yelled Tabby in frustration as they rolled to a stop and waited for the cab to clear.

"I'm starting to bleed again from all this excitement," said Grimes.

It made them madder.

When they hit the Berkeley wharf, the *Nostos* was headed out of the harbor.

*   *   *

The *Nostos* flashed out under the Golden Gate with Izzy in the
bow taking spray and Muscovado Taine at the tiller and Cookie
striding the deck, the puffin with his feathers streaming still on
her shoulder. They headed out west on a close reach and then
swung around to put the wind on the port beam. The coast
of northern California stood in its shawl of mist and looked out
to sea.

Cookie watched her opalescent Izzy. Her skin glistened with
saltwater, her dark hair was wet and shining. Cookie could see
the eagerness in her as she watched the sea and the shore. Izzy
drew into her eyes the future; she loved the future, she went to
it with an unreserved embrace.

It was simple, what Izzy wanted: the thriving on earth, by how
she lived, of all she loved.

Cookie came up to her. "You two meet me back in the cockpit in a half hour. We all got to prepare for what's comin' our
way." And she looked at Iz with her it's-goin'-to-be-a-long-day-
on-the-range look.

Renato and Maria-Elena and their eloquent unborn baby snug-
gled together in the front seat of the wagon. They cruised across
the Bay Bridge into San Francisco, then chugged through the city
on their way to the Golden Gate. Following this route, they got
to say good-bye to the Bay, and then a slow-moving salute and
farewell to the metropolis that shines with ocean light.

The painter and the Daughter of the Moon, who hoped so
soon to bear the thirteenth and last of the Daughters—making,
with her, one for every full moon in the year—drove their way
down along Lombard. When they got onto the bridge, they could
see below them, sailing out the Golden Gate, the *Nostos,* with
Izzy and Muscovado Taine in the cockpit conferring like a couple of old salts.

Maria-Elena, with her dark wisdoms, watched them.

"This is going to be so hard," she said quietly.

*   *   *

Homer and Francis were sitting in a courtyard in Mendocino.
Homer was working.

"How's the plot coming?" asked Francis skeptically.

"I can hardly believe it!" said Homer gruffly. "Why me? And
with so bizarre a cast of characters?"

"Relax. You're good with large battle scenes."

In the corral of her ranch in the Smoke Creek Desert, Beulah
stood with her bullwhip. On each fencepost, she had balanced
a target—a cup, a tobacco tin, a penknife, a cigarette lighter—
all around the corral. Then she uncoiled her bullwhip and,
slowly, methodically, turning easily in rhythmic practice,
whipped each target off the top of its post.

In Nevada City, a coyote padded into the Blue Dream Cafe and
went straight through to the back patio and sat down and looked
long with her golden eyes at Nattie.

"So it's time?" she inquired as she returned the coyote's gaze.
The minutes passed.

"Let's go, then," she said. And she rose from her bench and
went to make a call. In a shadowy garage in Nevada the phone
rang, and Nattie heard on the line the raspy voice of Antelope
on the Moon.

14

MUSCOVADO AND IZZY AND COOKIE bucked their way up the northern Californian coast. The puffin would sometimes fly from Cookie's shoulder, circle around the *Nostos,* and dive down into the sea; then to emerge and come glistening back to the gunwales. Whenever Izzy came near him, he gazed at her with the prolonged and amused curiosity of those who move between worlds.

Life in the next world, as everyone knows, is not subject to the delights and deteriorations of the movement of time. That is, the next world is spiritous, pure interior space that extends in uninterrupted splendors through the past and into the future, a silent and loving witness to the story of our lives.

And witness to more than our stories: those in the next world see what our stories mean.

Such were the subjects that Izzy and Musco and Cookie debated. This discussion was very much aided by Cookie's provision of a fine lunch of hot dogs, corn chips, and cold beer, followed by ice cream cones. Trying to lick the cones on the pitching sailboat created the most havoc, with Musco taking on the forehead a dollop of chocolate chip, and Izzy besmirched with a whole scoop of tangerine cream.

Cookie, of course, presided with her usual good sense over these proceedings.

"So, what's the story?" asked Muscovado in his journalistic way.

Cookie just smirked at him. "You're goin' to find out real soon. We got to go to Mendocino to meet up with the rest of this crazy troupe, and then Izzy, you got to set down with Homer and listen real close. He's got some news, you know, who's in danger an' how an' what-all. And he's in a fever to get on with it."

"Are you trying to suggest that Homer is eager to stretch out in bed with my mother and Ananda?" Izzy inquired in her evasive way.

"The fog would burn off early along Lost Coast," speculated Musco.

"It's a long way from here to there," said Cookie. "So as I was sayin': Izzy gets the story, then not long after we swing into action, our hearts pumpin' an' breath comin' quick—God, I love trouble! And if we play out a story we want, we move on to Lost Coast."

"And if we don't?" inquired Musco.

"Well, if we don't, Musco, then we'll be real lucky if we even have the chance to pass around some good-bye kisses."

"Hand-to-hand combat?" asked the reluctant Musco, who with his slow, warm tropical hands stroked Izzy's face and arms, he rubbed her feet, with his touch prayed for her and whispered to the sea winds a pledge of his life to her protection.

"Not the kind you're used to," answered Cookie.

As Ananda drove the pickup north, she was unaware of the tiny transmitter behind the rear bumper. It had been placed there by an ex-cop turned private investigator, from San Francisco, a man learned in tracking. He had used the device successfully many times. This was so obvious a case—a band of perverts running from the two good kids. Perverts! That young girl they had, what were they doing with her? Did they take turns on the beautiful thing? Bastards! The police couldn't arrest them, there was no reported crime. But most crimes weren't reported. You couldn't do what's right. What everybody wants you to do.

We need a way to deal with people like that. The police needed help, more people on the street, more guardians, more spirit, more hope. It had been such a thrill to read about Tabby and Grimes. Look at the way they had stood up against Tabby's own father. It must have been so tough. And the way they had caught the two who killed the sheriff in Downieville.

The investigator's eyes teared up when he thought of the two boys. He had met them and gotten all the details about the black and the girl. He had known the two boys would confide in him.

He had called the sheriff's office up in Downieville and pieced together the story of the Hurricane Troupe. Something stank. One of them, some big fucker, had gotten killed. That was the giveaway right there—they ran with scumbag killers. And not long after the whole bunch of them had headed to Berkeley— what a tip-off. Probably a small drug operation. They murdered the big guy, one of those inside power struggles, and then headed down for sickville to do more deals. And what can be done about it? What? Everybody wants to sit around and tell us about rights. Does puke have rights?

When he heard about the trouble on Telegraph, he knew that the two kids needed help. So he put out the word on the street to keep watch for the Troupe's cars, and he'd located the pickup. And tagged it with the transmitter so that it could be tracked.

The last part was getting a receiver to Tabby and Grimes.

The two boys, he'd had them out to his house. They were bigger than he had thought, standing straight, used to the spotlight. He could see how much they wanted to make things better. For years he'd been looking for some young people he could teach.

He was amazed at their weapons. But he saw to it that they got some backups: some beautiful laser-sight pistols with twenty-five-shot box magazines, an army carbine with a six-hundred-yard range and a barrel configuration where they could mount a grenade launcher. A new NATO design, very stylish, with a twenty-inch, chrome-lined bore and eight-hundred-round-per-minute fire rate. And to top it all off, a Peruvian buzzgun.

Not in twenty years of police work had he ever been so happy as when Grimes, so stocky and strong, had looked over the weapons and they'd talked about them. The kid was so knowledgeable! They weren't just do-gooder street kids. They knew their stuff. Both of the boys had shaken his hand. They'd said how he could be a father to them.

Tabby was excited about the placement of the transmitter.

The three of them turned on the receiver and watched the finder tune in. This brand-new tracker system triangulated off satellite systems and relayed to the screen the latitude and longitude of the criminals; then it searched a database for the right map and there displayed a little blinking, scarlet point of light that showed where the scum-suckers were.

Ananda and Chiara, followed by Renato and Maria-Elena and the thirteenth Daughter, were over the Golden Gate, past Santa Rosa, heading north at sixty-five miles per hour.

"I can get you an unmarked police cruiser," the investigator volunteered.

Saint Francis was looking incredulously at Homer. "I know you like to put together elaborate plots, but this is going too far! You can't be serious about the sea dragon?"

Homer looked at his text. "What, I can't have a little fun?"

"This is the twentieth century," Francis gently reminded him.

This reminder made even Homer serious. "Okay, okay, I'll redraft. How long do I have?"

"We need to tell them everything tomorrow."

"It's going to be mostly up to them, anyway. This is just a sketch."

* * *

In the Smoke Creek Desert, in the twilight of northwestern Nevada, the gristly and powerful rancher Beulah strode out into the hills behind her corrals. She headed for a big cave that was brimming with light, a thick light like gold melted and moving in the pools of its own heat.

"Bolt!" she said to the seething. "We got to go."

Cookie and Musco both watched Izzy, who could not seem to stay away from the bow, hanging there, catching spray. Her supple body was edged with silver light off the sea. She rocked easily and happily, as though taking into her flesh the salt, light, wave forms, weathers, powers—the whole symposium of sea beauties.

"Cookie!" exclaimed Musco.

"Heaven's sake, what is it?"

"Help us. You must help us."

Cookie turned the *Nostos* for shore, and with the wind astern she headed for Bodega Bay. "Shit, I don't know how to help. I keep on stewin' about those two boys. 'Bout all I know now is that we got to sail into Bodega Bay and find Nattie."

Dorothy Gallagher sat in the backseat of the unmarked police cruiser. Tabby was at the wheel, and Grimes sat with a receiver in his hands. The thing was incredible: the geographic database included street maps of even the smallest towns in the area. Right then, Grimes was following a blinking red light as it moved down a road toward Bodega Bay.

"I wish we had a warplane," commented Grimes in his strategic way.

"We'll follow them real slow," said Tabby calmly. "It's like fate, it's always following, following. They think that there will never be any consequences. The longer we wait, the more scared they'll be, because they know they have to pay."

Grimes smiled. Tabby was getting more and more eloquent. It was amazing how educable his friend was. He'd gotten decorous. Grimes was proud. A lot of people would have given up on Tabby a long time ago, but Grimes had seen that spark, the natural bravery, the longing for justice.

"When I get her in my arms!" exclaimed Tabby.

"Wait until she sees all our new clothes!" added Grimes.

"Are you getting all this down, Dorothy?"

Dorothy was still studying the map. "Why don't we go to Point Reyes? There's long beaches there, and I could take a walk by myself and think."

"Do you have enough cameras for when we catch these people?" interjected Tabby worriedly. "They need to have a lot of shots from different angles, so they can play different ones back in slow motion. It's in slow motion that you can see how graceful a man can be. Sometimes in the muscle shows you can feel that grace take you over. God-given, that's what it feels like."

In Bodega Bay, walking near the harbor, Ananda stopped Chiara and embraced her. "I'm not leaving your side."

"Do we have the throwing axes in the car?" asked Chiara.

"We do. Though we should remember what they did to Juha. Do you think an ax would have done him any good?"

Tabby and Grimes had changed to a pickup set up for towing. They hauled an enormous trailer filled with all the old and new weapons, and enough ammunition to incinerate Mendocino.

Grimes was irritated: "Everybody's so tired of the talking. All the chatting. Let's look at this way, let's look at that way, maybe there's a third way, maybe we can all jack off together. Let's wait for the guy in the suit to decide. Bullshit! How long do we have to watch all the talkers? Is any of that doing any good?"

Dorothy shook her head in wonder. This kid was really getting on with it, she thought.

The Police of Gentle Jesus had a following, and Grimes thought it was important to teach them. These were such good times. Even the sky was more beautiful, once you had the things you needed, like grenade launchers. Just knowing you could move down a block, taking out house after house, knowing who deserved it. But without getting all emotional and sloppy as you worked. Justice was a profession, and a professional never lost his composure. His calm was his joy.

All the same, Grimes had a problem to solve: "What are we going to wear in Mendocino? We need to set an example, you know." He looked at Dorothy. "How about the tweed? Maybe a nice tweed coat and the dark glasses, like FBI agents? You know," he went on, gesturing to the road behind, "these details are important."

Tabby and Grimes glanced back at their caravan—the other boys, they called them the Deputies of Gentle Jesus. And there were plenty of church groups in vans, and lots of young girls, the Pretty Girls of Jesus. Some more unmarked police cruisers.

Grimes gazed at the line of cars and was ecstatic. "It's just like I always said—"

"As you always said!" corrected Dorothy from the backseat.

"Okay, okay, it's just as I always said. Once they knew—"

"Once they knew we cared," Tabby broke in, his eyes glistening. He paused and watched the road. "Maybe we should find a meadow. We could get into some briefs and oil up and play some music and do a muscle show. There we'll be, all bright, the ocean behind us." He turned to Dorothy. "You could get it all on tape, no problem, right?"

"Let's do it!" Dorothy was thinking of how to frame the shots.

From the tracking screen, it looked as if the criminals had stopped in Bodega Bay; and so Tabby and Grimes had, in their zeal, gotten ahead of them. They could just take some time out, and wait to see where their prey went next. When justice and punishment are at hand, it's good to have a chance to savor their inevitability.

They were still on Highway 1, moving along the coast past Fort Ross, and Tabby turned off at the road into Salt Point State Park. The lane wound through wild rose and cypress brushed by the sea winds into the shape of clouds. Down by the Pacific, on either side of the creek, there was a meadow.

"Perfect!" exclaimed Tabby. And he jumped out and opened the gun-and-ammo trailer. They had put up big mirrors with lights at the back wall, track lights just as they're supposed to be. Everything was clean. There was a computer with software to edit and color videotape; Dorothy would take her shots and then work on them until they were right.

Police and gun magazines were everywhere; there were adventure stories, news clippings on how they had saved Angelica and found the killer of the sheriff in Downieville. The old trophies from weight-lifting contests were on a shelf, along with Grimes's self-help paperbacks. The shelf was starting to fill up now with novels, mostly crime fiction. Grimes wanted to understand the criminal mind.

Angelica had sent a tape that a cellmate in prison had made of Tabby's father after Tabby had pistol-whipped him. They kept the tape in the trailer. Great stuff! Sounded like the old bastard was sobbing and chewing on his tongue. Maybe he'd eat the fucking thing, thought Tabby, and a good thing too.

To know the right thing to do was so easy. Tabby couldn't understand why there was so much confusion and chitchat about the problems that everybody ran into every day—especially when it was so obvious that justice and punishment really excited people. It's such a relief to everybody. But it had to be left to professionals.

Tabby looked around, thumbed through an article on surveillance. He played some recordings of classical cello, looked over their clothes and clippings, handled the trophies, caught sight of himself in the mirror. He could hear the voices of the girls in one of the church groups as they giggled and huddled together, whispering excitedly.

In Bodega Bay, up behind a little restaurant called the Sandpiper, there is a wooden house facing the water. Painted cream with blue trim, the house has a splendid long porch that holds tables and chairs. When the fog comes in off the Pacific, it's the ideal place to have a hot brandy and listen to a story.

It was their last sanctuary. And so our travelers gathered around Nattie, just arrived from Nevada City. And old Nattie, she said, "Just take it easy! There's nothin' wrong with some last-minute storytellin'! Now is there?" And the old woman looked around belligerently.

"Okay, okay, let's have it," said Izzy.

And Nattie told them at long last the

The Story of the Joke in the Middle of the World; or, the Music of the Spheres

"Now, nobody would think, right off, that the celebrated Music of the Spheres holds a joke. But in fact, the joke is the first thing taught to us by the Music: which is, as you know, the singing and storytelling done by the earth moving through space, by the planets and all the stars moving through the beauties of day and night."

"You can learn about a joke from the Music of the Spheres? You sure?" This was news to Ananda.

"Sure as dirt!" said Nattie calmly. "Now the joke, once learned, has its ways; and they are the ways of liberty. Once the joke is learned, the world will sidle up to us, with whispers and asides and the most shameless rhetoric. The world will make its way delightedly into our days, our phrases, our reflections. And it is then we are able, wherever we may be, to hear the ancient and future Music. Such are the forces set free if you know the joke."

"Hey, we got to entertain," protested Musco. "Besides, jokes and love are married, aren't they? In bed together, no?"

Nattie cleared her throat. "If I may return to my story now! Has anyone ever told you that you're good listeners?"

"You want a passive bunch? We're supposed to sit here like rutabaga?" gibed Chiara.

"Please don't bring up food," riposted Nattie, "I'm already hungry, and I want to finish this."

"When you're done, I'll cook you up a pot of goat curry," offered Muscovado.

"I love goat curry!" said Nattie with salivary enthusiasm. "I like it with rum!"

"We're ready for the rest of the story now," said Iz, rolling her eyes.

"As I was saying!" boomed Nattie to cover the growling of her stomach. "Now, how did I find out that there is now widespread ignorance about the joke in the middle of the world? It went like this: I was out working in those days, taking different jobs, roaming around, trying this and that. Now, why was I so much on the move?"

" 'Cause you're a goddam vagabond, not solid, responsible citizens like us," guessed Renato.

"Nope. It's because I was dancing from place to place, dancing to the Music of the Spheres. What, did you think it was just some ethereal fluff?" Nattie asked roughly.

"Okay, okay, so yer two-steppin' around the towns, so then what?" Cookie demanded.

"And so I got to go shoot the breeze with everybody. I went to the tradesmen, and behind their counters I took a job and I would just improvise my way through the day, following the lead and the rhythm of the Music I could always hear. It was sumptuous and happy. Even when I was standing, still I was dancing. And everything would go forth in its strange, blessed ways until I noticed behind the counter that something was missing. First of all, no one could hear the Music but me. And I could see this was because they had never been introduced to it."

"How do you get introduced?" asked Izzy immediately.

"By learning the joke in the middle of the world! First you learn the joke; then you understand the Music! Just like I said! Listen up!" reprimanded Nattie.

"She has your teaching style," said Izzy to her mother Chiara.

"Now as I was saying," went on Nattie huffily, "I was all alone there. You ever try to dance alone? It was terrible. It was as though the air had died.

"But I was undaunted. Because when I stepped outside into the blue air of the afternoon, I could hear the Music again, I could hear all of it, and so I ambled my way down the road. I stopped in a computer company that was known as young and strong, smart and swift, rich and cool. And I landed a job there writing code and I loved it, the order and the finery and exactitude, and I was guided by the precise mathematics of the Music I knew best. But once again I saw that no one could hear the Music. I looked around me and I saw how everyone had lost the sense of the wink and unpredictability of things, the savor in the world that comes before and outlasts any fortune, and what did they think they were doing, anyway? This is what I asked them. And they drove me away—not savvy and disciplined enough.

"But outside I heard the Music again in all its fullness."

"This is getting to sound *very* serious—a homeless jokester," broke in Izzy.

"And so this old gal here went on with her itinerant labor, stopping in on booksellers, carpenters, physicians, plumbers, sheet-metal workers, farmers; on pilots, bartenders, lawyers, lumberjacks, teachers. I worked everywhere, and in some places everyone could hear the whole Music, and there everyone had long known the joke in the middle of the world; and where they didn't know, I offered to teach them. People said they would think about it, they told me to come back at a better time, they said that this was a year with a heavy workload but maybe next year, they pleaded pressing family responsibilities, they said that they would like to learn but could not because of bad impetigo, and one man said he was in just too bad a mood because of his clubfoot."

"Now wait a minute," asked Chiara, "did you visit everybody?"

"Not everybody," clarified the old woman.

"Why not? Who wouldn't want a chance to see a pistol like you?" asked Muscovado.

"Why not everyone?" pressed Ananda.

"Look, I'm just one old lady, okay?" Nattie explained irritably.

"What happened to all the people who sent you away?" insisted Izzy.

"Their next visitor was sorrow; and he will want to stay," said the old woman cheerfully.

"This doesn't sound so good. I better get to work on the curry," suggested Muscovado.

"We've had enough sorrow," said Cookie. "Tell us the joke."

"No question we could use this joke," added Renato.

"I'll get to it," said Nattie.

"I'd like to know myself!" said Maria-Elena's baby from the womb.

"Okay, okay! *We* are the joke. We are *ourselves* the joke. We are, each one of us, a joke. How do we know? It is the first thing you hear of the Music of the Spheres—for those harmonies have more than music. Listen—you will hear the heavens laughing at us. And where we cannot hear that laughter, where we are stuffed with our own serious selves—in those places work is extinguishing the soul."

"The world does have a kind of smirk to it," said Iz reflectively.

"So now what do we do?" inquired Ananda in her efficient way. "Now what?"

"This is what: love that laughter in the air—a movement of life inside all our lives, the beginning of celebration at the end of hatred: the first of what we learn, if we live. Once you know you're being laughed at, you can make use of it, for this is enchanted laughter: it will rid you of yourself and introduce you to a musical language at the midmost of the world. The Music of the Spheres! It don't sound so bad, now does it?" said the old woman impatiently. "So pay attention, goddammit! Now is the time. You're going to need what you're given." And she paused and looked at them.

"Why are you saying all this?" asked Maria-Elena.

"Because it's my best story and I might be telling you good-bye."

Muscovado got up and walked off by himself.

"I think I'm too hungry to talk anymore." And old Nattie stood up and went to help Muscovado cook.

And they would have thought about good-byes, they would have gotten more coffees and huddled together, they would have handed round ideas for the journey to come—but right there on a porch of a beautiful wooden house in Bodega Bay there came a sweep of music and a laughter.

It was just what the boys wanted: in briefs and combat boots, stalking around. They had camo-paint under their eyes. They yelled and ran and spun round and posed. They handled the guns rarely but lovingly. The wind touseled their hair, and the ocean ran up the beach, as though wanting itself to see them.

After the show and the speeches, the boys changed into blazers and white shirts. Dorothy had a little circle of chairs set up, where people could come and sit with Tabby and Grimes. Some hospital groups had come to offer thanks for the donations that Tabby and Grimes had made to the Surgery for Poor Children program. They had pictures of little ones who could not have afforded surgery they needed, but Tabby and Grimes had made it possible. Fathers and mothers whose children had died came and said how their young ones had loved playing with the toys bought with Tabby's donations. The toys were part of the program; they made the children laugh. The parents wept to tell their stories and hugged Tabby and kissed his cheeks. Tabby was quiet and respectful.

Grimes brought out a Berkeley evangelical group that used the boys' money to feed hungry people on holidays—Independence Day, Christmas, Thanksgiving, and Valentine's Day. But the evangelicals didn't take credit, they never did. They always told their beneficiaries the food came from God and that they didn't owe anybody anything. Some of them came to church and they were given hats that read I HAVE EATEN OF THE FOOD OF THE LORD.

Tabby bent his head and thought again of the innocent people in his father's congregation. He couldn't wait to start up the church again. And he gave the Berkeley restaurants more bucks for the holiday meals program. All the same, Tabby hoped they weren't feeding any whiners. You could have dignity even if you were starving. Everybody knew that.

The Policemen's Fraternal Aid Society came and talked about how hard it was to protect the public these days. Tabby and Grimes looked at each other and thought about these cops—all the hard work, all those who misunderstood them or didn't appreciate them.

The policemen went on to say how much good they could do with the ten thousand dollars Grimes had given them. They could buy special bullets: the big hollow-stemmed Cripplers, the Sunbursts, the Tickets to Hell, which had a shaped and barbed body that would carry off a big gobbet of flesh no matter where you hit your assailant.

When the storytelling was over, the followers and visitors spilled across the meadow and down onto the beach and some of them went into the woods—to whatever place seemed most full of blessings.

All except seven of a girls' singing group from a church. They were the ones who had shopped for the first uniforms that Tabby and Grimes had ever been given. The young men had since put them away in the trunk of memorabilia—it had some used weapons, a bloody sheriff's star, a lock of Angelica's hair, thank-you notes and invitations to speak—but the uniforms were special. They marked the beginning of a fated, new life of real service.

The seven were all blondes, sixteen to eighteen years old. They had been singing together for six years, making up songs for verses of the Bible. All kinds of social groups sought them out. Seven Little Sisters of the Lord, they earned money touring around in their white dresses and red-and-white hair ribbons, with the minister as chaperon.

They were all together at the beach. The blondes stood close with the bottles of golden oil. Over the remarkable muscular bodies of Tabby and Grimes the white hands of the girls moved with delicacy and affection and shyness; as though the two boys stood in a surround of butterflies.

15

COOKIE LOOKED UP the coast. She could see the Mendocino Headlands, and just beyond it Mendocino Bay, and the mouth of Big River. The misted redwoods floated on the ridges, the country ascended behind the headlands.

Farther up along the coast, she could see for the first time the beginnings of silent, incandescent Lost Coast.

"We're headed in," she said. And she turned the tiller and trimmed the sails and pointed the bow toward shore. In the little town of Mendocino, Ananda, Renato, and Maria-Elena and her loquacious unborn baby all awaited them.

Cookie anchored at the mouth of Big River. Chiara met them. "What's next?" asked our Izzy.

"We were thinking it would be nice to take a few hours of vacation before we all get back to work," her mother informed her.

And they roamed on into the quiet town, led by the stocky Cookie with the puffin still riding high and sassy on her shoulder. The bird, when Cookie strode aggressively down the streets, hung on rapturously. He leaned into the turns, ducked under bushes, braced himself firmly for the long straightaways—rather like a motorcycle racer. And when Cookie would stop, he would cock his head in a madcap and innocent way and look with a kind of gentle laser beam of curiosity at the passersby—as though he could see their stories. Of course, he could. And he commented to Cookie. This led to some loud expostulations by the tactless cowgirl:

"No, not with his dog! How little? . . . A weimaraner? No! And in the shower? He *perfumes* the dog? And dresses her up? A whole wardrobe of little nightgowns?

"He'll die next Thursday? A great white shark? Nothing left but his toes?

"Everybody in town hates her, but she will save twenty lives in two years?"

Then the puffin shut down his reading of events and characters and the future because the Troupe took another ice cream break. Now Musco and Izzy, it is true, had recently partaken; but we recall that eating ice cream at sea is more like a food fight than a sacrament. Here on solid ground, they could be more properly worshipful.

So it was that, outfitted with some rather elaborate cones, they returned piously to the streets.

So it was they licked and loitered, they hummed and sauntered, they flung barbs, traded cones, gazed at the world and whistled at the sea.

Chiara, to mock the peacock, decided to have a Proverbs of God contest. Whoever won got free ice cream for a year. She set up a little stand, and residents and visitors came in one by one to let fly their phrases.

From the first, a traveling salesman in a lavender polyester suit: "Even if you're selling the truth, everybody wants a discount."

"Not bad," commented Chiara. "Definitely in the running."

"A little materialistic, wouldn't you say?" said the peacock.

And Chiara gave him a flick on the side of his azure head.

The second applicant was a lumberjack of swarthy countenance, of fit and vibrant physique, his muscles knit together to make what Chiara guessed was an elegant fabric. The man, for his part, was taken with Chiara's comeliness.

He offered, "Before you cut down the tree, make sure it's not your own leg."

"How about," responded Chiara, "before you cut down the tree, make sure it's not holding up your soul."

"That's pretty good," said the lumberjack. "If we had about two weeks just to work together on it, I reckon we could come up with a whole set of real zingers. Lines so good you'd have to whisper them." And he looked with heat and hope at our Chiara.

She sighed. It really did sound splendid. But really, hadn't she been adventurous enough these last months?

"Moving right along . . ." said the peacock intemperately.

"Why don't you try following me with suggestions and enticements?" said our Chiara.

"I'll be very specific," the lumberjack promised.

"For the love of God! Why can't you stick to business?" reprimanded the peacock.

"For the love of God," replied Chiara very reasonably.

And the man went out smiling, to be replaced by a woman who just happened to be the mate and lover of Saint Francis. Chiara and the peacock knew something was up because when she moved her hand, she left in the air radiant drifting lines of light, as though the room were full of shooting stars.

Chiara got to her feet. "Who *are* you?" she asked urgently.

"My name is Clare. And my story is for another time."

"What can you tell us now?" shot back Chiara.

"I can tell you this: I know the syllables of wind, and what the flights of birds spell in the air."

Clare paused. But neither Chiara nor, for once, the peacock, felt like interrupting.

"I know how in a storm at sea there are sentences in the whitecaps, and by that salt eloquence we can learn to talk with the sweet meanings of fair days."

"And how about ice cream? How does that figure in?" Chiara wanted to know.

"I go for the classic double scoop on a sugar cone," the woman answered immediately. "In fact, ice cream in the middle of the afternoon puts me in that satisfied mood, just right for a meditation on the colors of heaven—the ones we understand when the shining of our eyes matches the workings on earth of the Wild Light of God," she said casually.

The peacock was stunned and did a somersault so clumsy that, to get back on his feet, he had to extricate himself from his feathers. "So *you're* the one I've been waiting for! You know how that light moves on earth! The light we can learn to see—I should have known!"

Chiara smiled. "I don't think you should tell him just yet the story of the Wild Light," she suggested slyly.

"I think you're right," agreed the woman. And she turned and walked out.

"What?" raged the peacock. "All this time waiting for my story to be told and then you let her get away. Is this the thanks I get for all my Proverbs? Huh?"

And the peacock went stalking out the door, fluttering and gazing madly about, and took off down the street in pursuit of the light-making visitor with her teasing wisdoms.

Eleven shining Daughters of the Moon—the sisters of Maria-Elena—walked in hope onto the sands of a wilderness cove along the Lost Coast.

In Mendocino, the light was marking the streets with minute late-afternoon dazzles. There was a slowing of the hours. Time pooled and eddied in the corners of the town.

Homer and Saint Francis were looking for Izzy. They found her out on the bluffs above the blue Pacific.

She was leaning back into the arms of Muscovado Taine. They had a ritual posture they used at such times: she would first undo the top of Musco's shirt, then turn around, and as she leaned back, Musco would gather up her long loose warm black tresses and let them trail down between his shirt and skin. And as they watched and whispered, he felt her hair turn over the skin of his chest, again and again.

Lustrous, Izzy watched the lustrous sea.

To interrupt such a scene was not the first inclination of the two helpers. But they had work to do.

"I will attend to this decorous young couple," offered Francis, "if you will gather the others of the Troupe."

"Meet you in the courtyard by the bakery," said Homer as he went off.

That evening, an unseasonable lightning storm broke over the peninsula of Point Reyes, dropping light on the beaches, over the marshes, into the sea. Bolt dropped again and again, glittering, inexhaustible, as if at play; as if in practice.

Beulah stood on the beach, watching, watching.

Tomorrow they would be moving north toward Mendocino.

"Well, well, I hope you all really are good onstage. I mean, really good," commenced the brawny Homer. "I've got just the basics figured out; it calls for a lot of improvisation on your part. And the ending, the ending . . . well, it's up to you."

And the poet told them everything: how many were being called, how the roles were given. How there was no escape this time; the confrontation had to happen now—this was the way of the world.

Sometimes he talked right at them in his deep voice. Sometimes he would whisper, sometimes he would sing.

All the while Francis moved among them, for he had tranquillity in his hands. He moved among them, touched them. The Troupe wanted him to come round, because of the sharp fear. It was so improbable. They all gathered around Izzy, wanting to touch her, to talk with her.

Izzy couldn't believe it. "You want me to do *what*? Here? Today?"

Cookie was outraged. She went to Homer and took him by the shoulders. "Wasn't losing Juha enough? Wasn't that enough?" she demanded.

A golden eagle high over the Central Valley canted its long wings, the feathers a burnt bright color. The eagle rode hot up-swelling fountains of air and soared toward Mendocino.

Tabby and Grimes and their caravan were an hour and a half out of Mendocino. The line of cars was longer now. Dorothy's tapes of the gathering at Salt Point had been a sensation in the Bay Area, especially on the talk shows: "a lurid but real depiction of citizen justice at work," said one. "A righteous and effective ex-ample of bravery, of two young men who got fed up with the know-nothing, do-nothing attitude of most citizens in this once-great country," said another. "These boys may scare us, but think of them: from difficult family backgrounds, they have trained themselves. It's a lesson of transcendence. These kids have beat the odds. And listening to them talk, so much without preten-sion, so natural a humility. The dreams of the future and the spirit of America are alive in these boys," judged a third.

Dorothy was fielding offers from other TV stations, but KICU had offered her rich bonuses, with incentives based on ratings of the news hour on those nights when they showcased a special report on the Police of Gentle Jesus. The ratings kept going up, Dorothy kept getting richer. On her portable fax in the van they towed, she was sent the numbers after each broadcast. She stud-ied these figures, she considered what worked and what didn't, and she used that analysis to shape her next segment. It was just like being a novelist, she thought, except that her work mattered to the world. All those slaving writers, what a joke. She was not describing life—she was creating it. She was the playwright of reality.

"So where is she? Where?" asked Tabby.

Grimes had had trouble for a while getting the fix from the satellites integrated with the database of street maps. But the military supply company had sent a technician, and now Grimes studied the crimson point that was the Troupe's car parked on the streets of Mendocino.

"They haven't moved for hours," Grimes said. "I think they're planning to stay awhile."

"They've given up!" exulted Tabby.

"Are you sure the girl is with them?" asked Dorothy.

"My bride!" exclaimed Tabby.

"She has to be with them," said Grimes. "Who knows how many of them are using her? There's no limit anymore on what people will do to each other. Once a person loses his pride and values, there's no going back."

Saint Francis took some time alone with Izzy and held her hand and spoke to her.

"I think it's a crazy plan," she said. "An absolutely fucking crazy plan."

"It's tough sometimes, but, hey, think of those stigmata."

"If we get through this, will you teach me to walk on water?"

"If we get through this, I'll teach you to cartwheel on water."

Muscovado and Chiara, Renato and Maria-Elena, Ananda and Cookie, and the coyote and the peacock, all took Izzy to the church. They walked in and looked around together, commenting, planning, reviewing. And then they led our Iz outside.

"They'll be here in ten minutes," said Cookie.

"Good! Time for another double scooper!" responded Izzy, and she turned to walk off down to the ice cream shop. Her mother caught her.

"Iz, for heaven's sake."

Mother and daughter looked at each other a long time.

"Is this tragedy or comedy?" Izzy wanted to know.

"I've lost track. I've lost track of everything."

"Good luck." Iz winked.

"Good luck." Her mother took Izzy by the shoulders and kissed her on the lips.

Iz walked over and stood by Muscovado Taine. He gave her a fierce embrace and whispered to her; and then another embrace.

"Where are they? Where are they?" demanded Tabby excitedly.

"The car is right by the church," said Grimes.

"Let's get there!" Tabby said. And following Grimes's directions, he came around the corner and saw her in a crowd of people. A jewel in a pot of bubbling scum.

"What luck!"

Dorothy shook her head. I'm riding a hot streak, she thought. And she got her camera rolling.

Tabby pulled straight over and, still in the cab, stripped off his sweater. He had on some tight pants and a formfitting jersey. He looked back at Dorothy.

"Ready?" he asked.

"Go for it!" she commanded.

Tabby and Grimes spilled from the cab and sprinted to the back of the big trailer. They traded high fives and had a brief, urgent, whispered conversation that ended with "Let's get it done! Gently, now! Fists only!" as they bent low and bolted toward the front. Tabby was in the lead and he burst into the open space in front of the truck; he could just see figures disappearing into alleys, along walkways, far down along the street. Running from them. The pavement in front of the church was empty.

Except for one angular, dark-haired girl.

Tabby straightened his shoulders and strode toward her.

There was silence, everybody was watching.

"At last!" said Izzy weakly, reaching out. "At last you've come." And walking unsteadily, with a pathetic expression of relief and gratitude, she went straight to Tabby and fell into his arms.

16

DOROTHY STOOD BEFORE the Mendocino church for the shot: it was another in her series of broadcasts, like walking from crest to crest. It fit together, it gave her a tingle.

"A Special News Report from KICU—Our News Is *the* News!" Dorothy held forth:

"In another feat of daring and persistence, Tabby and Grimes, the young citizen crime-fighters whose exploits we have followed across California, have recovered a young woman who was kidnapped by a traveling band of misfits. The cult affiliations and whereabouts of this band are unknown, and the police have been unable to get many details from the girl, who is still in shock. We know only her name, Isabella. We have to wait for the details of this young woman's ordeal; all we have at present are rumors of long, dangerous, secretive wandering, and hints of sexual abuse.

"But the story goes on: it's hard to believe that so heartrending a captivity could end in such happiness; sometimes during these past hours, I've felt like I'm living in a fairy tale. This is the news: Isabella refuses to part from her savior. And there is talk of a marriage in the clear air here along the northern Californian coast. It would be the return of a young woman to safety, and to society." Dorothy looks at the church.

"I hope by tomorrow to let you know whether we might hear wedding bells ring in this beautiful Mendocino church.

"From the little town of Mendocino, for station KICU, this is Dorothy Gallagher."

Dorothy and Grimes were trying to calm Tabby down.

"She *bit* me. After I saved her. They gave her up to me, the cowards. It was going so good, I showed her all the clippings, did a show for her in front of the mirrors with the lights and the music and everything, told her about my dad. I said I understood how hard it was. And that I just wanted a clean life, that I would always protect her. I told her she could count on me. Think of that! Having someone to count on! It's the best thing in the world. And I think she did know—she knew that I could be her . . . her rock. That's when she started to cry.

"So I let her cry, and I was crying too. Beautiful!" Tabby's eyes shone at the memory. "And I wanted to do something more. So I put on some of the cello pieces and turned down the lights and took her in front of the mirrors. I felt so close to her, so happy. And I told her to let me see her naked. So tenderly! It was so romantic! And she came up to me real soft and told me to close my eyes and I was so excited! And then she handcuffed me to the railing by the mirror, with my own goddam handcuffs, and she bit me in the arm."

"Maybe it was a love bite," suggested Dorothy.

"What did she say?" asked Grimes.

"She said I couldn't touch her except with the touch given grace by the sacrament of marriage. She wanted me to give her what she had dreamed of in her captivity. She wanted to wear a white dress, and everything had to be right and clean—everything. She wept and said over and over again that she was abused, it was hard for her to trust anyone, and that I had to prove myself. She was so scared."

"That's very well put," commented Grimes. "That's etiquette!"

Grimes felt a little jealous. This Isabella was like refined sugar, very pure. "She's providential, she's like manifest destiny, she's not lugubrious."

Dorothy looked at him. She was getting to be sorry she had given him all those vocabulary books.

"Put up with it, Tabby. It's good for the story."

Tabby was incredulous. "You mean it? No porking until after the wedding?"

Grimes and Dorothy looked at each other.

"She has to stand there at the altar knowing she can trust you," said Grimes to remind Tabby.

"She knows! She knows! I can tell because she's so afraid of the scumbags that have been keeping her. But it's good, because I can comfort her," said Tabby sternly as he thought of her captors. But then he softened. "It's exciting to have her. To love her. Exciting! Her eyes are such a funny color."

"She's a paragon!" said Grimes.

Dorothy thought: A wedding!

Tabby and Grimes got Izzy her own room in a bed-and-breakfast in town; she said she needed to be alone, to recover. She said she needed some books, she needed to be alone and to read. They gave her some comics and some gun magazines and adventure stories. Tabby bought her a nice cuckoo clock, as a love token.

Grimes had some of the choir girls meet with her so they could talk about the Police of Gentle Jesus. She needed to see how the judgments they made were judgments of love.

Grimes explained all this and even took over to her some of his books on the psychology of the criminal mind.

Tabby loved her so much that it was with great relish that he went shopping every day to buy her things: a book about movie heroes, a ballerina's dress, some classical recordings of the cello; fashion magazines—she would need to get dressed up more often, everyone would want to look at her.

Nothing had ever made him so happy as these purchases. It was no use being strong unless you were generous. It was as if she were already teaching him to be good—as only a woman can. He bought her flowers, lipstick, exotic creams that were specially prepared for application to face or thigh or feet, videos with tough exercise programs so she could keep in shape, and some church pamphlets about how to be a good mother. He got her some police training videos on firearms, even some advanced ones on SWAT team assault techniques. He gave her envelopes of money. He gave her photographs of sick children who had died holding the toys that the two heroes had bought them.

Best of all were his visits to her. Grimes went with him.

They took the visits seriously—choosing their clothes, trying on different outfits, having their pictures taken; sometimes they'd clean weapons together. They made sure Izzy saw the grenade launcher but they were casual about it. They sometimes delayed going because Tabby felt so shy and young and flustered.

When they were ready, they would walk out into the misty Pacific sunlight, just at the hour of the morning when the sun was showing the whole world to them: giving it all to them. Strong and tall, they would walk over to Isabella's room and take the lock off her door. And there she would be, with the clippings and videos and pamphlets spread out. Sometimes when they came in, she would be trying on different kinds of makeup, taking up and discarding one hair ribbon after another, dreaming over the pictures in the bride magazines.

One day, she had been tying her hair up in different kinds of buns. Just as she was putting the finishing touches on one she called the Tomcat Bun, because it looked like a cat was sleeping on her head, in came the heroes.

"Hi, babe," greeted Tabby breezily.

"Isabella," said Grimes gravely with an understanding nod.

And Izzy sat with her head bowed in a corner of the room where the lights were low.

Tabby knew what she was thinking. "The new hairdo looks so good on you. I like the way it spreads out over your head," he said kindly.

Izzy raised her head and smiled bravely. Grimes was moved.

"You two have to be gentle. I'm like the girl in the fairy tale

216

who was rescued—but they never tell you in those stories what happens afterward. It takes some time to learn to be a princess," she said charmingly.

"Aw, take all the time you want," said Tabby, going up to her and giving her a friendly sock in the shoulder, "but you've got to remember the wedding is coming right up." This worried Tabby. What if she wasn't presentable? What if she wasn't photogenic?

"I don't think I'm worthy of you," speculated Iz.

"You'll grow into it, sweetheart," rejoined Tabby.

"You're a man, out in the world, you have followers and respect and a future," she said. "I'm just a tramp. I've done terrible things. I didn't know how terrible until now, when I can see myself measured against all you've done, the way you're so devoted. The way you make things happen . . ."

Tabby and Grimes felt happy. With energy and verve Tabby rose from his chair and began to stride around the room with his natural grace. He was young, forceful, thoughtful.

"That's the secret. We *make* things happen. We got out! We could see it all in San Jose, how there was a trash compactor with our names on it. Step in here, everyone said, we can use your meat. We want to sell your meat. We'll feed you to your job. We'll put a rake up your ass and sit you down at a desk for fifty years, just be sure to give the rake back, sucker—"

"It's all part of the dialectic of violence," explained Grimes.

"It's like everybody's hypnotized! Don't they know how much pain is out there? Don't they know that nobody has any hope anymore? What do they hope for? They hope when they get old that they've got enough money for soap so they don't stink. They hope that one of the freaks won't rob them, even though it would give them something to talk about, something to cry about, better than nothing. They've got that stupid scared look. Morons. It doesn't have to be that way. It doesn't! We've proven it!"

"We want to lift them up into the empyrean," commented Grimes.

The sun roamed around in Izzy's room, playing over the new clothes and the magazines and clippings, over the neatly made bed and the wedding planners and photographs. Iz, attentive and wondering, watched them and thought about the way that so many had embraced with affection and longing these boys: handsome princes in one of the oldest kingdoms of history.

"Everybody's lost their dreams," said Tabby as though taking up a chant. "They don't just go out and make things different. It's such a good story! Me and Grimes, such a story! They used to come and dunk our heads in the sewage, saying, 'This is getting ahead. You'll get used to the taste, you'll like it.'

"But we didn't like it. And no one else likes it, either. Now here we are. Everyone who follows us understands us. It's their time. Because it's our time."

"It's the only politics that counts, the politics of salvation," summed up Grimes.

"Is this kind of like history as sport?" asked Iz.

"Just like that," answered Tabby. "It's the sport of men, a return to the days when men stood up and made a world for themselves."

"I can be a cheerleader. Maybe I need pom-poms."

"You don't need pom-poms. All you need is lipstick. Dark lipstick." Tabby even caught himself hoping she would bite him again.

"Wasn't the pastor coming to see you?" asked Grimes, to move things along. "He wanted to talk to you privately before the wedding. He says it's something he likes to do, to have these quiet talks in such an emotional time."

And there was a knock on the door, and in walked Saint Francis.

Along Lost Coast in the secret coves and at the base of unknown bluffs, atop black outcroppings of rock and along the sides of soft grassy promontories, the Pacific arced to show a treasure box of blues—molten lapis and topaz and sapphire; reflected big-city midnight neon blue, and the blue of dawn light over fragile and faraway atolls—gathering from all the world, the Pacific delivered its blue to Lost Coast.

Homer, on a beach just north of Mendocino, was explaining to Ananda and Chiara, "They were going to find you all, no matter what happened. What would you have preferred, a shoot-out? There were good reasons to make it a wedding. They'll be celebrating, which is just the time for us to strike. It fits with their story of victory, and no one is so vulnerable as the victorious. They're not going to take their weapons into a church; and besides, it's a beautiful church, there by the side of the sea."

"They have everybody on their side, and they have my daughter. What do we have?" asked the furious Chiara.

"Wit? Maybe?" answered Homer.

Francis shook hands courteously with Tabby and Grimes, then took Tabby's hand and led him over by Izzy. He sat him down, then pulled up a chair and faced them both.

"As the pastor of this church," he said with solemnity, "it is my role to make sure that the two of you are fully prepared for the obligations of marriage." And he looked at them with understanding and sympathy.

"Prepared? Prepared?" burst out Tabby. "I *fought* for her. I followed her. I dreamed about her, tracked her, rescued her, she was nothing but an animal in a trap. Prepared? Who do you think *you* are?"

"I am the pastor who is going to marry you," Francis reminded him gently.

Tabby tried quickly to recover. "There hasn't been any touching and feeling! None!"

"I'm very gratified to hear that. I have not in my life seen an example of respect quite like the one you demonstrate here for us in this little town."

Grimes smiled.

"You both need to tell me what this marriage means to you," Francis went on, "tell me how you will take these vows within and, as you live, let them lead you into a life of nuptial bliss."

Izzy looked into the clear eyes of the saint and said, "I will tell you privately, for these are just the subjects that have taken up my meditations as my wedding day comes near."

"I know just what to do!" broke in Tabby. He balled up his fists and pumped the air. "It'll be just like the spotlights in the shows, the music is all around you and everyone is watching you. It's fantastic. You can feel how they've been waiting for an example. Someone who will punish the ones who make us suffer. Someone to follow into the spotlight. Everybody loves it and they come to us, they know they can trust us, the choir girls come crawling just to have a chance—"

"They help us with all the mail," broke in Grimes.

The cuckoo clock struck the hour, and the cuckoo slid out and sang brazenly.

"My bride!" And Tabby gave Izzy a look of hope and admiration. "Bride! I need you in the light with me. The brave, the beautiful. The reporters will love it. It's a real life. Who can resist us? Who in this world?" Tabby got up and walked in front of Izzy and Saint Francis, flexing and posing, talking and pointing. He was formidable, full of conviction. "We're going to have a family, we'll show everybody how families once were. Close! Close! With a strong man and a safe wife, tough little boys and pretty girls. Pretty ones! I'll be honest and true. A husband. I'll come home and the little ones will run to me, they'll run to me. I'll throw them in the air. They'll laugh!"

"The family is a refuge," intoned Grimes.

"Something to defend! Everyone needs something important to defend." Tabby sat back down beside Izzy. The sun was banking in the window and highlighting his features and physique, and he said with passion and devotion, "I'll do anything for you! I'll fight for you! I love you! This is the end of your worries. You don't have to do anything. It's where everyone will envy you, but no one will be able to hurt you. Ever. I promise."

"The family is the foundation of the world," said Grimes.

And Tabby, having reached so energetic a pitch of affection, and being so full of love for Izzy that he imagined her shining with it—illumined in the beautiful stage lights of his love—Tabby went back across the room and took his seat next to Grimes.

"That was very honest and moving," said Francis. "And I am satisfied that you come to this woman with all the heart you have, and holding nothing back from her. And such is all that can be asked of a husband."

Tabby and Grimes beamed at him.

"And now you must leave this young girl alone with me."

Tabby got up to go. "Will you be okay, honey? I can stay if you want." He didn't want her to be anxious.

"Don't worry, Tabby. This pastor looks like a saint to me," said Grimes.

Tabby walked over and shook Francis's hand in a manly way. "Thanks, bud. Just let me know when to be there." And Tabby winked at Izzy, and he and Grimes pivoted and walked out.

Francis and Izzy were quiet for a minute.

"I didn't think a person could be so scared. It's like continuous electroconvulsive shock," said our Iz. "Am I throwing off sparks?"

"You are sparkling. As usual."

"I keep watching their hands."

In Berkeley, Festina, that companion of plants, met Laila, our compatriot of clouds, on Telegraph in the Cafe Mediterraneum.

"I don't know about this trip to Italy they want me to take. All the way to Rome just to have dinner with a guy named Lorenzo? Bizarre!" said Festina.

"At least they're not sending you off to be a farmer," commented Laila. "It just goes to show that a girl can sing her way to strange new friends. But who knows what will happen to us? I'm going to just go with it; Ananda and Chiara, they seem so sure."

"We'll probably both be back here in school next fall," guessed the skeptical Festina.

"In the meantime, we've got this trip to Mendocino. They said they'd tell us what we needed to do, when we got there. I'm hoping for a wild time."

"Let's head out," commanded Festina, just as a dozen of Renato's apprentices strode into the cafe.

"Mendocino!" one said. "Let's rock and roll—"

In a little cabin in the woods, Muscovado sat with old Nattie. She had gotten him a little organ, just like the one in the church in Mendocino, to practice. Musco played all day, and most of every night. He was playing for Iz.

He would be ready.

He missed her so much. The sky seemed drained of color.

He practiced a music of memory and hope.

Tabby and Grimes loved the fanfare. There was a constant stream of well-wishing and salutations—local politicians stopped in to shake their hands, interviewers came for short pieces for the Sunday papers, the presidents of the local gun clubs and the police association came. Best of all, the head of the union for California prison guards came by to offer a tour of the prisons in the area.

It was fantastic. The technology of restraint and punishment was taking brilliant turns, from the metal-mesh chokeholders and electric whips to the high-security facilities with their surrounding electrocution fences. Inside there was double-backup, multiple-camera, twenty-four-hour surveillance, with every cell an isolation cell and random body searches and wake-ups. It was so salutary for the Police of Gentle Jesus to see the energies of their companions devoted to the protection of society.

It was in such men—willing to risk everything for the sake of others—that anger was heated into wondrous justice.

Renato sat with Maria-Elena.

"Are you ready?" she asked.

"I will not leave your side," said Renato.

Maria-Elena had been quiet. "I don't know if Cookie is going to be able to do it. Even if we get Izzy free, everything will still depend on her. There's just too many of them."

The next days in Mendocino were a maelstrom of preparations. The television station had very helpfully sent up a celebrity wedding planner, Mrs. Penny Trencher, a toothy woman with a ferociously pressed wardrobe and social graces that shone in her face like rubbed metal. When she walked in to meet the bride—it took a while because the lock on Izzy's door had jammed—she shot one look at the dark-haired girl and said, "Just fine! You'll do just fine!"

Such a wedding! What an opportunity! And there is nothing more important for this ceremony than the right setting, the people and music, all the companions of feeling and stimulants of sentiment. Everything must be in place. And so did Penny Trencher take stock of the thrilled, imperiously hopeful Tabby, the increasingly eloquent Grimes, the accomplished, directorial Dorothy Gallagher; she set right to work.

The logistics were so complicated: a precise order of events, the need for monitoring, communications, and supply lines—it *was* like war. But she loved the sense of emergency and conflict; she thought of it as a battle won by love, a battle with a guaranteed peace at the end. And this wedding, in a hot crossfire of spotlights. She fell ecstatically to her labors.

Who would attend? Most of the guests were on Tabby's side. The bride could have whatever stragglers she wanted, what's the difference? For Tabby, it was simple: all the contacts they had in the media and charities and the Bay Area church community, the television producers and magazine writers, the police and security groups they had worked with—the whole fraternity of justice. They would be wonderful guests.

The only problem Penny had with Tabby as groom and Grimes as best man was that they were so happy. It was the kind of giddiness that men have at the end of exhausting work; it was as though they both had halos that held them upright, the circled attentions of society. There was a big payment for the movie rights to their stories, and a handsome sum for an exclusive series of network interviews.

Dorothy had just cut a rich deal with a New York publisher; she was having a writer put together the book. The advance publicity had already started—it was "the true-life story of the Police of Gentle Jesus. They fought for justice. They hoped for love."

Cookie sailed aways up the coast, to get as far away as possible from the killers of her husband. She needed to be alone, to gather her strength. She knew how much depended on her. Francis had gazed at her curiously.

It was so hard to think; her body was knit with fury at the two boys.

Juha had been silent.

Cookie hoped that Iz was all right, and that, somehow, the girl would be able to get away with some last flourish.

Cookie had traveled to the Land of the Dead. What she had to do now was more difficult.

Penny Trencher went in to Izzy to talk about her hairstyle and the design of her wedding gown.

Hair, especially, was so important to a wedding. It had to be just right, striking the balance between decorum and extravagance. This was just Mrs. Trencher's art. And happily, she found Izzy ready to plunge into contemplation of these important issues. In fact, when Penny walked in, Iz had a fashion show ready to roll.

"What do you think of this?" asked Izzy eagerly. She had bound up her hair in one of her remarkable buns, low and flat and tight, elongated back to front, so that it looked rather like she had a salmon on her head. But she was cheerful. "I think it has that je ne sais quoi!"

"That is the most astonishing thing I have ever seen!" proclaimed Mrs. Trencher in a spasm of truth-telling.

And Izzy stepped quickly behind a screen she had set up for this show, and she cried out, "Just wait until you see what else I've got! I'm so scared! I need to know what you think!"

So commenced the most elaborate exposition of hairdos Penny had ever witnessed.

"This is one I came up with this morning!" proclaimed Iz as she walked from behind the screen with her hair spiraling directly forth from both sides of her head in two long twisted strands held in place with knitting needles. The strands were long enough to prevent her from walking through a door unless she turned her head sideways, a maneuver that Izzy demonstrated gleefully. "I call this one the Antennae! Got the idea from insects!" she informed the dubious Penny Trencher, who felt herself going purple. But she recovered herself, because composure was her job.

Izzy, of course, knew this, and she retreated behind her screen once more, only to emerge after a decent interval with both of the long strands wrapped together, supported once again by the knitting needles, so as to make a long pointed horn that butted straight out from her forehead. "You guessed it! The Unicorn! You wouldn't believe the advantages! Watch this!" And she swung her head in such a way that the horn of hair struck the cuckoo clock, the little door slid back, and the cuckoo slid out obligingly to sing. It seemed to gaze directly at Mrs. Trencher.

Penny Trencher, though, knew she had a problem to address. It was time to intervene, in a way that made the young lady feel comfortable. And she animated her gestures with a starched courtesy: "I have heard, and now I see for myself, that you are a very creative young woman."

Izzy dove behind the screen once more. Mrs. Trencher waited. She heard grunting and swishing noises.

"The Hatchet!" exclaimed Izzy as she strode into view with her hair gathered in a bunch, shaped into a nice sharp arc, and then held out at an angle on a short stick at the top of her head. "I thought I might try something that fits with this woodsy area! I want to be sensitive to every social nuance!" Izzy strode back and forth—she had, after all, seen a good deal of striding and posing in this little room—she turned slowly this way and that, modeling the 'do, and giving Mrs. Trencher elegant, haughty looks. The lady sat with eyebrows lifted high. Very high. Satisfied, Iz retreated once more.

But Mrs. Trencher was now fully engaged. "We have to remember that the hairdo must work with the bridal veil. We do not, for instance, want the hair holding the veil aloft like a tent pole."

"No veil!" shouted Izzy with gusto from behind the screen. "I want to see what the fuck I'm doing in this wedding!"

Penny winced terribly, as though she had just swallowed down a whole kumquat. "We need to talk about that. I respect your needs, of course, in all of this. At the same time, we need to make sure everything *feels* just right."

Penny Trencher, ever patient, laid out some swatches of fabric for the wedding dress. And she thought, If I could just get this bitch to choose one, the seamstress standing by would put together the dress in a few hours.

"I'm really hungry!" said Izzy hysterically from behind the screen. "But I've got just the thing!"

Penny had to get the show on the road; she had incentive bonuses lined up if she could pull the whole thing off. Besides, they couldn't talk hairdos forever. "Come, be a dear, and choose a fabric for your lovely dress," she said coaxingly. But Iz had another 'do ready.

"The Lemon Meringue Pie!" hooted Izzy, and she swaggered forth with her hair wrapped around the outside of a pie tin, inside of which was veritable foamy lemon meringue. "It's in the spirit of the wedding. Everyone should want to eat the bride! Foamy!" Izzy smiled at Penny. "I'm so excited! Would you like a bite of pie?"

"No thank you," replied Penny firmly. "I would like you to choose a swatch of fabric for the dress."

"On one condition."

"The dress must cover most of your body," advised Mrs. Trencher, anticipating the worst.

"The dress must be big enough so I can wear my overalls underneath. I want to be secure and comfortable, and it's just not going to work without my overalls."

"Very well," agreed our Penny, thinking, Fine with me! She'll look like a damned blimp coming down the aisle!

"You are such a dear!" Izzy leaned over and gave the lady a big buss on the cheek, lodging a jellylike clump of meringue on the good woman's forehead. "Wait till you see this next one!" And Iz dodged away as Mrs. Trencher dabbed furiously with her hanky at the quivering egg white.

Surely there was an end to this, she prayed. How many 'dos were possible? Surely the girl would hit upon one decorous and dignified arrangement.

"I think we want to stay away from hairdos on the themes of animals or food," suggested Mrs. Trencher carefully.

"I've got it!" replied Iz, and she dove back behind the screen. This one took some time. Mrs. Trencher prayed for decency.

Izzy stole forth again and cried, "The Pap Smear!" She had a white tray on her head, held there by a complex set of chin strings and underarm straps. Extending from the top of this tray was a device consisting of two shaped metal flanges that, when inserted between the labia, would hold the vaginal walls apart to permit the sampling of tissue from the uterus. "It's education!" enthused Izzy. "Health education! It's kind of like my theme hairdo: a healthy pussy in a healthy marriage! What do you think, Mrs. Trencher?" And Iz looked at her expectantly.

"I think you're an insolent slut," she said cheerfully.

There is no stopping a planned wedding. It's like a trying to stop a horse in midpee. And so did Mrs. Trencher finish her labors on schedule. Dresses were sewn, flowers were ordered, a reception was organized to immediately follow the ceremony, with special catering by a company who had a serving they called An Extravaganza of Wild Game Meat. There was all through the town a bustle and a happiness.

Penny Trencher darted here and there like a serial killer of problems—the ring, cakes, ribbons, the right shoes for the bride;

the riffraff hanging around the church, the incendiary outbursts of Tabby, the weird pastor, the hubbub of the reporters, the pestering of Grimes, who wanted hourly reassurance that everything was being handled with the most deadly attention to the proprieties of matrimony. Penny always gave him her biggest smile, even when she was thinking that she'd like to poison him. But she understood: Grimes wanted everything just right for his friend.

On the beach, Ananda practiced with her trumpet. Chiara whirled a throwing ax into a tree, again and again.

Izzy met with the choir girls and giggled; she memorized the Book of Job and Ecclesiastes and the Song of Solomon; she swapped tales with Francis, who, she decided, had the most amorous imagination of any of the saints. She was especially interested in the tale of how Francis had expelled Augustine from Paradise, by exposing him as the fraud he was. It was obvious from the start, Francis pointed out—Augustine's conversion was merely the admission that he couldn't love this world.

17

TABBY WAS ALL ready. He was in his big van, in an austere dark-violet tuxedo with a crimson tie and hankie. When the coat was buttoned, the lapels flared in a striking arc over his pectorals. He was nervous, though; something about this whole thing just wasn't active and manly.

"Couldn't we have a twenty-one-gun salute or something?" he wanted to know.

"There are some times in life, I mean just every now and then, when you don't need weapons," commented Dorothy. And anyway, Izzy had insisted: no guns in the church.

"Fuckin' A! I'm in love!" protested Tabby in his jaunty way.

"She'll feel secure because of your gentleness and your grace," advised Grimes smoothly.

Saint Francis strolled around in the church as the final preparations were made. He thought of the woman he loved.

Just then, Clare was stepping along the sands of the wilderness beaches of the Lost Coast. The tracks she left behind her were of her choosing—sometimes the lightly touched signatures of seabirds, sometimes the marks of tides.

* * *

The wedding guests began to arrive. Penny and Dorothy watched them come into the church and take their places. On Tabby's side of the aisle there were just the guests expected: a collection of pastors, selected policemen sitting straight as fenceposts, and agents and reporters and writers and representatives of charities and police unions.

They were collected there with hopefulness and a sense of privilege. It was the community of people who earn a claim on the rest of us: the vital few, dominant, energetic. Their educated sensibilities in religious, journalistic, or security work—from the integrity of law enforcement to the dynamic free press to the distinguished sentiments of the charities and churches—their sensibilities earned them a place at the center of things.

Francis looked over them all.

At least, thought Francis, Izzy had had the chance to do her hairdo exposition.

Francis approached Penny and Dorothy.

"Who on earth," he asked with hauteur, "are all these hooligans draping themselves, quite without respect, over the pews?" And he gestured to the guests on the bride's side of the church.

"Well, I hope they make her feel better!" sniffed Penny Trencher. And Penny felt an overpowering urge to do a big snuffle, follow with a cavernous hack, and then really let go with some sputum. But—what was she thinking!—she mastered this irresponsible inclination.

"I presume they'll behave," commented Francis with venom.

The Troupe and their friends sat, readying themselves, watching the killers of Juha.

In the first row was Homer, burly, bedraggled, hairy, worried. He felt a little strange about this exotic piece. Why did love bring war?

Next to him, and nearly as brawny, sat Beulah from Nevada. Beulah had a bullwhip coiled under her coat; and, in a burlap sack, five folded rainbows that her son, the lightning bolt, had brought her as a present from his sojourns in the sky. The rainbows rustled in the burlap.

Behind Beulah sat Cookie, remarkably transformed by her hat, a big blue sailing cap. Cookie carried a satchel; inside it was a glowing halo.

By the side of the cowgirl sat Gus the Miwok. His sailing hadn't left him empty-handed: he held salt spray hidden in his right hand and oceanic winds tucked away in his left. By the side of Gus was Antelope on the Moon, who was still in his mechanic's overalls. He had an eagle feather in his hair.

Festina and Laila and a dozen of Renato's apprentices were there, taking time out from their labors. For who would want to miss this rock-'em, sock-'em, bang-up wedding? Renato's students were joined by Jamalia Sweets, whose rapping had so happily adorned his classroom. She had job responsibilities on this day, as would be expected at a wedding where life and death were going to meet and dance.

Next to Jamalia was Renato, who was tapping his foot and humming in the ear of Maria-Elena, so big with child that Renato could rest his head on her belly and listen to their baby rehearsing the sass she intended to use at the baptismal font.

Ananda was holding hands with Chiara. Chiara was calm, except for a sour, prickling, flesh-filling terror for her daughter. She and Ananda had hidden the throwing axes under the pew in front of them.

Tabby and Grimes were on the lookout for Muscovado Taine, but he was hiding out. He had his gig ready, though.

Chiara thought about Izzy, looked over at the sumptuously pregnant Maria-Elena, and tried to think of prayers. But Chiara, just like the others, couldn't stop thinking about the murder of Juha, in the beautiful North Yuba Canyon, just at the end of a summer that had held the highest of their hopes.

Chiara looked around at her fellow travelers. Their day had come.

* * *

As for Dorothy and Penny, they had progressed to that blessed attitude of those at the culmination of a long period of high-stakes labor: that is, they didn't give a shit. They just wanted to get it over with. And so they were happy when the appointed hour came round and they saw Tabby in his suit come out and stand with red face (he had been working out all morning) at the head of the aisle, waiting for the wedding to start. At his side, ready with the ring, stood the bristling Grimes, radiant with this chance for sanctioned celebration.

Saint Francis took his place at the head of the nave. And at the back of the church he saw Izzy, ready for her nuptials.

The wedding march sounded.

There was in the church an exhalation of longing and appreciation. Izzy, in a white silk dress, her hair down over her shoulders like a harvest of darkness, the way before her lit by the opal light of her eyes, was so beautiful that Tabby almost started to cry.

She came lightly and deliberately to his side, she was calm and respectful. She took Tabby's arm and turned to face Francis.

Grimes reached out and squeezed Tabby's arm. "Way to go, bud!" he said, and he gave his friend a big wink and a thumbs-up.

There was an appreciative chuckle in the church. Izzy took her place alongside Tabby, and with a sigh of happy anticipation, the church went silent. Dorothy could feel the joy of everyone whom she had brought into the story of these boys.

Francis began it this way: "It is customary in those moments preceding Holy Matrimony, to say a few words on the meaning of marriage in our times—how it bears two souls together into one house, how into that house the world comes with its beauties and promises."

Everyone in church was concentrating, Tabby most of all.

"This is the time of excitement," said Francis.

He's got that right, thought Tabby. Tabby stood still with just his rocketing hopes and his heart going like a kettledrum.

"But excitement will not make a marriage."

"Why not?" whispered Tabby involuntarily. There was another chuckle from the pews. Grimes, smiling, shushed Tabby.

"For marriage is more than the expectation of happiness, more than the blessedness of pleasure."

Now even Grimes was wondering: What did this guy want, anyway? A blood sacrifice?

"More than mere adherence to the vows, or the admiration of the beloved, more than the caretaking of the new souls brought into this world—none of these things by themselves will make a marriage."

There was a murmur among the wedding guests. This wasn't as purposeful as they had been led to expect. But still, for mumbo jumbo, it wasn't so bad.

Tabby gave Francis a wink of eagerness and friendship. The guy was such a thoughtful preacher. It was going to happen. "Moving right along!" Tabby said softly. He leaned close to Izzy. "Not much longer!" he whispered. What a good world!

"Let me continue," Francis said, "for we must know what makes the soul of a marriage, if not these things which I have so helpfully enumerated."

Cookie piped right up from the pews, "Well, fer chrissakes, shout it right out, would ya? It ain't such a damn mystery. I'll tell everybody myself, if you don't come right out with it." The cowgirl was strong, watchful.

"Could you put it in a song? So we could dance to it?" burst out Renato.

Everyone on the groom's side of the church stared resentfully at these outbursts. Tabby turned to glare at the offenders; but he was, after all, busy. "I'm getting married! Can't they all see I'm getting married?" he complained to Grimes.

But Francis was not to be deterred. "This is what I know: a marriage lives if it partakes of the marriage of heaven and earth."

"And why exactly is that?" asked Chiara in a clear ringing voice as she stood up and moved into the aisle.

"Because with our heaven-born souls and earth-formed bodies, we are, each of us, such a marriage. And so must we bring to our mate a life that holds a heaven."

"I really think I could tap my foot to this stuff," speculated

233

Ananda enthusiastically as she joined Chiara. "Why, I do think I hear music!"

That was it. Tabby turned to go after Ananda, but Grimes caught him by the collar and whispered furiously, "You're on-stage—onstage!" Tabby wrenched free, swung round to face Francis, and spoke in whispered rage.

"Do I have to shoot you to get you to marry us?"

"It's not the custom," mused Francis.

"Get it over with!" hissed Tabby.

"I'm with you!" exclaimed Francis. "Let's have some beat here." A drum sounded, the lights in the church darkened further, one spotlight drilled though the shadows. A heavy bass filled the building. A low, driving complement came from the little organ at the back of the room.

"Let me introduce the band," began Homer. "First, from Berkeley, the singer Jamalia Sweets!" And Jamalia came forth from the pews and took a bow.

"On the keyboards, with those well-known strong hands, from Kingston, Jamaica, Muscovado Taine!" And the spotlight picked out Muscovado, who winked and gave the church organ a few peals and sonorous blows.

"It's the ratty black bastard!" cried out Grimes. "Watch out for his knife!"

"On the trumpet, from Los Angeles, our bright Ananda!" continued Homer.

Izzy stepped over to Grimes and, in a deft move, handcuffed his right wrist to the left wrist of Tabby.

"You promised me!" shouted Tabby. "You promised me! You were waiting for me! You belong to me!"

"We've been set up!" yelled Grimes.

There was hubbub in the church. The door at the back opened and the coyote bolted in and bit Penny Trencher in the ass. Two of the policemen in the pews surged for the door, but someone had locked it from the outside.

Jamalia Sweets took her place at the head of the nave.

"I love services," observed Francis, "where the congregation bursts into song."

Homer smiled and cried out to Tabby and Grimes, "This is what we have on tap for you!" The old boy was having fun. "First, a short piece by our group, the Down Home Celestial Trio; then, especially for you, the Visitation of the Animals! What a day!"

Maria-Elena went to Cookie and got her up and took her into the aisle, near Tabby and Grimes; and all of Cookie's friends faced her, ready with music they had composed for her.

It was the prelude to their mourning the death of a man in love.

Musco leaned into the organ; Jamalia rapped in a rhythm that went from soft to raucous; Ananda blew out a gold and azure sound. They celebrated with music the journey they had made together with Juha. First, the melody took on the colors and dusty magic of the Nevada backcountry. Beulah got up and, touching Cookie as she went, hung at the head of the church her five rainbows. They were rainbows that on misty afternoons arch over the desert canyons where they had all camped and marveled. As the rainbows glistened and faded, the band played for the North Yuba River, and the meadow where the newlywed Cookie and Juha had built their cabin together; it was music full of hope and resinous shadows and tints of mountain wildflowers. And finally, for the cowgirl who had gone to the Land of the Dead to find the man she loved, her friends let go a music of desire, of one woman's desire; through the church it moved in power. And Gus turned loose salt spray and gusty ocean winds.

With Tabby and Grimes watching, Cookie went to the musicians; they each embraced her and whispered to her. They hoped for her.

Homer was momentarily silenced by the trio's cosmic riff. He cleared his throat. Now for the finale. But he didn't get a chance to speak, because—

Tabby, who, despite the instructions of Dorothy, was not so foolish as to go into church without a weapon, had drawn from a calf holster a featherlight pump-action pistol. He thought he'd quiet down the hoodlums who had taken over his wedding. He took dead aim at Saint Francis and yelled, "Everybody freeze!"

Beulah quietly took out her bullwhip.

"I will freeze," Francis assured him. "I won't even cock an eyebrow."

"You shut up!" Tabby said. But because he had yelled just then, he could not hear the whistling in the air of the whip, which tore the splendid gun out of his hand and stung and bloodied his fingers in a most insulting way.

But all hope was not lost: Grimes reached under the front pew and brought out a .308-caliber semiautomatic rifle, probably the best piece for what his police friends called "special purpose scenarios."

He pointed the rifle at Saint Francis.

"You're one of them," Grimes said acutely.

"They really are somewhat too rowdy for my taste," replied Francis.

"Have them come to the front of the church," said Grimes resolutely.

Francis turned to Homer. "For heaven's sake, what next?"

"This is next!" boomed Homer to cover the shouting from the wedding guests when they saw Chiara and Ananda wind up the big throwing axes and with a coordinated heave send them wheeling across the church. Grimes's rifle was blown out of his hands and fell in three pieces at the feet of Francis.

"Let me guess," mused Francis, "an emblematic gesture concerning the Trinity."

The Hurricane Troupe was starting to enjoy itself.

"So, gentlemen," said Francis to Tabby and Grimes, "it's time to finish the ceremony planned for this afternoon."

"Traitor! Wimp!" the two boys shouted.

There was more milling around and sharp exclamations in the church. Tabby and Grimes's guests huddled together, amazed, fearful, and hostile. Two security agents came up and took hold of Tabby and Grimes and hustled them away. The men surrounded them and began a series of rapid consultations. It would be quick work to round up these fanatics and display them for television, then haul them off to jail for attempted murder and kidnapping.

"Let the show go on!" cried Homer.

And Homer was winding up for another boisterous declaration when he stopped cold. Striding up the nave of the church he saw, resolute, irresistible, the Messenger of Death.

Homer, full of bitterness, sat down quietly to watch. Everything, now, was up to Cookie.

"What a joke!" Tabby said aloud. His fingers were still bleeding from his gun's having been whipped from his hand, and he knew he looked his best when he was bleeding. He looked around at his compatriots. "I'm ready to get this over with," he said decisively.

Renato put his arms around Maria-Elena. Musco raced to Izzy and held her close to him.

The Messenger knew what came next: darkness. He stood and faced them all and extended his hands. Darkness poured from them like water, a darkness that filled the nave and aisles and blocked the windows of the church and then fell back to let in enough light for killing.

Our travelers, lost on the coast of California, were all on their feet. Cookie walked out in front of them all until she was closest to Tabby and Grimes. She advanced toward the two boys, closer and closer.

The murderers of Juha were ready to finish their work.

Homer covered his eyes.

Francis was watching Cookie; he prayed for her.

Tabby went for Izzy. One of the policemen had jimmied the cuffs off. Tabby had bent down and ripped up from between the pews the kneeling board. He was going to wallop Musco across the face, but he'd miss with a few swipes and Izzy would catch it in the forehead. It was kind of a classical tragedy.

The Messenger of Death was watching.

Right there in a little church in Mendocino, it was the destiny of Izzy to die of her beating, to be carried out in Tabby's arms and displayed as the victim of an attack of degenerates on the holy ceremony of marriage. On the happiest day of Tabby's life too; everyone had seen how he had followed her, how he had found her, how the story of his life led to his loving her.

It was the destiny of her mother Chiara to die that day—had she not thrown an ax? An ax, for God's sake?—strangled by a San Jose police officer.

Maria-Elena, kicked by Grimes, would lose her baby. He didn't mean to, he was just trying to get her out of the way, it was an absolute emergency. The thirteenth Daughter of the Moon would never walk in the sunlight along Lost Coast.

There is no telling here of the destined trial of Muscovado Taine and the crowds around the courthouse that spat on him, and the triumphant testimony of Tabby and Grimes and their long, outraged interviews for the television cameras. Everybody knew Taine was responsible for the death of the girl.

What chance had our travelers with their little stories, against real stories, the ones that own the world? Those stories—that is destiny. Destiny had come to find our amorous band of wanderers, who from the high deserts of the Great Basin had come by the side of the Pacific to the end of their journey.

18

BUT WHEN TABBY went to kill Izzy, he had to reckon with a Nevada cowgirl. She had her own damn ideas about destiny.

Cookie stood facing Tabby and Grimes. In her hand was the halo of Saint Francis.

She was with her Juha and loving him. She remembered their meeting, their cabin; the life that, as they traveled, rose within them.

Francis, singing to himself, watched it happen.

With the rowdy joy of a woman in love Cookie stood forth. She was without hatred; she had nothing to hate them with.

Power streamed from the halo as Cookie shook out the ring into twisting currents of light, bright lariats: her shining work. The good thing about having a cosmic lariat is that it lets a cowgirl really show her stuff. She roped Tabby and Grimes and with a turn of the wrist upended them both over the pews, scattering as she did the men attacking Chiara. She threw another loop of light over the two big policemen threatening Maria-Elena, and another she dropped around the red-faced preachers besieging Muscovado Taine. When she was done, she had rounded them all up and gathered them smoothly back on their own side of the aisle where they belonged.

She left them there, ringed in sparkling light, and walked up to Francis at the head of the church. "I think I see the way these blame halos work. I am much obliged! Glad to get those beefy things back in the corral!" And, as she spoke, through a high window of the church flew a beautiful tufted puffin, who descended to settle on Cookie's shoulder. The bird clucked softly at the cowgirl and the saint.

Homer was tongue-tied.

"Could we jes' get on with it now? I done my part," said Cookie, to get him moving.

Homer swung to face Tabby and Grimes. "And now for the songs of Juha," he said quietly.

The Hurricane Troupe gathered together, their ceremony before them at last. They approached the boys and their compatriots, all in their corral of light. They stood close and looked them in the face. Cookie, the puffin on her shoulder, watched them all.

What is a man? What is it to lose him?

The church was dead quiet.

Our travelers conjured their music of loss, the only music left to them: the cries of animals.

The deep, drawn-out call of the gray wolf sounded in the church; Renato watched the killers, he thought of the sonorous Juha, and his throat was full of grief. Chiara had missed the gentle, hopeful Juha all these months, and that missing moved in her big and wild as a cougar; the church resounded with the big cat's screaming, over and over; strong with pain. Ananda thought of a cinnamon bear, and everyone could hear the thunderous huffing and roaring; Ananda wanted it to knock down the walls of the church, to have the heft of her sorrow to be without Juha, a bear of a man. Maria-Elena knew that Juha was so good and innocent even the singing birds of the desert missed him; and through the church moved the lament of meadowlarks. Muscovado Taine needed Juha because that big man knew what it was to want every gift of earth for one beloved woman; and in homage to our Juha there whistled and called a whole island of seabirds, a whole island—as though they sounded at the entrance to the Land of the Dead. And then Izzy confronted Tabby and Grimes and everyone heard the howl of her coyote; no animal knows more about death. The coyote howled with her bitterness in missing Juha; and in her young woman's blessing for so boisterous a man.

The quiet grew again in the church.

The little puffin took wing and flew around and around his fellow travelers; and then alighted back upon Cookie's shoulder and looked at them with shining golden eyes.

Francis smiled.

All the group watched Tabby and Grimes, in silence, for another minute; then they turned away.

The problem was that this was the world as it is, and not even a lariat of light was going to hold in forever Tabby and Grimes and their guests.

Big strong Beulah walked to the back of the church and with her forearms blew open the doors; and our travelers all followed and scattered in the street.

As Beulah was leaving, she waved and laughed and cried out in her raspy old rancher's voice, "Bolt!" And her son, the lightning bolt, with a single swipe blasted the big van that held the weapons and the dressing rooms, the clippings and the photographs and the videotapes of the Police of Gentle Jesus.

It made, in the middle of Mendocino, a wondrous fire. And the heat of it could be felt by Tabby and Grimes and their company, who, as the lines of light around them faded, did not move from their places in the church.

Along Lost Coast, the Daughters of the Moon readied on a beach the campfires and silence and celebrations that the country uses when she welcomes home her own.

They were not the only ones welcomed home. Tabby and Grimes, flushed and bruised, abandoned and beaten, came with their companions into the electric and delighted intimacy of the shared ordeal. The happiness of it was just proportional to the weight of sensation the story carried. And as cameras in helicopters were aimed at the burning van in front of the church, at the plume of oily smoke that ascended over the little coastal town, Dorothy Gallagher stepped out into the minutes that she would always regard as the most transcendent of her career.

"A Special News Report from KICU—Our News Is *the* News!

"In a gruesome attack in a church, the cultists that have been plaguing California have broken up the wedding of Tabby and Isabella, that so many have followed with such hope and celebration. In a terrible violation of the traditions of the church and the sanctity of the marriage ceremony, these primitives packed the church and forced the pastor to cooperate with them in destroying what promised to be the happiest day of a young man's life."

"Can you tell us yet exactly what happened?"

"I'll have a full account later. But this is what I know now. Pretending to be guests at the wedding, they first started yelling during the ceremony. Then they played some of their strange music; it's being said here that the music involved chanting that the group may use in their cult practices. And then they brought in one of their number from outside and taunted all the guests with talk about death." Dorothy shuddered.

"Are there any fatalities?"

"There's a number of guests being treated right now for shock; I'll have a report on their injuries soon. Just before the cult members took back the girl and fled with her, they did a terrifying thing. In a barbaric ritual, they sounded animal cries through the church; and then, in an orgy of destruction, they fled and set fire to Tabby and Grimes's van.

"Later, I'll try to get a statement from Tabby himself. In the meantime, we're just trying to contain the fire here in Mendocino. This is Dorothy Gallagher, in the war zone up here in northern California."

* * *

No one could trace the Hurricane Troupe. It was as though they had vanished into the sea. Most thought they had gone back to Berkeley; everybody knew they couldn't hide for long. They could be taken care of later; more important tasks were at hand.

The images—Tabby with the bleeding fingers and Grimes with burns from the fire, their emergence from the hospital to the crowd of well-wishers, some of them crying out the names of the boys, some weeping, the girls watching them in silence and adoration; the interview with the anguished Tabby, his anger not for himself, but for the desecration of the church; Grimes standing forth in righteous declaration in favor of the honor and future of his friend—all this was set forth with skill and sorrow to an outraged public.

JUST AT THE base of the sea cliffs, at the far corner of a wilderness beach on Lost Coast, Saint Francis of Assisi stood with Clare in his arms, and no will in heaven and no force on earth could have stopped him from kissing her. For she was the woman who had wandered with him through the centuries; who was always with him because his caresses had set into his hands the shape of her face. She was the one who had taught him to pray: on the wild beach, with the sea around their ankles, holding her face and kissing her eyes: that was prayer.

At the far end of that same beach stood Muscovado Taine and his Izzy, and because they had just been swimming together in the cold Pacific, just then together in the midday sun they held one another rapt with salt and heat and relief.

The sea sent its light around them, and they stood on the shore like two sparklers.

And in the shadows of the redwood were Maria-Elena and Renato, the mother and father of the thirteenth Daughter of the

245

Moon. Renato was shining. Maria-Elena was walking in a circle around him.

"If I were your wife," she was saying, "sometimes I would be a full moon to you, all my radiance I would give you. And then"—she moved a quarter of the way around him—"a half-moon, with half my light going off into a space you do not know, and then"—she moved another quarter way—"the new moon, dark to you, hidden always from you, never to be revealed to you, my love. And then"—she kept moving—"the first crescent on the western horizon, when you will know I am coming with all my brightness back to you." She extended both her hands to him. "Renato, will you marry me?"

Homer and Ananda and Chiara lounged around in that state of arousal and thankfulness that is only to be found at this strange intersection of narratives: they had turned back death, and the three of them were going off to bed together.

In a cove the *Nostos* was anchored, and Cookie strode around the deck, the puffin sometimes on her shoulder and sometimes flying up into the rigging. The dolphins were alive around the boat, leaping in arc after arc that left in the air a patchwork of rainbows.

Cookie was going to sail south, along the California coast down to the Sea of Cortés, then to Costa Rica and finally to the Galápagos. She was going with her Juha into the Pacific.

But Cookie could not sail just yet; for Renato and Maria-Elena had come to her first, to tell her; and she wanted to celebrate their marriage with them.

The next morning, everyone gathered at Needle Rock, in the heart of Lost Coast. There were important questions to settle.

Actually, only one important question: Who would marry Renato and Maria-Elena?

As in all matters of plot at this late date, everyone went immediately to Homer, who was used to arranging weddings. The poet was glowing with the extraordinary and learned embraces of Ananda and Chiara and sported around that morning with one or the other of them on his arm. Around noontime, though, he walked with resolution to the grass at the edge of the trees and lay down there and fell tempestuously asleep.

Ananda and Chiara would check on him every now and then, giving the old poet the encouraging caresses of mortal and beloved women.

Francis, luckily, turned up just then and immediately volunteered to marry our two vagabonds. For their part, Renato and Maria-Elena had, in a historic turn of events, decided to get practical. They needed a place to live.

Of course, there was only one house in sight, the old wooden house with its veranda overlooking the Pacific that was used as an office by the California Division of Forestry. In fact, a ranger was just then hanging over the railing on the veranda, watching them all carefully.

Renato went up to him. "We really need this house! We really do! I am a painter, and at the Jalisco Club in Gerlach I fell in love with the youngest of the twelve Daughters of the Moon. This was after we met the angels in Fallon but before we heard the Music of the Spheres in Bodega Bay, and I fell in love with her and now she's going to give birth to the thirteenth Daughter, the one all the sisters have been waiting for, and when we get married this evening—"

"Look," interrupted the wide-eyed ranger, "I'll go in right now and pack up my stuff. It's all yours."

Just then a golden eagle glided into the grasses in front of the house, stood still for a second, and then metamorphosed into Antelope on the Moon.

"No, let me explain—" went on Renato.

"Keep my stuff," said the ranger. "I'll just hit the road." And he did.

Jamalia Sweets did some wedding rap. Nattie threw in more of her celestial tunes. Three angels from Nevada sent the aurora borealis to hang in the air above the meadow, for that extra festive touch. Festina, with a simmering of garlic and olive oil and all things delicious, cooked up an Italian feast that made Saint Francis and his Clare faint with delight. Laila passed around some little thunderheads, very sweet, you could hold them in your hand and the rising and twirling would send through your flesh an atmospheric delectation.

Beulah sent Bolt out to sea to dance his happiness at the vows of Renato and his dark-haired lover. The peacock, improbably, tried to sing. And Gus the Miwok brought as a wedding present a secret word he had learned that allows a man to call breezes off the ocean. Renato would use the word in their wooden house, after lovemaking, to bring cool air to bathe the wet skin of the woman he loved.

Just at twilight, on the grass in front of the old wood house where they would live, the whole group of them gathered for the marriage of Renato and Maria-Elena. The coyote sat close.

Saint Francis stood before them, his Clare was near him, and he said, "Each one of us loves you two so much. And so it is proper that you come here among us to marry. For even as your love is alive in the daughter to be born here, so our love is alive in your family here by the sea. And so I ask, will you two go forth together into your wilderness, the one that belongs to lovers, the heart's whole birthright, the world entrusted to you?"

"Yes, we will," whispered Renato and Maria-Elena at once.

"And will you seek as lovers to learn the paradise here on earth?"

"I will," said Renato.

"I will," said his bride.

"I pronounce you husband and wife."

"I've got to see this!" said the baby. "I hope you're ready for me."

"I'll be the midwife," offered Clare. And she and Renato and the eleven sisters of Maria-Elena went into the house and everyone milled around to wait for the child.

It was dark. But this crowd was good in the dark.

Homer lolled on the grass with Ananda and Chiara.

"Can I at least come and read stories to my children?" he asked plaintively.

"Short stories, I hope," cracked Chiara.

"I'll teach them to improvise an epic," said Homer. "It's not that tough."

"You are welcome always on our coast, to our children. Come and teach them," said Ananda.

From the high desert of the Great Basin to the Lost Coast they had come, desert to mountain, city to ocean. And what will become of them, these men and women at work?

The sons of Chiara and Ananda, at play in the surf along the Lost Coast—what three secrets will they learn from the Messenger of Death? And is it true the Messenger, when pressed, can build an impressive sand castle?

What can a man paint in watercolors if that man is Renato and he learns how to dip his brush in the ocean?

How tough is it, anyway, to get whiskey in the wilderness?

What inexplicable love-gift will Muscovado Taine find in a clearing in the rain forest of Costa Rica, which he will recognize and take softly into his hands, then with celebration to set off at once on the way back to the embraces of Izzy?

And how did he find Izzy? For Cookie will have taken Izzy as her first mate. What will be their adventures among the great whales and the oceanic storm fronts and tropical cays?

When will the Hurricane Troupe settle down and do something important, like open a bar?

Why did Saint Francis and Clare set out for Sierra Valley, that meeting ground between the high desert and the Sierra Nevada? And why do they say that the reunion of the worlds will not wait any longer?

Who is that coyote at your door?

Francis was the first to return to the house; then the coyote and the peacock. Then, back from the beaches and out of the woods, along the road and through the meadow, everyone returned to the house of Renato and Maria-Elena. They gathered in the grass below the veranda. And they were quiet, even Beulah was quiet. All the lovers stood close.

Whatever they did in this world, wherever they went, whatever they learned, none of them ever forgot the moment Renato, in the ancient ravishments of joy, stepped out on the veranda with the baby in his arms.

The night streamed toward the house. Lightning leaned out of the clouds. The ocean rose silently along the shore.

Even with the little blanket around her, everyone could see the pale light around her head; for she had already begun to love this world.

Saint Francis was the first up the stairs onto the veranda, and he said, "Come with me, all of you. Come inside this house and we will each of us swear ourselves to this blessed child."

And they all came up, every one of them. They surrounded Renato and the baby, and he led them to the open door, and they followed and crowded quietly into the cabin. They touched and kissed Maria-Elena as she and Renato caressed their daughter and whispered to her. The night, gathered close around the windows, protected them; the child, in that surround of love, slept in the sure sweetness of their devotions; and the Lost Coast, which held them all, made ready to bring her the light of her first morning on earth.